Andrew Cotto

Cucina Tipica
An Italian Adventure

A Novel

Black Rose Writing | Texas

ISBN: 978-1-68433-123-9
PUBLISHED BY BLACK ROSE WRITING
www.blackrosewriting.com

Printed in the United States of America
Suggested Retail Price (SRP) $19.95

Cucina Tipica is printed in Georgia

To my father, Bob Cotto – the best man I know.

Acknowledgements

I'd like to thank my family, friends and other supporters of my writing over the years. Special thanks to those who encouraged me to finally write my "Italy book" and especially those who offered specific support of the effort: Christine Tidwell, Ken Golden, Dave Napoli, and Douglas Pinto. And extra-special thanks to CC Sofronas whose insightful suggestions and unbridled enthusiasm helped me, again and again, to keep the faith throughout the process. I'm also indebted to Leslie Schwartz and Lauren Deen for their generous professional advice and assistance.

Finally, I'd like to recognize all of my friends and acquaintances in Italy who inspired so much of this work.

Also by Andrew Cotto:

The Domino Effect

Outerborough Blues: A Brooklyn Mystery

Cucina Tipica

An Italian Adventure

"Our three basic needs, for food and security and love, are so mixed and mingled and entwined that we cannot straightly think of one without the others"

- M.F.K. Fisher, The Gastronomical Me

Chapter 1

Jacoby Pines arrived in the south of France with his fiancée of two years, six suitcases, and a secret from the previous century. He also had a hangover. Unable to get comfortable during the overnight flight from New York, his plastic cup was repeatedly filled with Burgundy by the Air France flight crew. Claire curled up next to him right after dinner service, and slept for the rest of the flight with her head propped on his shoulder. Five of the six suitcases, the leather Dunhills, belonged to her. Jacoby's piece of luggage was a crappy Samsonite filled with most of his clothes and a few other belongings, including his secret: a photograph from 1939.

On a bench in the parking lot of the Nice Airport, under a swimming pool sky, Jacoby tried to rub the nagging ache from his temples. Claire stood before him, erect and alert, her long hair, an auburn cascade spanning the slope of her slender back, blazed in the morning sun. She sucked a Gauloises down to its filter, flicked it to the curb and strutted, cocky as a house cat, into the rental car kiosk.

Through the window of the rental office, Jacoby watched Claire's hands flail as she spoke her fluent French, creasing quick smiles of charm and flashes of occasional impatience, pausing to toss her hair like a cape, gesturing towards the fleet of cars in the lot and the paperwork on the counter that connected her to a young male attendant whom she was surely turning to mush. Jacoby shook his head as Claire rolled out of the kiosk like a goddess of victory with her playful affectations on full parade. Jacoby was awed by her confidence and competence, not to mention her work ethic and ingenuity; he wasn't crazy about how dependent upon Claire he was, financially and emotionally, and especially since his recent collapse in New York that cost him his job and had brought them to Europe for what was to be a year abroad, of first escape and then recovery: both his. That was the plan, but he had the kind of doubts that kept people up at night, even after way too much wine.

•   •   •

Jacoby divided the suitcases between the trunk and the back seat of the sparkling, midnight blue, four-door Volkswagen Passat.

"So, whaddya think?" Claire asked as they settled into the leather seats and Jacoby aroused the purring engine before maneuvering through the parking lot. The new-car aroma was almost too much for his heightened sense of smell.

"Not bad, I guess," Jacoby said, adjusting to the feel of the standard transmission, slipping through the first few gears with ease. "If you're into, you know, really nice cars."

"Brand spanking new," she declared. "Just arrived from Germany yesterday. Or was it the day before..."

Jacoby laughed. And it really was an incredible car, feeling more BMW than Volkswagen to an American driver. The dashboard lit up like a rocket ship. The leather seats firm yet soft. The power and luxury inspired some adrenaline, which helped with his hangover.

"He wanted to give us a Ford Escort or something American," Claire continued. "Two-door. I told him that I was sorry, but considering the length of our arrangement, we needed an upgrade to the newest sedan in the lot or we'd simply take ourselves and our one-year of business elsewhere. I even threw in some absolute bullshit about choosing to rent in France over Italy due to our status as loyal Francophiles."

Claire smacked her thigh, and Jacoby smiled along with her silly pomp as he shifted into third, feeling the torque of the large engine made to European standards. They were getting along nicely, like they used to, and this soothed him some, eased his anxiety over the whole trip: his relationship with Claire, and his secret agenda with the hidden photograph.

"I can only hope you've taken care of your part of the planning with equal aplomb," Claire continued in her faux-majestic tone, touching Jacoby's forearm playfully, despite the decidedly un-playful manner in which she complained in the past about the renovated barn he'd rented for them in the hills just south of Florence, which Claire dubbed "no man's land" and nowhere near the area she wanted, 20 kilometers to the south in the heart of Chianti country where her English cousins had vacation homes in an area overrun by so many Brits that it was referred to sardonically as "Chiantishire."

Claire imagined some private apartment carved out of a Chiantishire villa, on a lush property with a communal pool and amenities (like laundry and Wi-Fi) and prepared meals made by local hands; a spot with easy access to a well-known village, equal distance to the cities of Siena and Florence. A Tuscan paradise.

Didn't work out that way. She'd put Jacoby in charge of finding a place, and he had generally chosen the hills directly south of Florence to avoid being neighbors with Claire's cousins and countrymen - he'd see plenty of them anyway - but his specific reason for renting in this area was the photograph recently found in a box of his mother's who had died when he was very young. He hadn't thought of her much when growing up, but her absence was present in the sadness that shaded his father; in the melancholy that tugged his face, slowed his walk, tempered his smile. He had died the previous summer from what Jacoby believed to be a 30-year case of broken heart blues.

Jacoby, the only child of an only child, handled all arrangements and matters of the estate, which were meager. His father was a fickle academic who moved them around a lot and never invested in property or saved much for retirement. He died in a cottage owned by the college in western Massachusetts where he'd been teaching classics for the past three years. And it was in that cottage, going through his father's things, that Jacoby found a small metal box which held some women's jewelry, letters too faded to read, and a worn photograph of a woman in an elegant dress furled out around her on the lawn of a grand estate. The back of the photo read: Villa Floria-Zanobini, 1939.

The metal box and its belongings were the only things Jacoby retained from the cottage. He gave the jewelry to Claire and kept the photograph to himself. It was all he had left, his inheritance. And when Claire, a travel writer, took an extended assignment in Italy a year later, he suddenly thought of the picture as more than inheritance: It was fate. Maybe.

Jacoby researched the name of the villa and found nothing: no family, no history, no address; only a reference on google maps to an unspecified location in the hills directly south of Florence. The area was definitely not a Tuscan paradise, only a smattering of small, unknown villages. The most luxurious accommodation Jacoby could find was a renovated barn behind a villa in the hills above a tiny village named Antella.

Claire hated the name of the village, and the idea of living in a barn; but she got over it for the most part as the trip loomed and other arrangements took focus, including a night in a swank hotel on the Italian Riviera she'd arranged for immediately after their arrival in Nice to pick up their car, which Jacoby steered toward the airport's exit, ignoring her quip about the barn and "equal aplomb."

Claire flipped off her flats and tucked her heels on the leather seat as she fished her phone from a Vuitton bag and attempted to program the GPS system. The airport's exit was marked with a maze of signs pointing to destinations in all possible directions. Claire punched away at her screen and cursed under her breath. Lack of cellular service made her bonkers. A car honked behind them. Jacoby lowered his window and motioned for it to go around.

"Christ," Claire muttered and poked away.

Jacoby resented Claire's impatience. To him, it was absurd and unproductive and the byproduct of privilege, though he had to recognize, painfully, that her impatience had increased in the months since he'd lost his job in spectacular fashion and failed to find another. The months he'd spent essentially in seclusion in Brooklyn, where his confidence faded and his rhythm faltered into a bleak morass which prompted the year they would spend in Italy as a way to change the scenery and inspire Jacoby to get his life together. The idea of a year abroad was amazing - not to mention ridiculously privileged - and Jacoby was grateful for Claire's support and inspiration, but he hated feeling like a charity chase. And he also feared how this was going to turn out if he couldn't get his shit together or find any long lost family in the hills south of Florence. Neither scenario seemed likely.

As Claire tapped at her cell phone, Jacoby scrambled to be of use.

"The highway runs along the coast, right?" he asked, turning his head toward the open window.

"Yes," Claire responded without looking up.

"Then it's that way," he said, motioning with his head to the left.

"How would you know?"

"I can smell the sea," he said with a modest shrug. "It's on the breeze coming from that direction."

Claire tossed her phone in the bag, faced Jacoby with a titled smile and wagged a single finger.

"You are an olfactory genius. Did I ever tell you that?"

"Once or twice," Jacoby said, feeling a bump of confidence as he released the clutch and shot the car down the exit ramp towards the crisp blue horizon over the Côte d'Azur.

It was a curious thing about Jacoby and Claire's relationship. Even though she was passionate about food and wrote about it often, the one who had eaten in some of the world's finest restaurants, he was the one with the fully developed palate, a gift of sorts he had for as long as he could remember but never really took notice of until Claire made such a fuss. His father liked fine food and loved to cook, so they took meals out together often and ate well at home, with wine at dinner since Jacoby entered high school, and these engagements were the most stable part of his adolescence, a regular experience of pleasure in an otherwise unpredictable and often lonely campaign; but, if forced to remember correctly, Jacoby could trace his first recognition of smell, and its connection to taste, to the Nabisco factory behind his childhood home, in the small hills beyond an open park that he would visit with his mother as a toddler. It was his only memory of her, not so much her appearance or her voice, but the pleasant aroma that lingered when they were together. And while he didn't consciously miss his mother, the smell of baking cookies always made him want to cry.

Chapter 2

"Whooooh!" Claire screamed as they joined the rushing traffic on the auto route which ran along the Riviera's French side.

Jacoby ratcheted up the gears and joined the flow. The road wound through the cliffs above the sea. It felt like a Grand Prix race event, with cars jockeying and rushing and blasting through the tunnels carved through the steep mountains. Claire kept her window down and her feet up on the dash as the wind had its way with her hair. Jacoby felt macho and European, shifting gears and switching lanes. His head began to clear.

The mid-morning, weekday traffic mellowed as they swept past resort towns officially still in the off-season, past the fairyland of Monaco. Claire soon tired of the road rally and curled up in her seat for a nap. Having been raised between London and Manhattan, Claire didn't like driving. She had a license, but never a car. When they went places on weekends, usually to the second homes of her city friends on the North Fork of Long Island or in the upper Hudson Valley, Jacoby arranged the rental car and did the driving, much of it while Claire slept, as she did now - while crossing the border from France into San Remo on the Riviera's Italian side. At least she didn't sit in the back.

Within an hour, cruising at a high speed along the Italian Autostrada, curling around the coast, past beckoning port cities of Savona and Genoa, Jacoby took the lone exit for Rapallo. He admired the baroque facades of faded pastel buildings that lined the quiet streets canopied by towering palms and umbrella pines. Slowed to a speed for observing, his first hard look at the beauty of Italy excited him so profoundly his teeth began to chatter. It seemed surreal - so casually spectacular.

Signs for the Excelsior Palace Hotel led to a tree-shrouded cliff under the horizon. After many stops and quick turns, the humming Passat with a sleeping passenger and a wide-eyed driver entered the hotel's property and maneuvered up a winding drive bordered by Cypress trees toward a majestic palace that yawned toward the sky. At the top of the drive, a box-hedged parking lot awaited, manned by a valet in a formal coat and top hat. Jacoby, awed by the depth of the hedge's green below the sapphire sky, dazzled by fatigue and pulsing awe, lost track of his feet and fumbled with the clutch as the tires crackled over the surface of sea stones. He panicked for a moment but recaptured his faculties, keeping the clutch in as the car rolled to a stop near the valet stand, where he, with great focus and attention to breath, turned off the ignition, slipped the gear-shift into first, and jammed the emergency brake. It felt like a moon landing. He inhaled and exhaled slowly, then gently shook Claire's leg.

"We made it," he said. "We're here."

Claire snapped from her snooze and stared through the passenger window, her eyes blooming like morning glories.

"Oh my God," she sighed. "So beautiful."

The lobby was wide and polished, of marble and light and mirrors. It smelled of flowers and citrus. The far end of the room was almost entirely of glass. Below the cliffs, the sea spread towards the horizon beyond a perched terrace and pool area. A jagged path led down to a small, stone beach. As Claire checked in, Jacoby stood by the wide windows and tried to make sense of the view. His rapid blinks could not alter the magnificence of what was before him. The light, in particular, seemed surreal, unfiltered, extending over everything. So peaceful. So beautiful was this world. He was afraid to move or it all might disappear.

Something poked the back of his knee. Jacoby broke from his

trance and turned around. Claire held the room key in one hand and a giant cellophane wrapped basket in the other.

"A gift from Mum," she said, her voice slipping into a selective British accent.

A handsome, uniformed bell hop stood behind her, their bags stacked neatly on a carriage.

"Shall we?" Claire asked.

Their room, on the top floor, was modern and modest in every respect except for when the curtains were drawn to reveal a staggering view of the property below and beyond, of cliffs and trees and hard blue sea. Claire snatched an ashtray from a night stand beside the double bed and slipped outside while Jacoby found the glistening bathroom, which he put to use, including his first encounter with a bidet. He came out shirtless and ready to pronounce his affinity for European bathrooms to Claire who sat on the bed in her red bikini, one of her five suitcases opened on the floor with its contents strewn around the carpet.

She tore open the cellophane with a sharp incisor and dumped the bounty of the basket on the bed cover: a bottle of Prosecco, vacuum-sealed prosciutto and cheese, olives, dried lemons and fresh figs.

Jacoby twisted off the seal on the Prosecco and eased out the cork. Pop! It hit the ceiling as suds roiled over the lip. He handed the bottle to Claire who quickly brought it to her mouth.

They ate with their hands and drank from the bottle, leaving stains and crumbs on the bed sheets, which Claire attempted to clear before removing her bikini bottom and crawling on top of Jacoby to kiss his neck and chest as he unfastened and lowered his pants, using his feet to remove them as Claire snapped off her bikini top and fell on him in a once familiar manner.

Jacoby considered Claire very sexy. Never a fan of boobs - which he found cumbersome and clumsy - Jacoby adored what Claire called her "pecs" and especially how she often displayed them through an opened-third button of a dress shirt or plunging neckline or barely covered in a bikini top that could fit most tweens. Claire in exercise gear of spandex tights and half shirt with her midriff exposed was often too much for him to bear.

The session in their hotel room above the cliffs of Rapallo was particularly vigorous and equally as rapid. It was the first time they'd had sex in a long time, and Jacoby felt a strong sense of relief at having bridged that gap. He also felt really tired - the physical and emotional exhaustion of someone who'd been drinking too much and sleeping too little not just the previous night but for the previous months - and as Claire climbed from the bed, sleep covered him like a cape.

He dreamed a familiar dream: a recollection of the actual moment, at home in Brooklyn, sitting on the side of his bed in his underwear, when he realized a text message he'd intended for a coworker had been sent to his entire team, including his new boss, who was the subject of a barb that in a rational world would be considered inappropriate and maybe unfortunate, but - in a hyper-sensitized, outraged America - destroyed his career and reputation. In his dream, still in his underwear, bedside at home while Claire snoozed behind him, Jacoby is besieged by a mob of social justice activists who would have once, and rightfully so, considered him one of their own. And before they pounce, just before he always shudders awake from his nightmare, Jacoby notices his father off to the side of the mob, in the corner of his bedroom, looking forlorn, as if his perpetual melancholy wasn't from being a widower but from his only child being a disgrace.

It was mid-afternoon when Jacoby awoke naked and alone in the room in Rapallo. He'd been asleep for three hours, though it felt like three days. The dream was still fresh in his memory, but it hadn't jarred him from sleep this time. He used the bathroom and Claire's toiletries spilled around the sink to brush his teeth and comb his dark brown hair, flipping the thick bangs sideways off his forehead and running his hands around the sides and down his neck, where phantom length still existed from his halcyon-hair days as a musician. He hadn't really looked closely at himself in a while. His lithe, hairless upper body, devoid of excess, showing muscle and bone, dappled with freckles, still held the form of an accomplished high school soccer and lacrosse player. People often thought Claire - four years his junior -

was older than him, which in some ways she was, at least in the ways that appeared to matter.

In the main room, sunlight gathered under the hem and around the edges of the curtains in front of the patio door. Jacoby separated them to the Technicolor world outside. Fishing boats were anchored just off the seaside cliffs. White birds circled the shoreline. Down below, on the hotel property, Claire was obvious in her red bikini on a chaise-lounge poolside, a magazine held with both hands. Jacoby pulled a pair of cut-off shorts and a fresh white V-neck T from his suitcase and went shoe-less into the carpeted hallway and rode the mirrored elevator to the shining lobby from where he followed signs for the "Piscina e Mare" that led him through a glass-framed corridor toward the "Pool and Sea" over a small gorge and into an adjacent structure that opened to the type of tranquility featured in upscale travel magazines or in ads for products purchased by the rich and beautiful.

The salty breeze blew back Jacoby's bangs and filled his nose. He wanted a dozen oysters. And sunglasses. He squinted against the brilliant light to reach Claire's side, next to the infinity pool, away from the shade of umbrella pines, immersed in a magazine while upright on a chaise, her soles together and her spine straight.

"Hey, baby," she said, before returning to her pages, which she flicked impatiently. "Such rot."

The blue, blue sea beyond the infinity pool was far more interesting to Jacoby than Claire's assessment of her contemporaries' work, so he wandered off towards a rocky path that staggered down to an empty cove below the cliffs. The stones hurt his feet, but he paddled on towards a smooth boulder that extended above the water. He took off his shirt and dove into the green-apple sea. Emerald light slanted through the clear water as he churned through the depths and onto the surface towards a wooden pallet floating 30 yards offshore. He glided on the buoyant water, soothed by its cool clutch. On the pallet, he faced the shoreline of high cliffs, the sun and wind drying the brackish water on his back. He blinked and breathed, listened to the rustle of the sea, feeling its gentle pull. Jacoby reclined onto the hot planks, closed his eyes and considered the contrast of the cool, cool water on his feet with the heat on his back and the sunshine on his face.

Sea birds screeched. Small waves lapped the sides of the pallet. Tourist boats skimmed the waters offshore. It felt like a dream, soft and serene. An image of Jacoby's mother began to emerge, a fantastic one of her in Italy, at the age of the actual woman in the picture hidden in his suitcase - a young woman playing with a toddler Jacoby in a meadow behind a villa. A connection to the photograph's history and significance began to take shape in Jacoby's imagination. Of course the woman in the photo wasn't his mother - it was dated 1939, more than a decade before her birth - but the woman in the photo could have been another relative, something he had assumed possible all along but had no real emotional significance until now, present in Italy with the sun of potential ancestors on his face and a sense of familial love warming him. He had no family left, as far as he knew for sure - his father being the last living relative that Jacoby recognized - and this was something he had somewhat successfully avoided since his father's passing, but the new reality of his orphan status, as if triggered by his firing in New York, lurked near his surface and even struck literally at times in panicked bursts of abandonment and isolation. And he fought off desolation by holding on to the fantastic idea that this trip to Italy was not merely serendipity but fate, a fate that would deliver him from the sense of displacement and disconnect which haunted him in modern New York and modern America, a baffling place of absurd politics and debased culture and rampant injustice: a place where he didn't feel welcome or wanted at all. It was like America had lost its mind, and while many were outraged and inspired to activism - and rightfully so - some of those without a firm sense of personal or national identity were sent spiraling adrift. Unemployment jacked Jacoby's plight. And maybe, just maybe, Italy was his place of redemption. He felt something already. Something beckoning and kind.

A familiar whistle, like a rock through a hot house window, shattered his magical thinking of salvation in Italy. He shot up. Claire swaggered down the path, her skin kissed by a few hours of sun, a sarong wrapped around her midriff, a coquettish purse to her lips. He'd kept this secret history from Claire, though he wasn't sure why. She stopped on the rock by the water's edge and made like a fisherman, casting her line at Jacoby and slowly reeling him in, her head down and eyes up, hips cocked to one side.

Jacoby knew what she wanted, and was happy to oblige. But he also sensed in a blinding moment of clarity that their love was faltering; that they might not last the year away together. And after the collapse, he would have no one, and nowhere to go, unless somehow the picture delivered him home.

•   •   •

That evening Jacoby and Claire walked into town in the rose hue of a seaside twilight. The last remnants of day gathered in the sky as darkness sifted down on the narrow streets of the regal seaport. Claire had read about a hole-in-the-wall seafood osteria near a marina by the hotel. The boats were all moored or on their way in from sea, flanked by seagulls and swallows. Jacoby smelled fish being filleted. A few turns and misturns inland, down a dark alley, through a low and arched doorway, local catch from the Tyrrhenian Sea was served on wooden tabletops covered in dark butcher's paper.

They sat at a shifted table in the dingy room among the indifferent locals and took a basket of lightly fried calamari, shrimp, bream and whole anchovy seasoned with salt and lemon followed by a pureed and garlicky fish soup, then steamed prawns dipped in aioli, grilled sardines, plates of pasta with pesto and plates of pasta with clams. They washed it all down with carafes of a local white wine known as Vermentino.

Even though Claire was intrigued by the place for a potential story, she did not - much to Jacoby's absolute delight - engage in her routine of announcing her intentions to the owner, chatting up patrons and staff, snapping pictures of the place and pictures of each plate, which she would post on Instagram, and generally make a show of things (while Jacoby sat there feeling like a tool). Jacoby hated those nights when their meals were interrupted by Claire's ambition and need to share.

They shared the meal of seafood by the seaside in the Rapallo back alley as completely as possible, holding hands under and above the table, kissing frequently, filling each other's glasses, sharing cigarettes outside, and laughing throughout the two hours of slow and utter indulgence. It was the type of moment when Jacoby's love for Claire was pure. When he got her and she got him; when nobody else mattered. They were alone, together. It assuaged Jacoby's fear and filled him with hope.

With the check, hand written on a napkin, the owner - a brusque man in a fish-stained apron - brought them a large piece of lemon cake with slivered almonds and congratulated them on their love.

They lurched home like honeymooners, drunk on love and just drunk. They passed out atop the bed covers and were woken by maid service who came to clean the room at 11:00 the next morning, prompting a harried check out and tardy departure for the hills south of Florence, where they would be late for a meeting with their new landlord in their new home that Jacoby had arranged for the year.

Chapter 3

Jacoby found the highway and jetted through the Ligurian inlands, away from the coast into the wild regions of northern Tuscany, through plains bordered by marble streaked mountains, past spa towns with sulfur baths perched on lofted peaks, and into the ramparts of greater Florence province where verdant hillsides were spotted with villas and lined with grape vines and shimmering olive groves that hid the sunken city from view. It was hard to imagine that a major city was so close to such a lush and rolling landscape. Jacoby liked it already; it felt like hidden treasure. He sensed a new beginning and a semblance of home.

Claire had spent the car ride diligently going through her composition notebooks, the ones meticulously filled by her flowing left-handed script, using her beloved Japanese pens in various colors, with information on all of their upcoming excursions throughout central Italy. Jacoby admired her preparedness, especially in this manner that was so old school. She had all the content scanned, of course, but still - just the point of a thoroughly modern woman engaged in such an antiquated act gave Jacoby a nice throw-back thrill.

Still high from their "honeymoon" night and the prospects of their new environs – Jacoby savored the adoration he could feel for his fiancée and remembered the wonder she was occasionally able to inspire, which began with their unlikely first meeting, a moment of serendipity that would change Jacoby's life.

•   •   •

Jacoby didn't want to go the Meetup in Midtown his PR agency hosted for travel writers. He handled music for the firm, using gravitas and contacts from his previous life as the guitarist in a well-known Boston band to secure a nice stable of music venues and festivals and record labels that outsourced their PR efforts. Travel was not his territory. He hated Meetups. Intimacy, one-on-one meetings, worked best for him, and he did well with clients over slow meals, long nights at music venues, the occasional round of golf or tennis match, cordial phone conversations and witty email exchanges. He could hang all day or all night; he just didn't like doing so in crowds. Everyone watching each other, jockeying for attention or eager for gossip. It made him crazy. Felt like high school. As a musician, Jacoby loved gigs but hated the fawning fans at the bar afterward who thought he was someone special because he could play guitar and shake his ass at the same time. His band mates ragged on Jacoby's reluctance to take all the action available to an attractive guitarist in a college town. Jacoby was no saint; he just found one night stands awkward and preferred women who didn't like musicians.

Jacoby had to attend the travel Meetup because his colleague, a recent Oberlin grad who handled travel and food, had hit a pop-up stand in a Chinatown back alley specializing in pork belly buns and ended up hospitalized with what doctors at NYU Medical Center suspected was the first case of trichinosis on American shores in over 30 years. Jacoby was tapped as her replacement and the reluctant co-host of the event. Oy. His soul churned as he stood at the entrance welcoming guests with a humiliating name tag stuck to his chest and a fake grin on his face until, near the events merciful ending, a stunning red head swept past him in knee-torn jeans and a Lily Pulitzer top. There was an ever-so-momentary pause in the clamorous room, as if everyone had noticed her at once, like a bride's first appearance in a chapel, before the event's swing resumed and the momentary object of everyone's attention abruptly stopped, spun around and approached Jacoby with a finger wagging and her mouth opened to an astonished smile. Jacoby's anus tightened and a streak of sweat crossed his neck and hairline as his feet seemed to lose contact with the ground.

"You were in that band!" she announced. "You boinked my friend!"

Jacoby knew who she was talking about; he blushed from embarrassment at his hypocrisy and her language.

But it was there, in that moment, hypocrisy and language aside, at the not-so-tender age of 31, that Jacoby Pines had his first encounter with the wonder that had eluded him through his motherless childhood and itinerant adolescence. He never had a home town, as his father chased elusive tenure-track teaching posts up and down the eastern seaboard, settling and resettling in small towns and cities where Jacoby enjoyed the trimmings of public and private schools but never the passion. He was the perpetual outsider, even after the requisite years of working his way into acceptance; at which point they'd usually move anyway, right after he found the boys he could confide in and the girl he thought he could love.

This emotional disconnect - it's subtle exclusivity - followed him into college where he was a somewhat spectral presence around the Emerson College campus, haunting more Boston music venues than college bars or house parties. He liked a lot of college kids but not really college life. Being a musician in a musician's town, though, connected him to an alt-rock diva from the New England Conservatory of Music and her expert rhythm section, and they embarked on an adventurous, post-collegiate, decade-long journey filled with promise but never full actuation, an eventual record deal with very little record sales. The disappointment of it felt inevitable to Jacoby. He liked his band mates very much, but he was not a musician's musician. Not of their tribe and willing to endure at any cost.

Convinced that life as an artist of any sort in the 21st century held little hope for life above the poverty line, Jacoby left the band and cut his hair, taking his Bachelor's degree in Communications, life experience, music contacts, and interpersonal skills to New York for a new gig as a PR person that provided much-needed stability yet very little magic until Claire St. James, a beautiful and revered travel writer, a younger woman of hypnotic presence, swept across the room which she owned at the moment to stand too close to Jacoby and fawn over him for the rest of the night and make him feel – for the very first time, at the not-so-tender age of 31 – what is was like to be awed by the wonder of being alive.

And it was the dizzying wonder Claire inspired that night which led, ten months later, to a Spring proposal - broached by the bride-to-be who would wear no ring - and a late September engagement party at Cipriani's in Manhattan, lorded over by Claire's fabulously wealthy and affected mother, an English travel writer of great renown, where guests of the bride-to-be outnumbered guests of the future groom by, at least, a 20 -1 margin. But who was counting?

Jacoby moved into Claire's Fort Greene floor-through in a Brooklyn brownstone where the engaged couple struggled to come up with a wedding date or maintain a marital-like bliss, especially after the death of Jacoby's father, which was followed the next year by his being fired under shameful circumstances. After six months of unemployment, frequent bickering and genuine concern about Jacoby's emotional health and employment potential (not to mention his lack of interest in socializing and sex), Claire decided the remedy to their woes, and his in particular, would be delivered by a year in Italy, where she would write and Jacoby would prepare himself for a big comeback in New York. And this year abroad would all begin with a stay on the Italian Riviera before arrival at their temporary home - that Jacoby had arranged and Claire resented - in the unfettered hills just south of Florence.

•   •   •

At the Firenze Sud exit of the Autostrada, Jacoby nudged Claire, and she put her notebooks away and put on a quaint smile. She rested her fingers on Jacoby's forearm and studied the countryside as he shifted gears on a rural road towards their new home in the immediate hills. The road was bordered by grape vines, twisted and gnarled, but still manicured. Faded Fascist-era buildings spotted the foreground. They passed a bleak hospital and a shuttered gas station. Claire slouched a little in her seat. Jacoby started to suspect why this area was not on the map.

He downshifted into a turn that curved around a park and fed into the small village of Antella. A narrow road bordered an empty piazza with a statue of a man in the middle and rimmed with small shops closed for the afternoon respite. The church bells at the far end bonged three times, and Jacoby navigated the perimeter road to zip past the church and up the hill beyond the village that swooned with olive groves. Smoke billowed from a roadside farm house in the sparse Tuscan countryside that opened before them. Claire sat up when they breached a ridge and the immediate skyline of Florence appeared as out of nowhere. Jacoby trolled the ridge road, lined with high walls and overgrowth, searching for a cement arch past a cluster of small shops and a Casa di Popolo. He slowed and turned on a pitched dirt road jabbed with stones. The car bounced beside an Etruscan wall strung with drapes of rosemary, buzzing with insects. A valley to their right was sown with red poppies among knee-high wild grass. It was beautiful. Isolated villas appeared beyond the cypress trees high on both sides of the valley. Jacoby stopped in front of a high wooden fence and got out. Claire joined him. They held hands and looked around. A wide terracotta roof hung above the trees beyond the fence. The air smelled of wood smoke. Jacoby took a half-breath and pushed a button on the side of the fence.

A rifle shot exploded across the valley.

"What the hell was that?" Claire asked, squeezing Jacoby's hand, panic flushing her face.

Jacoby shrugged and tried to appear calm as he pushed the button again. He knew what a shotgun sounded like from his years living on Maryland's eastern shore where duck hunting was one of the pastimes. He wondered what they hunted in the hills above Antella.

Probably not duck.

Claire got back in the car. They waited, separately, in the silence. The environment seemed to shiver around them, alive and beautiful yet unfamiliar. A viper slithered across the dusty road. Jacoby pushed the button again, glad Claire hadn't seen the serpent. Finally, a voice called out, from over the fence.

"Allo? Allo? Ja-co-bey?"

"Yes! Paolo. It's me. It's me. It's us."

Relief flushed through him as the door shuddered and then lurched open mechanically, moving in toward the property, where a short, rock-strewn driveway ramped up to a thatched carport behind a stone barn. To the right was a modest villa with a Spanish-tiled roof, faded-pastel facade and big red shutters. Ivy scrawled down the side. A high, solid fence of fresh-cut wood separated the barn from where a dog barked with ferocity on the other side.

An elderly man with no hair and bright eyes stepped forward, work gloves stuffed in the tweed cap he held which matched his elegant work clothes.

Jacoby shook Paolo's calloused hand. The older man bowed slightly and clasped Jacoby on the shoulder with thick, dexterous fingers.

"I am sorry," he said with measured words. "I am in my trees. Cutting."

He gestured toward the olive grove beyond the barn and produced a pruning shear from his back pocket as evidence.

"It's OK," Jacoby assured him. "I'm sorry we're late."

Claire got out of the car, smiling as she approached.

"Buongiorno, Paolo," she chimed. "Sono Claire St. James. È un piacere incontrarlei."

They shook hands.

"Tank you," Paolo said slowly and turned back to Jacoby. "You wife?"

"Yes. No," he said. "Claire is my fiancée. We will be married. She speaks Italian."

"Fidanzata," Claire proudly translated 'fiancée.

Paolo nodded and motioned toward the carport, speaking slowly to Jacoby in his broken English.

"That is the place for you car. The barn door is open on other side. The key is in the door. I leave things for you on the table. There is bell by the fence. Make it when you need for me. And do not have fear of the dog. He only for albanesi."

Claire got back in the car and slammed the door. Paolo didn't seem to notice.

"OK," Jacoby said. "Thank you so much."

"And you can meet with me for dinner tonight. At the hour eighteen. Use the bell. Bring you wife."

Paolo lumbered up the drive, putting on his hat and gloves and disappearing behind the barn into the grove beyond a staircase of stone under a plunging fig tree. The dog stopped barking.

Jacoby got back in the car and bumped up the track to the carport. Claire didn't speak. She stayed where she was and brooded, cross-armed, as Jacoby unloaded their belongings, dragging them two at time across the terracotta terrace to the small patio in front of the barn's entrance, marked by a metal table and four matching chairs. A non-functioning fountain adorned a structural stone wall near the stairway leading to the olive grove. The barn doors were ancient and ornate and well-maintained. They opened on both sides, revealing glass doors that allowed light to veil a round table in an open area that fronted a small kitchen behind a wooden counter. Exposed roof beams crossed the ceiling. There were two stairs to a side room and a spiral staircase in the far corner that twisted towards the upper level.

Jacoby sighed and let the relief wash through him. He'd been fearful that the barn would be a dump and that Claire would refuse to live there. But it looked just like the photos Paolo's son, a banker who worked in New York, had shared on his iPad over lunch with Jacoby in Midtown. They looked at pictures of the barn before the renovation and after, and spoke of Paolo's status as a retired widower who tended to his olive trees and kept to himself. There was no mention of the dog. Or hunters. Or danger from Albanians. The down payment of only one month's rent was provided, and the lease was signed during dessert.

Jacoby opened the glass doors and left them parted to allow in fresh air as he fetched Claire from the passenger's seat. Annoyed by not only having to live in no man's land but on the property of a bigot and sexist for a landlord, she scowled when Jacoby opened her door and extended his hand, but she took it with a reluctant huff. The fig tree caught her eye, as did the small balcony outside the closed wooden doors above the entrance. They entered. Claire's eye sought imperfections: tacky decor, unacceptable conditions; but the room was sparse and functional. The table was strewn with a welcome of local products: a capped fiasco of ruby red wine, a shank of prosciutto, a round of fresh Pecorino cheese, cured sausage, fresh figs, a box of podded fava beans, and a glistening decanter of olive oil. The room to the side, where Claire would work, had a Formica desk on shiny, wide planks of oak, a couch, and tons of light. The spiral staircase was solid and functional. Upstairs, Claire fingered the fine linens on the king-sized bed before opening the doors to the Juliette balcony and a sun-splashed olive grove. Paolo waived from a ladder leaning into a gnarled branch adorned with leaves shimmering green-gray. Just beyond that hill lay the city of Florence.

Downstairs, the suitcases had been brought in by Jacoby and a small feast hastily arranged on the table. Jacoby felt like a real estate agent trying to please a reluctant buyer.

"How do you like him now?" Jacoby asked with a curious smile as Claire descended the spiral staircase after her thorough inspection of the upstairs.

"Oh, he's a sexist and racist, that's for sure," Claire said. "And I'll have nothing to do with him, but he does do nice work. And the food looks amazing."

"What should I tell him about dinner?"

"Tell him that I have to prepare for a trip, or won't he believe that I'm the one who actually works?"

Claire could be cruel when on the defensive, though Jacoby understood. She was an accomplished woman who did not deserve slights, yet she was often objectified or underestimated, to which she, rightfully, took issue, though her reactions - to Jacoby - seemed inflated and loaded with darts aimed at the undeserving, especially him of late, which he would try to deflect with deprecation or dash.

"I'll tell him that you've stayed home to iron my underwear and unpack my bags," he said with his hands out and a salesman's smile. It occurred to Jacoby that his sense of humor was returning.

"Perfect," Claire said with a small yet conciliatory smile. "Do that."

Chapter 4

They spent the afternoon unpacking and familiarizing themselves with the functions of the barn, including the bed, which led to a nap interrupted by the clanging of the bell. Jacoby dressed quickly in jeans and an un-tucked oxford, and, from the terrace, motioned down to Paolo that he would be there momentarily. A plume of wood smoke, infused by rosemary, billowed from beyond the fence.

Jacoby went next door alone. He explained that Claire had to leave early in the morning for an assignment, which was true; and that she was tired from all the travel, which was not. Paolo shrugged and welcomed Jacoby within his fence. After a vigorous sniffing from the giant German Sheppard, the guard dog laid down in the shadows of a long wooden table under a canvas umbrella in the center of a terracotta terrace. Around the periphery, potted lemon trees dangled fledgling fruit. A hot house bordered the property's far end. Gardening equipment leaned against a stone wall beneath a hedge of rosemary which sequestered the terrace from the fields beyond. A wood burning oven bordered the fence that separated the barn from the villa.

In the fading light, the villa was dark. The back door was open, a light on somewhere deep inside. Jacoby sensed that he was not welcome in the big house. Paolo motioned towards the outdoor oven and handed Jacoby a thick branch of rosemary, which he was instructed to insert into the flaming mouth. A renewed aroma of piney-herb rose from the oven along with the crackling and snapping sound of licking flames devouring wood. Jacoby noticed a foil-sealed tin tucked inside the oven, away from the direct heat.

A flour-dusted marble counter secured to the side of the oven held an assortment of products for making pizza. Paolo led Jacoby over and demonstrated his technique, rolling out a rounded ball of dough into a disc which he ladled with tomato puree and adorned with strips of fresh mozzarella torn from a ball removed from salted water. He then sprinkled pitted black olives on top and carefully distributed anchovy fillets. The pie was lifted from the counter with a wooden pizza peel and shoveled into the center of the oven.

Paolo smiled at Jacoby and assigned him, through a cupping motion with his hands, the task of making the next pizza.

"Pronto. Pronto," he said. "We have two minute only."

Jacoby hurried his way through an oblong disaster while Paolo disappeared behind the hothouse for a handful of basil stems before slipping the first pizza from the oven and putting it on a cutting board centered on the wooden table. He anointed the pizza with olive oil and a pinch of red pepper flakes before finishing with a confetti of basil leaves snipped with kitchen scissors. Paolo sliced the pizza into quarters and poured red wine from an unmarked bottle.

The crust snapped between Jacoby's teeth as his mouth flooded with a blend of familiar flavors ratcheted by freshness and perfect balance. The anchovies and olives added an element of tang. The ruby wine washed it all down with rounded fruit up front and a hint of spice at the finish.

"Amazing," Jacoby said.

Paolo nodded.

"What kind of wine is this?"

"Our wine," he said, talking with his mouth full. "From the church."

"What church?"

Paolo pointed toward the fading horizon in the west. "For the village, there is a cooperative, a place was once a church, on a hill, where we make the wine, the oil, the other prodotti. You will help with the harvest?"

"Sure."

"You will see then."

Jacoby ate more pizza, inspired by the romantic idea of a harvest and the amazing quality of the flavors he enjoyed. He wanted to find an excuse to get Claire, to share this treasure. The lights were on upstairs in the barn, and they could hear drawers opening and closing, smell the occasional waft of cigarette smoke. Paolo paid no notice. And, ultimately, Jacoby did not want - despite the extraordinary meal - to expose Claire to marginalization. He would, sadly, not be able to make dining with Paolo a regular event, but he also sensed - with or without Claire - this was a one-time offering. The big, new fence was there for a reason.

The pizza that Jacoby made looked like an aborted version of the one produced earlier. Too much sauce left the crust soggy, throwing off the balance. They fed most of it to the dog. Paolo patted Jacoby's hand and smiled. He handed him a newspaper and directed its distribution over the tabletop. Jacoby, curious, performed his task while Paolo returned to the oven with the pizza peel and retrieved the covered tin, which he carefully carried to the table to set down. Wearing thick oven mitts, he removed the foil. A plume of heavily scented steam arose from a cornucopia of meats and root vegetables and herbs. Paolo dumped the tin onto the table. Jacoby's taste buds sluiced with carnivorous splendor. Paolo stripped a thick rosemary sprig and let the leaves fall on top. He anointed with fresh olive oil and sprinkled with coarse salt flakes.

"Misto arrosto," he said. "Mixed roast. From the village macelleria."

Paying a visit to the village butcher became a top priority. A sense of tortured anticipation seeped over him as Paolo left to secure plates and silverware from inside the villa as Jacoby sat on his hands, overwhelmed by the vision in front of him and its killer aroma. Paolo put the frenzied dog inside and returned with dining ware and bread from a loaf that he tore into thick pieces and dropped on the table. He slowly poured more wine and raised his glass.

"Salute," he toasted to health. "And welcome."

Jacoby nearly smashed both glasses with his enthusiasm.

The two men set upon pieces of roasted lamb, sausage, rabbit, liver in caul fat, guinea hen, halved-potatoes, heads of garlic, caramelized carrot and fennel. The bread, spread with softened garlic and swiped through the juices was almost as phenomenal as the tender meats coated in the balm of aromatics. The wine proved its versatility as an accompaniment. In the silence, as darkness sifted down, they finished the entire mixed roast and went through two bottles of wine.

They took local grappa for dessert.

Jacoby felt as peaceful and inspired as he had in months. Maybe ever. The best two meals of his life had been had over the first two days in Italy. The country itself was more beautiful than pictures could capture. The people spoke a lovely language and wore elegant clothes. It was all good. And he wanted in.

.   .   .

When Jacoby got home, Claire was asleep, snoring slightly. Two of her bags were ready for the upcoming trip; the rest of her stuff neatly tucked away in the antique furnishings. Jacoby slipped one of her cigarettes from the pack and went out to the far side of the barn to blow smoke at the black sky rung with stars, trees quivering around him. The earth seemed to move, as if he could feel it growing, shifting, restless. A rustle and grunt came from the darkness, just beyond the hedge. The beastly sound increased in volume and proximity. The hedge shook. Jacoby - high on food and wine and well-being - didn't register the enormous danger. He snuffed out the cigarette and went inside to arrange his own belongings for their three-day excursion into Umbria and Le Marche, which would begin the next morning.

Chapter 5

Claire was a very successful freelance writer. She constantly pitched and frequently scored assignments for major magazines and popular websites. She wrote about travel with an emphasis on food. Continental junkets to fabulous places - New Orleans, Miami, Northern California, Vancouver - were frequent. In New York, she was a regular contributor to *The New York Times'* Metropolitan section. Her own blog, Girl in Brooklyn, drew heavy traffic and many comped meals at places both hip and established, anxious for her digital blessing. She'd appeared twice on as many Food Network TV shows. She worshipped Anthony Bourdain and one day aspired to follow his model, traveling the world with a camera and crew to eat and explore every corner, though she still seemed, at age 28, most inspired by New York.

The job in Italy would be her first step to broader territory. She took it on contract, a paid ambassador of the British travel guide Haxby's, started in the 70's by Alistair Haxby, a moneyed Londoner with wanderlust and a terrific appetite. *Haxby's Guide* was published all over the world and considered the bible of European excursions focused on haute accommodations and gourmet cuisine. Claire's mother had been one of their primary correspondents (and its first female one) for 30 years, and the young Claire - during her childhood in London - often accompanied her mother on trips throughout the continent, eating and sleeping well in major cities and resort towns.

Claire's assignment in Italy differed. The guide, in need to adapt to a world with a shrinking population of super wealthy, was to publish an alternative, online guide dedicated to a more rustic experience, one still aimed at financially successful clientele, but featuring places where one could stay and eat well at more reasonable rates, destinations slightly off the gilded path that could offer exemplary stay and dining experiences to the new-money types of Asia and America and Europe who didn't necessarily need high thread counts and fine china, but wanted to eat well and stay well in places where others have not yet been. It was the new frontier of high-end travel. Less pomp; more circumstance. Jacoby called it four-star slumming.

Claire was anxious to please and eager to begin. She did all her own exhaustive research, reading magazines and travel blogs, filling her notebooks with names and notes and addresses. She was after the unexplored, the hidden gems of central Italy, which would not be easy to discover since central Italy, especially Tuscany, had been explored plenty. But Jacoby had faith. Whip smart and well-educated, Claire's determination and professionalism were just as impressive as her pedigree. She fought and fought and went down swinging on those occasions in which she didn't triumph. Her notebooks overflowed with places to visit in central Italy, so much so, that Claire, in her ambition, had arranged their first excursion to begin the day after arrival in the hills south of Florence.

The morning light was lemon-tinged and soothing. After packing the car, Jacoby wandered into the grove of birch trees on the property's edge, near a listing shed, from where he'd heard the grunting noise the night before. At the base of the trees were rounded holes, clearly the work of a large and nocturnal forager with a serious snout. He thought to ask Paolo about it but not hip Claire to the fact that grunting beasts hung around their new backyard.

The work plan in Italy was for Jacoby to accompany Claire on her excursions, not just as her driver but more importantly as her counsel. An expert and additional opinion on the quality of the places they visited and especially the quality of the food and wine offered

(Jacoby's specialty). Claire lovingly called Jacoby her "Royal Taster" and "Her Man with the Golden Palate" and on blue occasions of double entendre, her "Magic Tongue." Jacoby didn't mind. He loved food and wine (and cunnilingus) and didn't feel condescended to whatsoever, though the reality of the Italian trip - his role and its need in the first place - still played on his insecurities since he had - inadvertently - brought them there.

Jacoby was fired for a crude work-related text, sent too late at night, to the wrong people. The text was a joke, intended for a singular audience - a close work friend - but received by many - his entire work team - including the object of a barb who just happened to be Jacoby's new boss - a flamboyant Persian from Los Angeles, the spoiled nephew of the wealthy Iranian who had recently acquired the firm - who had tried to assert his professional authority and sexual identity throughout their first team meeting via the insistent refrain that he was the "new cocksucker in charge."

The meeting was a disaster. Everyone left late and angry and worried about losing their job. Jacoby hurried to meet Claire for dinner at a new whiskey bar / barbecue joint in Bushwick, where he finished Claire's brisket sandwich, ate a piece of shoo-fly-pie and downed two-flights of new American rye as Claire made eyes with the pearl-buttoned guitarist of a newfangled honkytonk outfit. They arrived home after midnight, Jacoby with a sour stomach and a spinning head, annoyed with everyone and everything. It wasn't until he crawled into bed that he noticed the text from the new boss that had arrived at 10:00 p.m., insisting upon the presence of the entire team in the office at 8:00 a.m. the following morning.

Jacoby, now beyond annoyed, fumbled with his phone, shooting off a text intended solely to his openly gay work friend whose direct authority had been usurped by the new boss.

I prefer the old cocksucker :)

The next morning, Jacoby awoke to a curt text from his new boss advising him not to report to work and to wait on word from Human Resources. His hands shook as he scrolled through the texts in his boxers on the bedside, as Claire quietly snored, uncovering the trail of his awful mistake. "Oh, no. Oh, no. Oh, no. Oh, no. Oh, no," he babbled under his breath. He'd been disappointed by life many times - broken up with or told "no" or informed by his father that they would be moving once again or reminded in small and frequent ways that his mother had died when he was very young - but this was his first experience with visceral rejection and staggering regret. A sledge hammer between the eyes. His pores opened and burned across his hairline and the back of his neck. His throat clamped shut. A small animal with sharp claws clutched the inside his chest. His father had died the prior summer, and Jacoby had struggled ever since with the loneliness and insecurity of being an orphan, of being without relations anywhere on the planet, but he had kept this quiet, suppressed. Getting fired released the hounds of his latent insecurity. He scrambled into clothes and walked out of the apartment and took to the street so Claire wouldn't see him cry and cry and smash his cell phone into a thousand pieces.

It didn't matter that Jacoby had paraphrased the words of his new employer. Or that his words were meant as a joke. Or that his openly gay friend at work, the intended sole audience, was not bothered by such language. Or that his performance on the job had been exceptional, without a trace of insubordination or indiscretion. And that he had put in 60 hour weeks and outperformed his colleagues with regard to client acquisition and retention. He was fired. And humiliated. Marked homophobic. Slandered as such in the industry daily and on Social Media (he had to cancel all of his accounts due to the vicious attacks). His work friend and former colleagues were too afraid to support him for fear of association and retribution. He received three month's severance and banishment from the professional world of America.

Claire vigorously supported Jacoby throughout the ordeal, offering comfort and relentless criticism of the sophomoric circumstances which led to his dismissal. "Complete bullshit," she spat. "Fucking cowards," she called his former friend and colleagues.

She even arranged for a family acquaintance and high-powered Manhattan attorney to represent him, pro bono, in a law suit for wrongful termination. Jacoby loved Claire for her vigilance on his behalf. Her passionate support was reassuring and particularly welcome at a time when their relationship, in its second year, had begun to simmer down from its roiling boil. There was a phase in Jacoby's aftermath where he believed all of it had been for the best - a blessing in a brutal disguise - though, eventually, impatience surfaced on Claire's part once it appeared Jacoby's hopes of legal redemption and - more importantly - future employment began to dim. He'd sent out a ton of resumes, but there wasn't much interest in the work place for a 33 year-old white, male, Communications major, ex-guitarist turned shamed PR exec. He was finished in the professional world. Death from text message.

The burden of humiliation and hopelessness weighed on him as he sat day after day in their Fort Greene floor-through as Autumn faded, and the cold and darkness of winter bore down upon Jacoby like twin fists of depression, though he never really thought of himself as depressed. Defeated was more like it. Sucker punched. Piled upon by an absurd world, a world where it seemed he had no place, and this is what scared him most of all. The displacement. The way everyone seemed to now look away or see right through him, like his immediate surroundings were an ex-girlfriend who was so over him that she barely registered his existence. It was terrifying.

But he would come out of it, surely, eventually. When the time was right. The trauma passed. But his three months of severance elapsed quickly in expensive New York, and Claire started to complain about money. And other things (like the absence of sex and his reluctance to go out at night). And then everything, it seemed, until she came home after a dinner meeting with a contract in her hand. She had been with her mum and Alistair Haxby himself, taking the tasting menu at Del Posto and finalizing the arrangements of Claire's new deal: One year in Italy as the central Italian scout for Haxby's forthcoming travel guide, *Off the Gilded Path*.

The pay, including all expenses, was damn generous. Their floor-through in Fort Greene would be easily sublet for additional revenue. They would leave at the end of Spring. All Jacoby had to do was find them a place to live in Tuscany. This is when Jacoby dug out the picture he'd found in the box of his mother's belongings and began to research Villa Floria-Zanobini, but all he found was that the property was located in a secluded area in the hills just south of Florence. Jacoby couldn't decide if this was fate or the desperate dreams of a failed man. He did know that Italy had always intrigued him and that his mother was of Italian descent. And he also knew that he had to get his ass out of New York and do something. Accompanying your stunning fiancée around central Italy with a chance of finding distant relatives in a grand villa? Can do.

Chapter 6

They pulled out of Paolo's driveway for their first excursion, onto the dirt track alongside the valley and onto the paved road that coursed downward toward the ramparts of Florence proper. Before the city line, Jacoby turned onto an unmarked two-lane road flanked by withered vineyards, crumbled farmhouses, and empty fields: The official and modest beginning of the famous Chiantigiana highway that connects Florence and Siena through Tuscany's fabled wine country.

After a few quaint hamlets, the countryside opened up. The road dipped and dived, twisting past enormous pastures spotted with white cows taking green grass. Fluffy cumulus clouds with flat bellies cast shadows on the rolling and verdant hills in every direction. Groves of olive trees soon gave way to slanted hillsides spiked with endless rows of manicured vines strewn with grapes maturing in the late Spring sun.

Claire stared out her lowered window, breathing in the crisp morning air. Jacoby focused on the road with the fervor of a formula one racer, feeling electric and alive, immersed in experience, navigating sharp turns with increasing expertise. He felt like a kid at a go-cart track. The roar of the engine was the only sound as they rocketed through the ramparts of Chianti country, the gateway, Jacoby sensed, to many upcoming explorations.

The topography increased in depth and drama as they entered the heart of Chianti, hilltop towns of stone and low-lying villages surrounded by the plush landscape leading to the Val d'Or (the Valley of Gold). They swept past Greve-in-Chianti, the first tourist destination, and were soon, after a long and winding incline, upon Panzano, the postage-stamp village, dead-center bulls-eye of Chianti, the perfect distance between Florence and Siena with a stunning view in every direction. As he slipped through town, Jacoby was kind of hoping that Claire wouldn't recognize this as pretty much exactly where she would have chosen to live.

"Oh, Panzano!" Claire yelped. "This is where we're meeting Dolores on Friday night, on our way back."

"Awesome," Jacoby said, hiding the sarcasm.

"Yes," Claire continued, leaning towards the front window for a better view. "She says there's someone I absolutely have to meet. Could be a great story."

"And who's that?" Jacoby asked as they passed through Panzano toward the narrow road east out of Tuscany into Umbria.

"Some butcher who fancies himself an actor," she said, tapping her first cigarette of the day out of a fresh pack. "He just opened a restaurant behind his shop. Apparently the meat is the most amazing in all of Italy."

"You don't say," Jacoby said, already fostering cynicism with regard to the reliability of Claire's cousin, Dolores, a British lollapalooza who was as man crazy as she was crazy-crazy.

"Yeah," Claire added, "and he's supposedly quite a character."

"Let me guess. He happens to be hot, too."

"She didn't say," Claire responded, blowing smoke out the window.

"My ass," Jacoby said.

Claire chuckled as Jacoby downshifted into a curve and attempted to accelerate away from the slight sense of foreboding that slithered through him as they tore through the valley between two fortress-cities perched safely atop Tuscan hills. He envied their walls.

• • •

Their first stop, located in the high countryside beyond the Umbrian city of Spoleto, was a rustic agriturismo, a dozen miles down a winding dirt road of a sprawling farm nearly overrun with chickens and pigs and sheep. A fenced in pool area overlooked a rich valley and its surrounding hills, a nice respite from the bustling farm life, but not enough, Jacoby knew, to meet Alistair Haxby's demanding aesthetic. Way too rural for that crowd. Claire complained about the website having misleading information and doctored photos.

They took off early the next morning and arrived before lunch at a place that felt to Jacoby like a Wild West settlement, an old outpost in the Umbrian badlands north of Perugia. They stayed in a modest cabin near the main building, a wooden hotel with a front porch and tables in the pedestrian street where tenants and locals gathered in the makeshift public square of dirt that had been hosed down at the first sign of dusk. Claire wasn't particularly pissed off at this failure since she knew it was an outlier. Still, going 0-for-2 right out of the shoot had her grumbling about the job and questioning her own judgment.

The drive the next morning to Le Marche required a steep climb over Mount Sibillini, a subrange of the Apennines. In a plain at the crest of the mountain was the Comune di Norcia, a small village known for its devotion to the abundant wild boar, called cinghiale by the Italians, that roamed the surrounding hills and hollows. Nearly every store was fronted with stuffed small-eyed, wiry-haired, sharp-tusked beasts, backed by rounds of Pecorino, nuggets of black truffles, ceilings hung with cylinders of cured meats and rows of fat prosciutto legs. Hell, even the fucking shoe store had a cinghiale in the window. At a local groceria Jacoby took a porchetta sandwich, slow-roasted pork flavored by rosemary and fennel, made crunchy with crisp pig skin and chunky sea salt. Claire had a salad of wilted wild mushrooms atop bitter local greens. The pleasing lunch soothed Claire and lifted her spirits, especially since she was confident in the next destination.

The elegant agriturismo had been recently renovated into a modern accommodation. The farming venture was separated by an entrance road and a new fence from the residential grounds dotted with quaint brick quarters for guests and an administrative area complete with a spacious yet cozy room for dining. The far reaches of the property led to a play area for children and a tiled-pool bordered by sweeping valleys that listed towards the nearby Adriatic Sea. After checking into their well-heeled quarters, a spacious brick bungalow with modern amenities, Jacoby and Claire drove a short distance to the salty Adriatic, where they spent the afternoon frolicking in the gentle waves, lounging on rented chaises, and taking small plates of briny crustaceans and carafes of Vernaccia at a seafood shack posited on the sand. The sun and sea, all the amazing food and abundant beauty, was making Jacoby feel strong again, fortified somehow by the magic of it all.

Dinner was a semi-formal affair which began promptly at eight. Jacoby and Claire arrived late with wet hair and fresh clothes. They ate by candlelight at a small table near a window, taking a charcuterie plate of house-cured meats, followed by a silky thick noodle topped with a generous shaving of black truffles. The main plate was a lamb roast so tender Jacoby tried to blow a rose in its supple surface. The prim waitress, and daughter of the owners, informed them in practiced English that everything they'd consumed had been produced on the premises, except for the Rosso Piceno they quaffed by the carafe which came from the vineyard on the neighboring hill.

"Did you guys make the ceramics, too?" Jacoby joked, touching his oven-forged plate.

Claire laughed.

The waitress looked puzzled. "No," she said. "We get them from a fattoria in Toscana."

Claire went to the patio to smoke. Jacoby watched her through the window, her hand on a hip, blowing smoke at the black sky. Her wheels were turning, and he knew this place would make the cut. That she would be happy, and he wanted her that way. His reconnection with Claire provided a sense of security with an undercurrent of joy, though pragmatism remained about their potential to last the year and beyond together.

Claire returned to share a plate of mild Pecorino drizzled in house honey. After dinner, they roamed the silent grounds and made love on a pool-side chaise lounge after skinny dipping in the cool water that rippled with shards of silver moonlight. Back in the bungalow, Claire slept with her head on Jacoby's chest, her hair covering his torso like a fine sheet.

They slept in late the next day before taking the long drive back through Umbria and into Tuscany on narrow roads leading to Cortona, where the modern American fascination with reading about Italy had begun nearly 20 years earlier with Frances Mayes' *Under the Tuscan Sun* - a book that Jacoby enjoyed but Claire couldn't stand.

Chapter 7

The Tuscan sun hung high over the Val d'Or when Jacoby and Claire rolled into Panzano and parked off the tiny and shaded piazza that surrounded a small fountain full of koi. They had just toured the walled-in city of Radda-in-Chianti and walked the small high-hilltop circumference of Volpaia, a fortified town of one restaurant, one inn, one cafe and a modernized wine/oil/prodotti collective hidden within the town's ancient architecture and sold under the same brand at the village's only shop. The concept appealed to Jacoby's sense of totality, of having all that you need in one place, under one brand.

Jacoby sat alone in the small piazza in Panzano, thinking more about the insular and independent environs of small Italian villages. He wanted no more than comfort without complication. And he had noticed that the complications came when more was sought: more income or more status or more pleasure. His father always chased new positions when it was clear that the department chair or tenure-track was not to be had, having to move and adjust and navigate the unfamiliar once again. It had complicated the hell out of Jacoby's adolescence. As a fledgling adult, the band he played in was best during their early days, when expectations were low and the creative continuity pure. Once they gained attention and made tip-sheets at music conferences and got a hot shot manager, things began to unravel. A record deal ruined them since it never delivered on all the expectations. And what was the world of business, certainly in America and even more so in New York, but a massive cluster of desperate people working away their most vital years on earth in the counter-intuitive pursuit of more, more, more. Jacoby craved less.

It seemed simple enough, but elusive all the same, against rational thinking in modern times, and it had Jacoby pondering not just the world in which he lived but his possible place in it. He couldn't actually say in a job interview that what he really wanted was a quiet life of simple pleasure, nor could he honestly project where he saw himself after five years of dedicated labor. *I dunno...retired*? He'd been in Italy all of one week, and he couldn't imagine leaving the pleasing confines, yet he knew he had so few options, so little control over his circumstances. The reality gnawed at him though he kept it at bay by focusing on the moment. And by holding out faith in fate.

Claire walked out of an enoteca that bordered the piazza. Two enormous goblets of purple wine swayed with her as she crossed the cobblestone street and joined Jacoby on an iron bench beside the koi pond. She had touched up while inside: brushed her hair and doctored her eyes a bit. She looked so beautiful. So at ease.

"Brunello di Montalcino," she gushed, handing Jacoby a goblet. "By the glass!" She crossed her legs and looked around. "I love this place."

Jacoby put a hand on her thigh. The smell of the wine alone nearly lured him into a trance. He loved those big Italian reds, but they were ridiculously overpriced in the States, especially at restaurants where they were a rip off - too expensive and too young. But the wine Jacoby held was at least ten years old and in no need of breathing. He took a small taste, followed by a quick breath, and he knew instantly that he was experiencing the best glass of wine he'd ever had: silky yet complex with a blast of fruit and wood, heavy tannins and a poke of spice. Holy shit.

"Wha'd this run you?" he had to ask.

"Eight Euros a glass," Claire said coyly. "I thought I'd splurge a little, you know."

Jacoby smiled. In the States, even if it was available by the glass -

not likely - the cost would have been closer to $40 per glass (and a small glass, at that), sucking the pleasure out of the whole thing. It drove him crazy thinking of how really nice things in America were only for the rich.

Claire tucked into Jacoby's side and put a foot up on the bench against the back of her leg. They silently swirled the wine and took small sips, staring at the valley beyond the village that burned gold with smoldering sunshine of a fading afternoon. Jacoby savored the apple smell of Claire's radiant hair and the feel of her lithe body pressed into his. He thought that they, in that still pose, would make a great statue, like a modern Apollo and Daphne, frozen in marble so that their love would always last.

A fantastic idea occurred to Jacoby: He and Claire might survive the year, and that maybe the year would be infinite, and that they could live on local food and local wine and their own love in the Italian countryside. Claire could write about all of Italy, and all of Europe, and they could open their own inn that Jacoby would operate and promote and prepare the meals and tend to the olives and grapes they grew and turned into their own house wine and their own house oil. And maybe have marmalade from figs that fell softly on their lawn, a lawn where maybe their children would...

"Coo-coo!" a voice called from across the small piazza. "Coo-coo!"

Claire leapt from Jacoby's side to greet her cousin with a grandiose hug and affected kisses on both cheeks. Dolores was plus-sized and outrageous. Glamorous and uninhibited, platinum and wonderfully curved, she devoured life. In New York for a graduate fashion program, she met Claire and Jacoby bi-weekly for dinner, where she loved to flirt with waiters and then blithely declare after the check arrived that it was too bad she didn't "fuck the help." He was happy for the servers of New York when she finished the program and returned home to torch London once again, though he was sad to see her go because - despite her excruciating snobbery - Dolores was about the most fun person he'd ever met. He envied the way she indulged in her privilege without being completely obtuse to the outside world. She also made him and Claire a better couple when she was with them.

Jacoby walked over to where the cousins stood in the center of the piazza, complimenting each other in various ways. Dolores was dressed in a patterned Chanel romper and reeked of a perfume shop.

"Why hello, Jacoby," she declared, removing her Anna Wintour sunglasses. "I heard you went and got yourself fired."

"Yeah, Dolores, I did. Thanks."

"No. No. I should thank you. You finally got Claire back on the continent. Well done you homophobic cocksplatt."

Jacoby sighed and Dolores dropped all pretenses to give him a colossal hug around his neck, smothering him in bosoms and perfume. She released him and broke into her "Katie Holmes face" - the greatest recurring gag among many shared by Jacoby and Claire and their favorite cousin, one which began on a wintry evening when Dolores showed up at their apartment with a bottle of tequila and the first season of *Dawson's Creek* on DVD that she'd found on a stoop. Dolores declared that the three of them do a shot every time Katie Holmes made the face - the mix of coy, bewildered amusement she used in nearly every situation requiring emotional response through facial expression. They were dead drunk by episode three.

Jacoby missed Dolores, though he was also relieved to see her go since she could be too much to physically bear, particularly for Claire who struggled to keep up with her cousin who lived on the fringe of lunacy. Still, if it had been only Dolores who vacationed in "Chiantishire" (and he didn't have his own secret agenda in the hills just south of Florence), Jacoby would have definitely found a place nearby, but other cousins from London also owned homes in the area, and they were a humorless, mean-spirited bunch of snobs who made Jacoby feel like he'd stepped into a Jane Austen parody novel.

"It's wonderful to have the band back together, isn't it?" Dolores asked rhetorically, taking a hand of Jacoby's and a hand of Claire's. "Shall we go to see the magic butcher then?"

They strolled as a threesome through the small piazza and across the two-lane road which the highway had been reduced to in order to pass through this tiny village. On a quiet lane slanting toward a knoll, they stopped in front of a small shop, a white-washed plaster facade with its door and windows open to the street. A bull's skull hung over the entrance.

"This is his shop, though I imagine he's gone off to the restaurant which lies behind, just over this hill."

Jacoby walked inside where a young boy of color was mopping the floor behind the counter. On a narrow table along the wall was an open fiasco of wine, beside a lone glass and platters strewn with crumbs and grease. There was no odor whatsoever except the antiseptic in the cleaning substance being splashed around the floor.

"He has a magnificent feast in here every day," Dolores said, "with roasted meats and bottles of wine just out for everyone. No charge. People hang about while he works, drinking and eating and toasting the host. I've been getting shitty here three days a week. It's remarkable. On some days, he breaks into long passages from plays in front of everyone."

"Is he any good?" Jacoby asked.

"Fuck if I know. I'm here for the wine and eye candy. But apparently he'd been up in Bologna getting rave reviews in some production when his poor father passed away. So, the young son did what any good Italian boy would - came back home to look after his mama and pick up papa's trade, giving up his dreams of being on the stage."

Claire poured wine from the fiasco into the last glass as Jacoby studied the small storefront, noticing, among the typical butcher-shop bric-a-brac, the minor theater motif, including a framed picture of Sting as Hamlet high on the wall between the counter and the space for patrons. He hoped it was sarcasm.

Dolores and Claire passed the glass back and forth, and polished off the remnants of the bottle while Jacoby looked around, oddly curious. There was a picture of a handsome young man in clean butcher's garb being interviewed by a faux-hipster in front of an MTV Europe tapestry.

"He's becoming quite famous now as a butcher," Dolores said before adding. "And he's about the best looking lad I've ever laid eyes on. Too bad I have two dates tonight."

Cucina Tipica

Jacoby thought Dolores was referring to him and Claire as her two dates until they walked up the hill and approached the entrance to the restaurant where two dark Italians in tight t-shirts and American jeans leaned into Ducati motorcycles and smoked cigarettes. Both had sunglasses turned back on their necks - a sure indicator, to Jacoby, of serious douche bag status.

"Ah," Dolores said. "My two Marcos await."

Chapter 8

The Marcos stepped on their cigarettes and straightened off their bikes. Dolores swaggered toward them with her hands above her head.

"How do you know them?" Claire whispered, a few steps behind her.

"Met them at the Autogrill," Dolores said over her shoulder. "You know, the filling station and eatery over the Autostrada."

Claire stopped. "Picking up boys at rest stops, are we now cugina?"

Dolores kept going. "Perchè no? C'è il posto cui tutti gli uomini vanno."

Jacoby tugged Claire along, imagining clever Dolores perched at the rest stop cafe, sipping a latte, eyeballing motorcyclists and sports car aficionados who stopped for breaks during their weekend rallies. One trip down the Autostrada was enough for Jacoby to know that driving was a recreational sport for Italian men, and one week in Italy was enough to know that the overwhelming majority of Italian men were damn good looking. No wonder so many English women came to Italy.

Introductions were made in Italian. The two Marcos ogled Claire, gave Jacoby indifferent nods and hard handshakes, whispering to each other as they went inside. The one-floor restaurant of cobbled stone was alone on a knoll flattened for a parking lot above the village. The open interior had white plaster walls, polished-plank floors and a wood-beamed ceiling. Wide windows allowed for views of the spectacular valley that horded the last remnants of daylight in the sky above the hills. The tables were modern and communal, wood with metal legs and matching metal chairs, adorned with place settings, carafes of red wine and a single and sarcastic fennel bulb as a centerpiece. Along the width on one side of the rectangular room, a wide iron grill lay over a pyramid of split wood under a massive ventilation shoot. Aside the indoor grilling area was a stool and microphone on a three-foot stage.

"Hey," Jacoby said to Claire as Dolores spoke with the hostess. "Maybe they have karaoke."

Claire patted his shoulder while studying the room. Crap, Jacoby thought: It's going to be an Instagram night.

There was one sitting for dinner, which began at 8:00 and lasted many courses. All meat. It seemed promising to Jacoby but contrived, somewhat, especially for Italy. Still, even with the two assholes tagging along, he was happy to be there, together again with Dolores and Claire in a band-back-together kind of way.

The room, soon full, held a pre-theater tension. A peroxided hostess in leather pants and tattooed shoulders sat them at a long table for eight near the grilling area but not directly in front, a prime spot secured when Dolores spoke to the hostess upon entry, mentioning "giornalista americana" numerous times. Jacoby appreciated the extra space, so he was able to separate himself from the Marcos in a zig-zag formation that left him at the far end, on the left side of Claire who sat directly across from Dolores, with the Marcos side by side to her left. One Marco filled the glasses at his end, including those of the ladies while Jacoby secured the carafe on his end to fill his glass alone, his isolation tempered somewhat by his personal quantity of wine.

The grill flamed and the scent of wood smoke filled the room. The kid from the butcher shop arrived, winded, pulling a huge metal cooler, which he left near the grill but beyond the range of heat. Servers appeared. A high table near the heat held a huge mallet, long tongs, jars of coarse salt, pepper grinders, branches of rosemary, unmarked bottles of olive oil, and a bowl of fresh lemons.

Dolores flirted with the Marcos, who paused from her attentions to shoot Jacoby occasional looks of disdain. Why didn't they get that they were the fucking interlopers? Jacoby was really starting to hate them and their arrogance. He thought meat-heads were an American only thing. These guys seemed like the direct descendants of the morons in high school who called him faggot because his hair was long.

Claire explored the room, her iPhone out for photos, her charm out for conversation with guests and employees. Jacoby quaffed his carafe and began to feel sour in his stomach from too much wine and not any food. A ping of anxiety appeared somewhere under his rib cage. He pulled at the skin in front of his throat and fought the burning sensation in his gut.

Baskets of bread appeared, and Jacoby gobbled enough to soak up the acid in his stomach and partake in the refreshed carafe in front of him. Claire returned and noticed his boozy countenance.

"Slow down, cowboy," she said playfully. "The show hasn't even started yet."

The cousins turned their attentions to Jacoby, who was sulking a bit, when the Marcos went outside to smoke. They returned as the young man from the photo in the butcher shop entered. The hostess whispered in his ear and pointed at Claire. He nodded in her direction and then waived to the room and approached the high table. Silent attention was paid to the young man with light brown hair and deep brown eyes and the short-sleeves of a butcher's jacket rolled high on his muscular arms. He opened the cooler and retrieved a giant T-bone in each hand.

"Ladies and gentlemen," he announced in a grand voice with broken English, raising the slabs of meat over his head. "I am Fabrizio Franchetti. And it is a pleasure to *meat* you."

Jacoby sighed cynically. Dolores growled. Claire, along with the rest of the room, broke into applause. And so the show began.

The cooler was stuffed with bistecca fiorentina, a three-inch thick porterhouse from local cows, simply prepared. Probably the single most recognized dish from the region, the crown jewel of cucina tipica (typical cuisine). After the large grill face was lined with dozens of steaks, the host - on a platform in front of the grill - theatrically salted and peppered the steaks, then chopped lemons and minced rosemary. The steaks were quickly flipped by an assistant wielding long tongs, and delivered to the cutting table to rest before being surgically hacked into chunks and placed on ceramic platters where they were dressed with local olive oil, coarse salt, squeezed lemon and sprinkled rosemary. A large pot on a burner to the side held stewed white beans with baby tomatoes which were ladled into ceramic bowls and given a swirl of fresh oil. A small crew of waitresses ferried platters to each table, though the host himself, the fabulous Fabrizio Franchetti, delivered a specially chosen platter to the table of the American food writer, Claire St. James, and her four guests.

He put the enormous platter of meat and the bowl of beans directly in front of Claire.

"I hope you have hunger, Americana."

Claire played along and smiled politely before moving the platter and bowl to the center of the table. She stood up to introduce herself professionally with an extended hand, but the butcher held up his own, as they were not clean enough for shaking.

"We will talk after the meal. No?"

"Yes," Claire said. "That would be great. Thank you."

The butcher smiled and nodded and then turned to the rest of the table.

"Please. Enjoy. It is a pleasure to have you with me here."

Dolores wiggled her fingers in a coquettish hello. The Marcos nodded with respect. Jacoby leaned forward to take in the smell of the steak, which reduced him to nothing more than his carnivorous instincts. Drool pumped from his saliva glands.

The butcher motioned for a server to refill their carafes and returned to his post center-stage as Jacoby sucked on his own tongue.

"My, my," Dolores purred. "Of all the babes in babe-land."

Jacoby grabbed the utensils and portioned hunks of meat onto the plate of his cousin and the plate of his fiancée before serving himself (fuck the Marcos), but Dolores' point - even in a meat-induced frenzy -

was not lost on Jacoby. Italy was a country full of beautiful men, but that butcher just might be the best-looking of them all. Still, Jacoby felt no jealous threat. Even with enough alcohol in him to inspire irrationality, the butcher struck Jacoby as silly, and Claire didn't seem too impressed either beyond the potential for a freelance story. Jacoby was more concerned with the Marcos, who leered at Claire in a swarthy European way and said things that she swatted away yet made Dolores laugh, but Jacoby couldn't even attempt to translate due to distance and the dialect of the Marcos who were on holiday from Calabria. Animosity for Dolores and her tendency to impose strange men upon them began to rise in Jacoby until he forked a piece of meat and placed it in his mouth.

The flavor was as profound and complex as any beef he'd ever tasted. Steak in the States was bland, in need of sauce, but this simply-prepared choice cut was perfectly grilled - seared on the outside, rare and warm internally - helped by hints of lemon and rosemary and coarse salt while letting the flavor of the meat itself dominate. Amazing. Transcendental. Good fucking lord.

Jacoby was aware of the ambiance around him, chatter in English and Italian, and the sound of the grill as flames licked more meat, the butcher bellowing somewhere to someone about something, but he was immersed in the pleasure of the bistecca, which even changed the way the wine tasted as an accompaniment. The beans, toothy and savory, made for a perfect match and Jacoby vowed to never eat potatoes with meat again. He remained lost in the moment until his plate was empty.

When he looked up, the plundered, original platter was being replaced with another, hosting a hunk of meat fresh from the grill and delivered by an attentive server. The Marcos pulled the plate towards their end of the table, but a smiling Claire moved it back to the center as Jacoby and the Marcos stared at each other like junk yard dogs ready to battle over a bone.

"Calma, calma," Claire begged sarcastically. "Ce n'è abbastanza per tutti."

She had assured them there was enough for everyone before going outside to smoke.

Dolores stayed put and carefully doled out portions of the meat to the three men. The Marcos ate and talked to each other, consulting Dolores sporadically, while Jacoby ate in silence, contemplating the majesty of the beef and drinking his way through much of another carafe until his mouth began to pucker. When Claire returned he was full and drunk and over the whole scene.

"So, fiancé mine," Claire said, loping an arm around his shoulder, clearly aware that Jacoby was half-drunk and wholly-isolated, "tell us what makes this meat so exquisite."

Dolores translated for the Marcos, also informing them of Jacoby's famous palate. They looked more skeptical than impressed, but Jacoby appreciated a little attention from the table and the arm of Claire over his shoulder. He was about to share his culinary diagnostic when Dolores leaned in towards the Marcos and said something that involved the word lingua, which meant tongue. The three of them burst out laughing, and Claire held a hand over her mouth to shield her smile. One of the Marcos turned to Jacoby, put split fingers in front of his mouth and wiggled his tongue through it. The other one pointed at Jacoby and laughed. Claire stopped her smile and stared a dagger at Dolores.

"What?" she responded, showing some tipsy herself. "The man has a magic tongue, and he puts it to good use in more ways than one. It's nothing to be ashamed of. It's quite valiant, if I might say so myself..."

Jacoby's face flushed with embarrassment, and he wished Dolores would shut the fuck up, but he knew she would keep on blathering once she got on a roll, so Jacoby stood up and stared at the end of his nose like a punch drunk boxer. Claire grabbed his arm, trying to get him to sit. Humiliation heated his face as he directed a stare at one of the Marcos, who looked back with mocking eyes. Jacoby made a quick move around the table, to take a Marco by the neck and shove him to the floor; but when the butcher appeared in his peripheral vision, Jacoby pivoted and bolted for the door, his feet wobbly and nearly detached as he struggled through the blurred room that seemed to direct all of its negative energy at him.

Chapter 9

The low sky was devoid of stars, and the cool evening air on the high country knoll soothed Jacoby's frayed nerves. He clenched his fists, blinked and breathed and wandered off toward the parking lot to lean against a car and get himself together. He knew he'd overreacted, but the malice and mockery from the Marcos reminded him of all the shit he dealt with as the fresh-faced new kid throughout middle school and high school. His inherent insecurity always set off a violent response, which he fully intended for the nearest Marco when the butcher came into view and changed his mind. He was actually happy with the way it worked out - always regretting the messy aftermath of fights (win or lose) - but after a few minutes of standing outside alone, he wondered why Claire hadn't come out to check on him and make the matter of his return more normal. He would go in, shake a hand, say he was sorry, and use it as an excuse to call it a night.

What was she doing in there anyway? He tried to see inside the restaurant, but bodies blocked the view of their table. The happy sound was of a party going on without him. From the light of the entrance, one of the Marcos appeared. He lit a cigarette and walked up to Jacoby, who was startled by the lack of space between them and more so when the Marco began to speak solid English.

"Why don't you go home? I will take care of your woman. I don't eat the pussy, because I don't have to," he said, grabbing his crotch.

Jacoby smelled stale smoke and beauty products. His heart thumped. He looked down and away, his breath quickening with anticipation. The Marco huffed and sought witness to the American's cowardice. He crouched to look up condescendingly into Jacoby's eyes.

"Huh? You here what I say, pussy-eater man?"

Jacoby waited, a plan of attack set in his head. He focused on his breath, in and out of his nose, poised to strike, but when the Marco pushed him in the chest, when the provocation was clear and retaliation appropriate, Jacoby didn't do anything. He froze. His heart skipped a beat, and then, in an instant, it roared back as a sense of panic came over him. His head spun; he couldn't find his breath. He thought he might faint. Or puke. Or cry. It was all he could do to lift up his feet and stagger away.

Chased by the Marco's cackle, Jacoby lurched through the parking lot and into the darkness. As his feet found purchase with the ground, he nearly tripped down the hill, along the quiet street, passing doors lit by small lights or gated storefronts. The butcher's shop was dark. He crossed the main road in town and found their car off the square in the silence under a lone street light. Without hesitation, he climbed inside and drove off out of town, in a direction from which they had not come. He blinked and fought the rushing breath that matched his slamming heart. The road twisted, under a wall of thick trees, and it was dark as a dog's nose, barely penetrable by headlights. He jerked the wheel when it rumbled off the track and only had seconds to react to every bend in the road. An oncoming car nearly blinded him with its brights. He lowered both front windows; the crisp night rushed in and made him shiver but kept him alert.

Jacoby's head spun, and he felt the terror of being completely lost. Alone. And drunk. His collar was soon sweat soaked. His eyes burned no matter how much he blinked. But he couldn't stop. There was nowhere to stop. No signs. No turns. Only darkness and wind and the swarming panic of life threatened. Thick bugs splattered on the window. And he drove on, terrorized by the night and all the pain that it held. All of its harm and regret. If he came upon a cliff, he would not have bothered to turn. Or slow down. But there were no cliffs in the hills and hollows west of the Chiantigiana highway. And soon the roads smoothed and industrial areas emerged with flats traveled by trucks past dark prostitutes dressed in denim pants and denim jackets, standing on the cold and dusty shoulders of Italian byways. He thought of stopping and paying one to help him home, but he lacked the courage to even speak, much less slow down, so he kept driving, a little calmer than before, driven by a desire to survive, studying signs along the industrial route, looking for familiar towns but only finding strange names like Scandicci and Poggibonsi. He'd heard of Livorno but knew it was on the coast and far from home.

After a half hour of aimless driving, he came across the Siena-Firenze Highway, the straight shot connection between the two Tuscan cities, but it took Jacoby entry into the outskirts of Siena before he realized he'd been going the wrong way, so he turned around and drove 60 miles back toward Florence, noticeably more collected but so thirsty and fatigued, his head cleaved by a sharp ache, and still too rattled to think clearly beyond getting somewhere where he could get out of the fucking car. At the Firenze Sud exit, he recognized some buildings and found himself in known territory. He took a few wrong turns, but eventually, through the desperate perseverance of trial and error, bound down the track toward the village of Antella. Being anywhere close to a place that resembled home brought him comfort.

But it occurred to him, as he got closer, that going home wasn't an option. He feared arriving so late, after midnight, waking Paolo and his patrol dog. He also did not want to have to explain, if Paolo woke up, why he had come home alone. So he parked in one of the open spots that lined the village's piazza. Turning off the roaring engine brought some relief. The piazza was dark, save a few night lights in front of shuttered shops. The church's bell tower seemed to quiver in the stillness as Jacoby approached and sat on the steps. A single bong startled Jacoby and then prompted a deep sleep after curling on his side, hugging himself in the fetal position.

He woke a while later, shivering and frightened by the feral sounds and baleful squawks coming from the darkness beyond the village square. He got back into the car and slept in the backseat until the first light of dawn appeared above the village's low roof line. His body felt as wrinkled as his clothes. He smelled of body odor and sour breath, his whole mouth dull as Styrofoam, but a semblance of serenity existed from having survived the long night of potential danger and awful emotions.

Jacoby climbed out of the car and went to the oxidized statue in the piazza's center, a replica of the town's founder - a bald man in Renaissance costume, looking forthright and noble. Jacoby stretched his legs on the precipice that held the statue and then walked over to a cafe on the piazza's far corner. How he wished it were open, to take a giant glass of cold water followed by a caffè and pastry. The simple act of having a small and pleasing breakfast seemed decadent after the night he'd been through, the challenges of his shame-hangover spoiling any ideas of pleasure. He ached for happiness. For relief. His stomach growled like a trumpet's prompt. A ping of optimism inspired Jacoby to wait for the cafe to open, to take his simple breakfast and move on from there. After cleaning up, he would return to Chaintishire to find Claire and try to explain what happened. The thought sickened him but he was still too frazzled to entertain regret.

Metal chairs out front of the cafe were strewn across the patio space, strung together with a coiled lock, under a black canopy. Jacoby straightened the last chair and sat. Light appeared in tiny bursts above the piazza. Promises of daylight warmth came through the breaths he took through his nose. Birds serenaded him into a light sleep, a mixed-state of half-consciousness where one is aware of the fact that they are sleeping, like the time Jacoby had dozed off at the opera but still followed the songs that informed the most wonderful dreams. In his dream-state in front of the cafe, he felt the atmosphere surround him and lift him over the village to a meadow behind a large villa, where the woman in the hidden picture - one who resembled his mother - kept eye on a young Jacoby who wobbled in the cut grass, picking up leaves and twigs, peaking behind trees.

A blast of water splattered across Jacoby's chest and under his chin, waking him instantly. He jumped up from his chair. Frightened and furious, he stood and stared at a small and younger woman with a face curled mean like a fist and a hose in her hand as a weapon.

"Vai!" she hissed, her mouth and eyes both moving, her demeanor more feral than human, motioning with the hose toward the piazza. "Vai!"

Jacoby held up his hands as if to plead his case, but he had no words to counter the impression he gave as a vagrant, the kind that people in the area build fences and get dogs to deter.

"I'm sorry," is all he could muster. "Sorry."

The woman's face, at the sound of English, grew softer, somewhat. She titled her head as Jacoby hurried away across the piazza. She watched, the hose limp at her side, as he climbed into the shiny German car, backed out of the spot, and chirped away, around the bend and up the hill.

Jacoby's heart pounded as he raced up the hill, feeling chased by the whole world. He took great care to give wide berth as he passed a gray-haired man in a down vest wagging a stick in the growth that bordered the road. He didn't need to start piling up enemies. Or bodies. The sun crested the horizon as he bumped up the rocky track toward the villa. It was still too early to enter the property, so he parked the car in the divot in front of Paolo's fence and sat on the hood, facing the valley as the soft lemon-light coated the expanse sown with poppies and wild grass. The smoky light of sunrise shrouded the forest of cypress and umbrella pine beyond the valley

Jacoby wished he'd had breakfast, and realized the fierce young woman with the hose must own or run the cafe, and that he'd have to find another place to take a morning coffee and pastry in the future since she scared him far more than he had scared her. He thought with self-pity of how he wasn't making very many friends in Italy so far. At least he hadn't run over the old man foraging on the side of the road. And then he thought about Claire, and how he was going to save that relationship, for he felt - sitting alone on the car after a frantic night on the run from his own demons - that he needed her more than ever. And without her, he was alone in the world.

Would she be angry or worried that he'd left like that? Had he ruined her story-in-progress? How could he explain why he ran or his cowardice when confronted by the Marco? That he just didn't have the fight in him, even though Claire knew better. His surprising physicality had intensified their early relationship. On their third date, riding the F train, way after midnight, back to Brooklyn from an East Village music venue, the train stopped at 2nd Avenue where a young and drunk Latino in matching top and shorts, twisted hat and a tall boy can of beer got on and got in the face of every male aboard, one by one, slurring shit about white bitches and gentrification. Everybody looked away. When he approached Jacoby, a seething Claire stepped forward, but Jacoby held her to the side while delivering a front kick to the sternum of the wobbly loudmouth, which sent him flying through the car, his margarita flavored Bud Light spilling all over some stunned passengers at the same moment the train approached the East Broadway stop. The doors opened and people poured out, including Jacoby and Claire who ran out of the station and into the streets of Chinatown, holding hands, frantic yet laughing, and didn't stop running until reaching the shadows of the Metropolitan Building at the mouth of the Brooklyn Bridge. They walked the bridge, nearly alone, except for an occasional night biker, stopping at landings to kiss and grope each other over the moonlit water, in front of the sparkling skyline of Lower Manhattan, which seemed to shimmer just for them. Later, in Jacoby's studio apartment in Vinegar Hill, just on the other side of the bridge, they had sex for the first time, vigorous, adrenalin-boosted, hero's sex, which would set the tone for their physical life in the days and months ahead that led to their engagement.

Jacoby never mentioned to Claire that he only embraced violence out of insecurity and a history of being bullied. And that he'd only learned a few self-defense kicks and not real fighting because he didn't like fighting, and his fledgling guitarist's hands were too precious for punching anyway. He let Claire believe what she wanted, that her boyfriend-cum-finance was a clandestine bad-ass, because it made their lives better. But now - in the wake of the Marco incident and the certain interruption of her story-in-progress - Claire was likely to have a much less inspired view of Jacoby's masculinity. He'd have to manage the right manner of contrition, offer a sincere explanation - one that also explained why he hadn't felt the need to essentially defend himself - and come up with the way in which to do so before finding her, hopefully later that day, probably holed up at Dolores' house, wondering what was up with her pain in the ass fiancé.

An engine roared from across the valley. A plume of dust rose above the trail and wended down the road toward Jacoby. It was a dark Jeep, traveling quickly, top off and loaded with olive men and a black spotted border collie. The gate behind Jacoby opened, and Paolo appeared with an ax drawn back over his shoulder, his face red, his eyes wide. He ignored Jacoby and stood on the side of the road. The Jeep passed, and Paolo raised his ax and yelled something at the men, who yelled back at him and made hand gestures. They were young, wild-haired, dressed in camouflage. A dead beast was tied to the hood, tusks extending upward, blood dripping down the front of the Jeep, leaving a trail on the road after they passed in a cloud of dust.

"Cacciatore," Paolo said to Jacoby. "Hunters."

Jacoby felt like saying "No shit," but he said "Oh," instead.

"From the comune," Paolo said, gesturing with disdain towards the village. "They are not to be here, but they do because the cinghiale come to our hills for tartuffo."

Jacoby knew from his trip through Norcia that cinghiale meant wild boar and tartuffo was truffle. He also now knew that the noise from outside the barn, heard on their first night, had been a wild boar in a nocturnal search for delicacies. Even the animals eat well in Italy, he thought.

"Oh," Paolo said. "You ragazza is home."

He pointed towards the barn, where Dolores' car was parked in his spot.

Chapter 10

"Where have you been?" Claire screamed when Jacoby walked in through the barn doors. She'd been on the couch, still in her clothes from the night before. A line from a cushion creased the side of her face. Her hair was a mess. She stood with her arms now thrust to her sides, like a rocket ready to launch or a child set to stomp.

"I'm sorry," he said. "I got lost."

"Sorry? Lost?" Claire heaved. "My god! What the fuck?"

Jacoby closed the barn door so as not to be overheard. He couldn't come up with any sort of strategy. It was the only place he wanted to be, but he really didn't want to be there either. He went to the kitchen for a glass of water, which slid down his throat like quick silver, its momentary pleasure squashed by the undeniable fact that he was about to get his ass handed to him.

"Aren't you going to say anything?" Claire asked, a sense of incredulity rising as her face turned apple-red. "Explain why you just abandoned me?"

"I was trying to do you a favor," Jacoby lied.

"A favor?" Claire laughed with disgust. "By leaving me worried sick?"

Jacoby grew angry, and he sensed a line of defense.

"You didn't seem all that worried when everyone was laughing at me. Your fucking cousin and those two pricks. I went outside to avoid making a scene, to not interrupt your precious deal with that ridiculous butcher. You saw the whole thing. You couldn't even bother to come out and check on me?"

"I meant to but Fabrizio came over to chat just as you were leaving, and I had to engage him for a few. It's my job after all. I am here to work, you know that, don't you?"

"Don't make it out like you're on some sort of U.N. mission."

"Oh, that's rich," Claire fumed. "Coming from the guy who gets to spend a year in Italy, essentially on holiday, living off someone else's wages."

"It wasn't my idea to come here."

"But it was because of you that we had to come. Remember? Right?"

"Fuck you."

"Fuck you."

"Oh, hello cousins," Dolores said, descending the spiral staircase with one hand on the railing and one hand in the air. "If anyone should be pissed here, Jacoby, it should be me."

Jacoby clenched his jaw and raked his tongue along the back of his teeth as Dolores crossed the floor and plopped herself on the couch where Claire had slept.

"I had not one but two cylinders of primo Italian sausage that you ran off, leaving me alone for the evening, having to mash my own button."

Jacoby and Claire exchanged looks and held them hard for a few seconds before breaking into laughter as Dolores waived them off in a faux-imperious manner. Her colloquialisms were often as vulgar as they were hysterical, and Jacoby and Claire agreed on the interruption of laughter since the fight was taking the shape of those that happened on occasion since their engagement and often in the last months before leaving New York: Claire being high-minded and impatient; Jacoby being defensive and insecure.

The trip to Italy was to remedy this riff, though the flaw in this solution always loomed, and a Dolores-provided distraction from reality was welcomed in that moment by both, after such a long and awful night.

"I've got a case of Prosecco in the trunk," Dolores said. "What do you say we have a bubbly breakfast and then go kick around Florence for a bit? I'm dying to see what they've done with the Mercato Centrale."

•   •   •

Jacoby took Dolores' Audi to a small groceria just off the main road that ran along the ridge, happy to avoid the village below and its malevolent cafe owner. He purchased eggs and a loaf of bread. With the Audi's top down, the cool, herb-scented air and the sunshine on his face, and the topography of rolling hills studded with majestic trees and olive groves, lifted Jacoby's spirits. He was back, once again, to believing a split with Claire was unavoidable, and he was weary from the emotional games he played with himself and her, but it was such a beautiful day, the colors so vibrant, that it felt like being immersed in a three-dimensional, senses-evoking cartoon. He'd enjoy the moment for what it was and deal with the awful truth as far down the road as he could kick it.

Back in the barn, the yolks were huge and orange, and Jacoby hummed as he whipped a half-dozen eggs together with some chopped prosciutto left over from Paolo's welcome bounty. He added some sage taken from a bush behind the barn. He scrambled the eggs and prosciutto then slowly reduced them to a creamy consistency over a double boiler (one of the many culinary techniques his father had taught him). Jacoby loved cooking for people, then sharing the meal and mutual pleasure of being together. Eating the same food; drinking the same wine; everyone on the same stage. It was like sex when sex was good and mutual. What people called "making love."

Dolores popped two bottles of Prosecco, and they ate outside on the terrace, slathering the egg and prosciutto on chunks of fresh baked bread. The quality of the eggs was so apparent, and the meal so delicious that it rivaled Jacoby's favorite breakfast: steak & eggs. He especially loved it when the band was on the road, and his vegetarian band mates would cobble together meals of old fruit and gummy starch at roadside diners while Jacoby took steak and eggs with home fries and buttered toast, feeling empowered by the protein and the pleasure of eating, something he was currently immersed in when Dolores slurped down a mouthful of Prosecco and declared Jacoby to be brilliant.

"No, I'm serious," she said after Jacoby and Claire chuckled at her random statement. "You're so talented."

"Don't start that again," Claire demanded.

"No. No. Not that. Though knowing your way around a clitoris is a real talent, you know? And you should probably have an instructional YouTube channel for the rest of the sad blokes out there, but that's not what I meant."

Claire's face flashed with anger, but Jacoby didn't sense one of Dolores' outrageous commentaries coming, and he sipped Prosecco, sort of anxious for her to continue.

"I'm just saying that the man can do so many things magnificently. He's a wonderful cook, and obviously an accomplished musician. He knows more about wine than both us lushes combined. He's smart and well read, and he makes wonderful company, really. And the fact that you're nice to look at makes it even more remarkable since every decent-looking fellow I come across seems to be fairly satisfied with just that fact alone. That's all I'm saying, really."

"Why, thank you, Dolores," Claire said sincerely.

"Fuck you thanking me for? I wasn't speaking of you. You're a twiggy bitch can barely scribble a sentence. Was talking about 'im."

"Thank you, Dolores," Jacoby said with feigned formality but also a true sense of appreciation. It was so easy for him to forget, after so many defeats, that he was - on paper, at least - quite accomplished. And a good guy.

"You're very welcome, dear cousin-in-law-to-be," Dolores said with a hand on Jacoby's leg. "Now, let's wash our bums and get to town."

Chapter 11

The drive into Florence was fast and spectacular. Dolores insisted on driving and that Claire and Jacoby sit in the back, like an important couple being chauffeured, though Claire insisted on the top up to keep her hair from tangling. They went away from the village on the ridge road and swooped down into the ramparts of Florence proper, past low-slung and colorless apartment houses and commercial enterprises of stone and cement. Soon they arrived in a shaded, rolling area of elegant villas behind high metal gates on a winding, Cypress-lined road. At the top, Dolores quickly pivoted into a parking lot crowded with tourist buses with an open expanse beyond. She parked in the far corner, yet Jacoby could already sense the elevation by the sweeping views of the hills and valleys to the south. He wondered which hill their little village was nestled beyond.

"This way lovelies," Dolores ordered.

On the other side of the lot, beyond the corroding replica of "David" that fronted the piazza named after his creator, lay the city of Florence, a spooned circle of terra cotta and stone and pastel, split horizontally by the nearby River Arno and surrounded by verdant hills like a lush hood framing the face of a movie star.

Jacoby felt wonder rise through his sternum and out his nose. It seemed like a model, a tiny replica of plastic pieces, of a make believe place, not a real place in real size made by the hands of men many centuries ago. A city of domes and towers and palaces, of ceramic tiles and stone, of four bridges that spanned the Arno, including the famous Ponte Vecchio, lined with shops of pastel facades. From high above, Jacoby wandered through the tourists who snapped pictures and pointed. He stood atop the paved slope that led down the hill toward the magnificent city, but he held still, fighting the current of enticement, the beckoning, savoring the feeling of anticipation like a child has atop a long water slide above an enormous pool. He thought of Sara Sherman in the 8th grade, and the moment the bra straps fell from her shoulders. He felt kinship and profound love for Claire and Dolores since they were there in the moment, and the reason he discovered the city of Florence.

"Don't just stand there," Dolores chided. "Get moving, ass hat."

They took the switchback path of dirt and stone and sometimes gravel, laughing as Dolores tried to fight gravity and unsure footing in her well-heeled outfit from the night before. They made it to the landing by the San Niccolo tower and wandered a silent cobblestone street of the city's sleepiest quarter on the side of the river where tourists seldom go. They emerged on the two-lane, busy with autos and bicyclists, which bordered the Arno, and walked its parapets towards the bridges and city center that appeared even more grand from ground level. Jacoby glided along as if on a moving sidewalk, peaceful but fully aware of everything around him. He was like a calm kid in a candy shop.

Dolores refused to cross the tourist-choked Ponte Vecchio, opting for the quaint Ponte Grazie which connected its passers to a shaded two-way with narrow sidewalks squeezed between the high walls of stone buildings with modest storefronts. Motorini and tiny cars zipped past, honking and humming, only feet from the pedestrians who overwhelmed the sidewalks.

"My god, the fucking tourists," Dolores bleated without irony.

They stopped in Piazza Santa Croce for breathing room and a gander at the piazza's opposite end where a statue of Dante Alighieri stood on the stairs in front of the white marbled Basilica facade, accented with green and pink, entered through enormous doors of wood. While Jacoby and Claire studied the church, Dolores disappeared into a leather shop and returned with a pair of red suede flats on her feet that directed them down a side street, away from the crowded lanes of tourists, from where they emerged behind the Duomo and its massive, red-tiled cupola and its own facade, albeit much larger than Santa Croce, of white marble with green and pink trim. The line for the main doors or into the bell tower snaked around the block. Dolores whisked them past the hordes of tourist groups following guides who held unopened and colorful umbrellas high as beacons for their flock.

"Good lord," Dolores declared as they got snarled on a side street. "What day is it anyway?"

Jacoby shrugged, and Claire began to search through her hand bag for her phone.

"Mi scusi, signore," Dolores implored of an old newsstand operator."Che giorno è?"

The man, dumbfounded in his tiny kiosk, smiled politely and said, "Mercoledì."

"Ah," Dolores sighed. "Damn."

She turned to Claire and Jacoby, patting her ample bosom in contrition. "I should have fucking known. Wednesday. It's the day when the cruise ships dock in Livorno and all these imbeciles descend on Florence on excursion. Christ. It's worse than ever."

Jacoby started to feel fatigued from the previous night's adventure, which informed a sense of claustrophobia and mild anxiety as his breakfast buzz wore off and the uncertainties of his reality returned.

"Let's come back another time," Jacoby offered. "When it's less crowded."

"No. No. No," Dolores insisted. "We're here already and really through the worst of it. The majority of these groups don't have time to do anything beyond wait three hours to wander a church or gape at David's johnson. They rarely go beyond the historic center. We should be fine at the Mercato, which is just a little way, where lunch shall be on me."

Claire took Jacoby's hand and implored him on. He knew she was thinking of an article about the refurbished Mercato Centrale and its symbolism of modernity coming to Italian dining. She'd been questioning Dolores on the way to town in the car.

"Fine," Jacoby playfully deferred, "but I'm picking the wine."

"Well, of course you are, Jacoby," Dolores said with harrumph. "I wouldn't have it any other way."

•　　　•　　　•

The Mercato Centrale was an ugly and enormous mart. According to Dolores, it had been entirely dedicated to local vendors: meat and fish and cheese on the first floor; fruit and veggies and dried goods upstairs. But now, after the renovation, the first floor held all the markets it could fit while the second floor had been converted into an enormous food hall, with pop-up shops from local eateries and open tables to take food on plastic trays to be eaten with plastic forks off plastic plates. It was supposed to be some sort of gourmet cafeteria, which made Jacoby think of such places in Manhattan and Brooklyn. He didn't like it.

It was a noisy faux-warehouse space of white brick walls and funky neon or hand painted signs, packed with tourists and fabulous locals, practically bouncing off each other trying to get tables or navigate the tight spaces while carrying trays of food and bottles of wine or pitchers of beer. Dolores plopped herself down at a table just vacated by a tow-headed Scandinavian family of four and declared that she felt like having pizza for lunch. Claire joined her, and Jacoby set off with Dolores' credit card for the line that waited to order pizzas from pretty girls in paper hats behind an open counter where men in smocks kneaded dough and rounded out pies to be topped and fed to the flames of an open oven.

Jacoby hated waiting in lines. It made him feel insignificant and mindless. He spent the time studying the techniques of the pizzaioli and practicing his order. Jacoby spoke Spanish proficiently, and had worked on his Italian once their plan for Italy was set. He had some working knowledge and was eager to improve, though speaking in real life and studying alone were very different things.

"Tre margherita e un bottiglia di Moralino di Scansano," he said too fast when faced with a pretty girl in a paper hat, her eyes wide and brown.

"Scusi?"

Jacoby took a small breath and repeated himself, slowly, or at least, more slowly than the original attempt.

She repeated the order back to him in English. Jacoby's face flashed with a bit of shame. She took the credit card and rang it up, quickly handing him a bottle of wine over the counter along with a corkscrew. Jacoby popped the wine and stuck the cork back in the bottle just as the three piazzette came from the oven. He stuck the corked bottle in his back pocket, cupped three inverted glasses by the stems and carried them under the tray stacked with the food carefully across the dining hall and to the table where Claire and Dolores seemed to be discussing the latter's new shoes.

"Oh, thank God," Dolores said. "I'm famished."

Claire wrinkled her nose at the presentation. "At least the glasses aren't plastic."

Jacoby passed out the plates while Claire poured the wine. Dolores' plate held the receipt, which she gave a quick glance before doing a double-take.

"For fuck's sake, Jacoby," she cried with mock-horror. "Did that hussy in the hair net stroke you off as well?"

"Nope," he said.

"She should have for these prices."

Smiling, he began to stand but Claire pulled him down by his arm while swallowing her first bite.

"It's damn good, though," Claire said, turning to Jacoby. "Don't you think?"

He took a bite of the classic pizza of cheese, sauce and basil over a thin, crisp crust. Of course it was good; it was Italy, but he didn't have the heart to tell them that both the pizza and wine at Paolo's house had been much, much better.

• • •

The threesome cafe-hopped back to the Piazza Michelangelo, taking grappas at three different corner bars off serpentine streets which twisted through quiet quarters beyond the historic center. The sun slanted as the afternoon progressed and stores on the city's outskirts began to shutter for the afternoon riposa. With Claire and Dolores each holding an arm, Jacoby strode down the middle of narrow streets, wobbly but happy, feeling secure for the moment, in-step with the adventure in progress.

The walk up to the piazza was tough, especially on Dolores, over-sized and over-dressed, tipsy and temperamental as the buzz started to fade, but Jacoby held her arm and helped her up the steady incline until they reached the top. The city looked different under a higher sun, but no less spectacular. The river rippled with shards of light, and Jacoby felt like he was falling in love. A tour bus blocked the car in, which Dolores didn't mind since she needed a quick rest before driving, so she put the top down and the three sat quietly in the car and fell asleep like cats, one after another, in the afternoon sun, with Jacoby dropping off first.

So much had happened since meeting up with Dolores nearly 24 hours ago in the small piazza in Panzano. With the soft light on his face and the arduous events now behind him, Jacoby did not doze. He slept soundly until they reached the bumpy dirt road above the valley sewn with poppies.

"Oh, you're up," Claire said from the front seat.

"Yeah," he said, taking a big breath of fresh air and rubbing his chest with one hand. He started to think of what they would all do for dinner.

Dolores kept looking over her shoulder and then to Claire, who cleared her throat, and turned to face Jacoby in the back seat.

"So, Dolores and I were just talking...And I was thinking that maybe she could go with me on the next trip for old Alistair Haxby."

"Why?" Jacoby asked, feeling more curiosity than rejection, and a thread of relief.

Dolores was checking his reaction in the rear view every few seconds.

"Well," Claire continued in her most diplomatic tone, holding her hair over one shoulder to keep it from blowing in the wind. "You could spend some time getting acclimated to the area, that little village and whatever else is around. I'm sure there's some hidden treasures lurking. Who knows - maybe there's even something for Haxby or an article somewhere else. Anyway, we need to know where to shop and eat out and whatnot. And you're the perfect man for the job. Don't you think?"

She put a hand on Jacoby's knee. He splayed his fingers out on each thigh and considered the possibilities, scanning the idea for potential threats. He was curious about the village (beyond the crazed cafe owner) and the consortium Paolo talked about. He could also use a few days alone to start searching for the villa in his picture, though he feared the dead-end that would probably come of it. Still, it had to be done. No sense in delaying.

"Alright," he said. "Sounds good. When you leaving?"

"Tonight," Claire said as she turned back to the front of the car.

"Oh," Jacoby said as he spied the cousins exchange sideways glances.

Chapter 12

Claire and Dolores left early that evening, and Jacoby sat around bored and wishing he'd brought a guitar with him from America. He missed the feeling of the instrument in his hand, its comfort and familiarity and gift of sound. He vowed to stay away from playing after leaving the band, but like an old habit or a lost love, his thoughts returned to something he had dedicated so much of his time, the blessed solitude of hour upon hour of practice and its eventual actuation in a band on a stage, on the road, in a recording studio. A little taste of fame. It was all worth it, no regrets, but all he had left were memories and a guitar. And only the latter could address the loneliness he felt now.

He thought to ring Paolo's bell, to see what his neighbor was up to, practice some Italian, but he didn't want to seem intrusive, and he really wasn't craving Paolo's company anyway. The remaining eggs, cobbled together with some fresh herbs, made a decent dinner which he washed down with the red wine left in the fiasco. The barn, lit by dim bulbs and completely surrounded by darkness, felt isolated in wilderness. A cool wind blew through the half-opened kitchen window. There were no electronics whatsoever and, therefore, no sound. Jacoby wanted music, so he dug his phone out of the suitcase along with the only book he brought, a noir by Nic Pizzolatto, which he planned to read by lamplight, accompanied by his favorite Dylan album, *Love & Theft,* tucked up on the couch in the room off the kitchen that was to serve as Claire's office.

His phone's battery was dead, and Claire had taken their only adapter on the road, so Jacoby stretched out on the couch to read in silence. He opened the book where the picture he had hidden appeared tucked inside the front cover. He studied it like he had hundreds of times before, trying to feel some connection. The woman still bore no obvious resemblance to him, but he felt closer to her now, more hopeful yet still decidedly level-headed. He'd take the picture with him to the village tomorrow on his mission to get acclimated, trying not to put too much faith in what he might find, if anything, about its overwhelming yet unlikely potential connection to him. Despite his ever-changing moods and outlook, his outright desperation at times, Jacoby managed to be somewhat pragmatic through it all.

After reading for more than an hour, Jacoby dozed off. The story was of an outcast, a big-hearted, bone-breaker in the underbelly of New Orleans, on the run from once-friendly cohorts. The protagonist reminded him, in a far more dramatic fashion, somewhat of himself: unfairly run out of town and displaced without many options for hope or redemption. With the book flat on his chest, Jacoby dreamed of being chased through the bayou, under canopies of live oak and Spanish moss, toward pungent waters over fecund earth, pursued by malevolent hipsters and PC warriors.

Jacoby awoke at some point much later, bemused by the absurd dream, with no clue of the time but a sense of being deep into the night by the darkness beyond the windows. He lifted his weary body from the couch when the sound of grunting from outside penetrated the silence. His body constricted. The hell hounds had come to get him. He moved cautiously toward the window and pressed his face as close as it could get, letting his eyes adjust to the darkness, braced for a horror movie moment when the demon or beast pops up out of nowhere. But nothing moved; all he could see was the thick hedge. Then it rattled as the grunting returned. A bolt of fear shook Jacoby's body, and he hurried from the room, tripping into the front area and scurrying to the barn door to make sure it was secured before rushing upstairs to bury himself under the comforter, safe from the predators outside and the demons of his dreams, to continue his much-needed sleep.

•   •   •

The morning air welcomed Jacoby as he split the curtains and opened the balcony doors. Blue skies with a hint of smoky morning mist stretched over the olive grove and the knoll at the far end of the property. He leaned over the balcony to spy on the noisy hedge from above, but the necessary angle was not available. He was happy in the sober morning light to abandon his dark fears.

The new day brought optimism and a sense of well-being, of purpose. He quickly dressed in a t-shirt and jeans, and grabbed some belongings to bring to the village. At the last minute, he decided to leave the car and walk the mile down the winding road that lead to the square, to be alive in the beauty and promise of nature.

The dirt road was more fun to walk than drive, with insects buzzing on the curtain of flowers and herbs that draped the Etruscan wall. The valley on the other side provided depth and color and a sense of serenity. At the ridge road, under the cement entrance arch, Jacoby checked the mirror hung high on a telephone pole that provided a view up the hill and around the bend. With only road in the reflection, Jacoby hustled across the street and walked the narrow shoulder up towards the groceria and Casa di Popolo, where there would soon be a turn for the village.

Morning birds chirped and larger ones began to search from the sky for food below. Small cars zoomed past on their way toward Florence. Soon, an olive grove emerged, with a worn trail that angled through the grove and toward the road Jacoby would eventually take. He chanced the short-cut and took the dirt path through the grove of slate-green leaves shimmering in the morning light. It was well enough into the season that many branches showed fledgling black fruit, some of which had already fallen to the ground. The aroma of olives made his stomach growl. He so wanted an espresso in town and so hoped there was another cafe besides the one run by the scowling woman with the hose.

The path through the grove connected to the road towards Antella, and Jacoby walked the edges, looking through the high grass and wild growth for bounty sought by the old man in the vest - the one he had carefully avoided with the car on his escape from town the prior morning - but he spied nothing edible. Past a ramshackle farm house with withered grape vines beyond and beside, and laundry draped over a listing clothes line, the road turned toward the village in an abrupt angle, opening almost immediately to the town square which was a rectangle to the left of the road, beginning with the small frutta e verdura (fruit & vegetable) market on the near corner in the shadows of the church to its left. On the opposite corner, across the worn stone surface, was the newsstand and general store manned by a dapper middle-aged man with a waxed mustached, neatly parted hair and a stitched, down jacket over a Merino sweater.

"Boun giorno," he said with a gracious bow as Jacoby entered.

Jacoby returned the greeting and held out his cellphone and power cord. The man took them and looked quizzically at Jacoby who made a plug-in gesture.

"Non funziona."

"Ah," the man said. "Aspetta."

Jacoby waited as the gracious man went to the back of the store, past the racks of magazines and stacks of newspapers, between the three aisles full of various household needs, and returned with an adapter, which he unwrapped and plugged into an outlet beneath the counter.

"È morto," he said of Jacoby's dead phone. "Trenta minuti."

Thirty minutes. The man smiled at Jacoby; he smiled back. The man tapped his wristwatch. "Trenta minuti," he repeated.

Jacoby started to leave but stopped, the man's kindness inspiring courage. He took the picture out of his wallet and showed it to him. Jacoby's heartbeat ticked up as the man studied the photo. It was as if in a void, where time and breath stand still, like when waiting for someone special to answer "Yes." Or "No."

The man shrugged and looked at Jacoby with confusion. His heart sank, but then he motioned with his hand to turn the photo over.

"Ah," the man said. "Floria-Zanobini."

"Lo sai?" Jacoby confirmed the familiarity and asked where. "Dove?"

"Sulle colline," the man said, twirling his pointer finger for some reason.

Jacoby couldn't translate the words nor the gesture.

"Che cosa?"

"Colline," the man said and now made wave motions with his hand.

Jacoby squinted from lack of comprehension.

"Ah," the man said, throwing his hands up in an 'of course' gesture. "Vai in albergo. Per vedere l'americano."

Jacoby got the 'vai' part meaning 'go' but the 'albergo' was beyond his limited vocabulary. He incorrectly assumed that the 'americano' was him.

"Scusami?" Jacoby asked, starting to feel embarrassed. "Mi dispiace."

The man smiled and came around the counter. He gave the picture back to Jacoby and took him by the wrist, marching him out of the store into the piazza. Jacoby felt like a child and was happy no one was really around. A few buildings down from the corner store, the man stopped in front of a three-story sandstone structure with a large wooden door adorned with ornate metal shapes and a small plaque beside it that read: Hotel Floria-Zanobini.

"Albergo," the man said. "O-tel."

Jacoby pulsed with excitement. A hotel. Same name. He wondered why it never came up in his google searches.

"La stessa?" he asked if it was the same family name.

"Si," the man confirmed. "La stessa famiglia,ma solo l'americano è qui ora."

The kind man rang the bell and waited. Jacoby rubbed his hands together, confused about the 'americano' comment, but thinking that a long lost ancestor might just open the door. And that his life might change in an instant. But no one answered. The store owner looked at his watch and then gestured a recognition.

"Lui è sulle colline."

He was in the 'colline' - whatever that meant. Jacoby had to look that word up.

"Aspetta," the man advised with his hands up and then palms together in prayer. "Presto."

Jacoby had no problem waiting, especially since the man assured him it would be soon. But who was he waiting for? He wished he had the words to ask. Instead, he thanked the man and assured him he would return for his charged phone in trenta minuti.

The man nodded cordially and went back to his shop. Jacoby leaned against the facade of the hotel. The sun had yet to clear the hills, and the piazza was cool and draped in diffuse light. The cafe was open, across the piazza in the far corner beyond the statue, which Jacoby used to block himself from view. He should have asked the shop owner about another place for a caffè. He craved a small comfort, something to tide him over until potentially bigger discoveries arrived, even if his pragmatism whispered that they probably never would.

Getting tired and restless, he sat down with his back against the hotel, feeling forlorn and lost and kind of silly. He craned his neck around the statue, to check on the status of the cafe when a voice from the opposite direction took him by surprise.

"You look like a man without a country," an older man said, approaching Jacoby with a newspaper under his arm, his native English delivered in mezzo-baritone with some Southern twang at the bottom.

It was the man Jacoby had seen foraging by the side of the road. He wore a vest over a dress shirt and khaki pants. He was a modest-sized man with a remarkable presence, a face like Hemingway's, only smaller, gentle and slightly ruddy, with a bulbous nose and insouciant blue eyes, squinted against their intensity. A crown of gray hair flecked with black had a trimmed beard to match. He held out his right hand with a ring on the third finger. Jacoby stood quickly, scratching his back against the wall.

"Bill Guion," the man said. "I understand you're looking for me?"

The sun crested the hills and blanketed the piazza in orange light as the two men shook hands. The contact warmed Jacoby. The gates of a storefront squeaked open. A dog barked. Morning doves cooed. Someone called a greeting across the piazza.

Jacoby took a breath and opened his mouth to share his name when the malevolent cafe owner appeared from the other side of the statue, stomping toward them, her hands karate chopping the air, her words a staccato string which felt, to Jacoby, like machine gun fire. He put up his hands as if begging her not to shoot. The word "inglese" was repeated by her again and again, with a tone that was not pejorative but slipped in between such rapid phrasing and animated gesturing that Jacoby had no ability to decipher the message beyond its apparent hostility. He wanted to run, but his feet wouldn't go.

Bill smiled and put a hand on the woman's shoulder. She took her diatribe to him, and he put his hands together in front of his chest, praying for her to stop talking and calm down. She did and spoke in an animated yet controlled manner to Bill.

A moment later Bill turned to Jacoby.

"She's attempting an apology."

"Really?"

"Yep. Says she feels horribly about what happened the other morning. She thought you were a vagrant not an Englishman."

"I'm American," Jacoby said to her.

"Nicoletta," she said, offering her hand like a penance.

In the new morning light, she looked soft and tawny. Her small, calloused hand that Jacoby held, the only remaining toughness. A head shorter than Jacoby, a pelt of thick hair the color of wet sand framed her face and rested on her bosoms within a cream cashmere sweater, propped like a continental divide above a compact torso and lower-body in boyfriend jeans and blue suede Puma Clydes.

Bill spoke to her rapidly in Italian, and Nicoletta released Jacoby's hand.

"Goodbye americano," she said. "Mi dispiace."

"No problema," Jacoby said, bowing his head. "But my name is Jacoby."

She creased a puzzled smile and walked quickly on solid legs back to the cafe.

Bill tilted his head. "Should I ask what happened the other morning?"

"Please don't."

"Then I won't."

Bill gestured toward the seating area around the statue; they walked over and sat as pigeons fluttered down to peck and beg.

"Jacoby is it?"

"It is."

"Going to be here for a while?"

"Maybe a year."

"Then you're going to want to change that."

"Change what?"

"Your name."

"Why?"

"Because it's too foreign for the people around here. They're far too provincial to adapt to an American name beyond the handful they already know. Hell, I've gone by William my entire adult life, but even that was too much, so I've been Bill since I got here."

"And when was that?"

"Five years ago."

"Five years?"

"Hmm-hmm. I think they're just starting to get used to me."

Both men laughed.

"Why?" Jacoby asked, composed and comforted by the gentle conversation.

"Because these are people who do not adapt quickly. Their whole lives are pretty much within what you can see. Generations pass with very little change."

"No, I mean why'd you come here?"

"Ah, now that's a story. How are you on time?"

Jacoby looked around and huffed. "Pretty good."

"Good then, come to the hotel for breakfast. We can discuss what has brought us both to this most unusual place."

Chapter 13

The Hotel Floria-Zanobini had no awning or any indication whatsoever of its purpose except a small bronze plaque mounted on the facade next to the buzzer by the door. Bill opened the door from a ring of keys and led them through the spacious and empty lobby with comfortable seating and potted plants and reading materials. The walls were hung with oil on acrylic landscapes of the Tuscan countryside all done by the same artist.

Adjacent to a darkened wooden stairwell was a front desk for check-in and a small table with an office chair and a desktop computer. Natural light illuminated the open atrium in back and overhead, spaced with wooden four-tops and dark floors that helped absorb the abundant light. Bill disappeared through a swinging door after pointing to a table near the frosted glass wall in back.

Jacoby sat still, listening to the cacophony from the kitchen of clanging and chopping and sizzling. Aromas of pork and herbs wafted until Bill came through the door with a plate in each hand.

"I've been an ex-pat for 35 years, and the only thing I miss about America is breakfast."

He motioned with his head toward the glass door, and Jacoby opened it for Bill to pass into a courtyard of slate shaded by a wooden trellis strung with wisteria vines. They sat at a wrought-iron table with matching chairs, streaks of blue sky overhead, beside a long and lush garden of dark soil marked by a dozen separate patches.

The ceramic plates steamed with sausage and eggs and stewed tomatoes. Bill slipped back inside, on separate trips, to fetch a coffee pot and two demitasse cups along with cutlery and napkins.

"This is great," Jacoby said with a mouth full of sausage and tomato. "Thanks so much."

"My pleasure," Bill responded, wiping his mouth. "I'm happy for the company. And the chance to speak English."

Jacoby, too, appreciated the comfort of a native language; he was also loving the breakfast, clearly the work of a skilled chef, so he tucked into his plate and encouraged Bill to tell his story.

Bill came to Italy as a journalist working for the AP as a young man. He met an Italian named Fillipo at the bureau in Rome, where they fell in love. Bill quit the bureau and ingratiated himself with an American university in the Trastevere neighborhood as a caterer, student of art history, and finally a professor of art and culinary history courses. Bill and Fillipo lived together near the university and within the university community for 30 years of romantic, cultural and social bliss before retiring to Fillipo's hometown in the hills south of Florence where they would run the family hotel and eventually be buried together in the mausoleum of the family's estate outside the village.

"How long has he been, you know, there?" Jacoby asked, after a moment of cloying silence, his throat choked and dry.

"Four and a half years."

"You'd just got here?"

"Basically, yes. We'd been here just about six months before Fillipo got sick. Stage four pancreatic cancer. He died two weeks later. His family never forgave me."

"Why?"

"They assumed it was my fault."

"Was it?"

"No," Bill laughed before taking on an orator's tone. "This was once a very noble family. Their lineage extends back to the Roman Empire. Some settled here, in Florence, after the collapse; some stayed in Rome. In both places, they were well-established, powerful and incredibly wealthy merchants, though their status in all regards has decreased steadily over the centuries as the family numbers dwindled and members dispersed. The last patriarch, really, Fillipo's father, left his mother for a Venetian countess. They lived in Monoco until their deaths. Fillipo visited on occasion but grew up, essentially, without a father, and he was deemed a failure in many respects because of his lifestyle and work as a mere journalist. His mother assumed, like all good Italian mothers do, that their sons are perfect and any flaws are caused by the hands of others, which is where I come in. The depraved American, Texan no-less, who corrupted her innocent son, made him prefer the company of men and kept him from having children, extending the line. And now there's really nothing left. A rundown estate in the hills and this hotel."

Bill finished the coffee in his cup and stared at withered vines twisting around the trellis. Jacoby exhaled through his nose as his heart began to race. Birds chirped and fluttered in the secluded courtyard. Bill looked stoic in the silence of a conversation he thought over.

"Is she still alive?" Jacoby asked, hoping not to betray the currency which freighted his words.

"Who? The mother?"

Jacoby nodded.

"I believe so, yes. I haven't heard otherwise. She must be pushing 100 at this point."

"No other siblings or relatives?" Jacoby asked, his teeth chattering a bit after he finished speaking.

"Actually, yes," Bill responded, sitting up quickly, drumming his thighs. "There was a sister, much older, rarely mentioned, though she disappeared after the war. It was the dark family secret. Basically, an heiress gone missing. Never to be heard from again. End of story."

The fact that the story might not yet have an end flooded Jacoby with head-spinning awareness speckled with doubt. It couldn't be. It couldn't be her in the photograph. Fillipo's sister? Goose bumps raced up his arm as he reached into his wallet and removed the small, black and white photograph of a young woman sitting on a great lawn behind a villa, an elegant gown spread on the ground around her. With a shaky hand, he extended it to Bill who had leaned back to sip coffee and let his sad narrative fade away.

"Is this her?" Jacoby asked, afraid in so many ways of the answer.

Bill, dubious, took the photo and studied it. After a moment of furrowed staring, he turned it over, where on the back it read in barely visible script: Villa Floria-Zanobini, 1939.

"My heavens," Bill gushed. "Where on earth did you get this?"

Chapter 14

Jacoby barely had time to explain the photograph before Bill whisked him out of the hotel and on to the back of a rusted motorini. With Jacoby clutching Bill's torso, they raced down a narrow road bordered by dense woods on the far side of the village which Jacoby had yet to explore. There was nothing in the low-lying areas spotted with small hills beyond the occasional farmhouse and forests of chestnut and oak. Bill turned onto a wide, dirt road and pointed toward an abbey and cloisters surrounded by dormant industrial equipment and three-wheel vehicles backed with flat beds. The air smelled musty as they bumped past, up a hill and toward a knoll where a great property spread.

The road joined a high fence of metal bars, speared at the top and lined between buttresses of stone. Between the bars was a large expanse nearly as overgrown as the area outside the fence, with wild grass and felled trees and swarms of gorse. The villa was faded into a jaundiced yellow with tilted shutters and a roof of shifted and missing Spanish tiles. Jacoby, still a little stunned by the urgency that erupted in Bill, resigned himself to the position of an observer of someone else's story.

Bill cut the engine and glided up to the entry gate, 50 yards down a sparse gravel path from the faded front door. An arch above the gate had a family crest and the etched title of Villa Floria-Zanobini barely visible.

"What was that?" Jacoby asked.

"What was what?" Bill snapped, pinching his chin and pacing.

"The church or whatever you pointed out, just back there."

Bill gathered himself with a breath and stopped moving. "That's the village consortium, where our prodotti, our products, are made. Wine, oil, vinegar. It's quite an operation, though they refuse to let us expand." Bill motioned cynically with his head toward to gate.

"Do they own everything around here?"

"Used to. Pretty much. Now it's really just this villa, the abbey and all the land you can see. And, of course, the hotel, though it really isn't a hotel as much as it is a pensione, a very high-end one, for relations and acquaintances of the family who may be passing through Florence. It's not like we advertise or welcome tourists."

"But they pay you?"

"Not exactly. I've never had the pleasure of meeting Fillipo's mother or even speaking with her."

"Never?"

"No," Bill responded, trying to maintain a tone of rationality while explaining the absurd. "Fillipo intended to bring me here when we first arrived, to make peace with his mother, to live on the grounds and restore them, but she flat out refused to meet me. Refused to acknowledge my existence. She'd grown far more irrational and bitter than even Fillipo recognized. So, we lived essentially alone in the hotel. Fillipo managed the affairs and I prepared the meals for guests, kept up the property. We talked about going back to Rome, but then he got sick. When he passed, I stayed on alone. I had nowhere else to go and no idea what would happen. Guests eventually returned, on occasion, without warning, as they continue to do, and I take care of them as we once did. Except, now, I do everything. I don't get paid, but I have a place to live."

"What do you do for money?"

"A check comes for expenses, which the bank will cash for me since they know the family. I use what I need sparingly and live off the rest."

"It is enough?"

"Hardly. All of our money was in Fillipo's name. I'm technically an illegal. I came here on a temporary work visa and never left. My income at the university was off the books. I forwarded the checks to Fillipo's accounts. The country doesn't know I exist. Fillipo's mother basically controls my assets, but she refuses to recognize me."

"She might now," Jacoby said, pulling the picture from his wallet.

"She might now," Bill said, smiling. "But first, she'll have to recognize you."

Jacoby felt electric and alive, like he mattered.

•   •   •

Bill rubbed his hands together then pushed the button on a box beside the gate. Both men held the rusted steel bars and stared at the villa's front door. Nothing. Bill rang the buzzer again. They waited. Bill rang the buzzer for the third time, his once visceral enthusiasm fading into dejection.

"I don't know," Jacoby gently broached. "It looks abandoned."

"No. No. Someone's here. People tend to the fattoria, to the production site, year round, even before all the seasonal workers come for the harvest. They live in quarters way beyond the villa, but within the property, closer to the fattoria. Someone has to tend to them."

He hit the buzzer again; the front door slowly opened and a figure emerged.

"Allora," Bill sighed. "Signora," he yelled kindly to the elderly woman in a house coat who peeked her head and shoulders from behind the great door. "Per favore. È la donna qui? È molto, molto importante."

The woman wagged her finger, no, and began to retreat inside. Bill put his head down, then quickly raised it high on an extended neck. "Bruna?" he shouted.

The woman reappeared, the door a little further open, more of her upper body exposed.

"Bruna?" Bill inquired again.

The woman stepped onto the vast landing in front of the door and tilted her head.

"Bruna. Vengo dall'albergo. Sono l'amico di Fillipo. Lui ha parlato di te con me."

The woman began walking slowly toward them, slow enough for Jacoby to piece together a translation of what Bill had told her, particularly the last sentence stating that Filippo spoke of her to him: Lui ha parlato di te con me.

Bill held his breath and crossed his hands under his neck as the woman hobbled up, her face soft and brown and rutted like a walnut shell. She reached through the bars, took Bill's hands and spoke with great warmth.

"E lui ha parlato di te con me."

Tears streamed down Bill's face. Through the bars, Bruna comforted him in a way that Jacoby had never experienced but recognized as maternal and particularly Italian. He felt a little jealous but also tremendous relief at some progress and something so meaningful to Bill. He fought back his own tears just from being there, a witness to so much emotion.

"Vuoi vedere il posto dove si riposa?" Bruna asked.

"Si," Bill said quietly but with great urgency.

They spoke for a moment, passionately yet too rapidly for Jacoby to understand. When finished, Bill released her hands and broke for the motorini.

"How do you know her?" Jacoby asked. "Who is she?"

"She took care of Fillipo as a child. Practically raised him. He'd told me about her. They kept in touch through letters, and he had told her about me!"

"So where are we going?" Jacoby asked, following.

"Around back. This gate can't be opened, but there's a way through the back of the property, through the fattoria."

"But what for?" Jacoby asked. "Where are we going?"

"Vedere il posto dove lui riposa. To see where Filippo is buried."

•   •   •

The road to the abbey was bumpy, rutted by the three-wheelers and watershed from the surrounding hills. The front doors of the abbey were open; men on ladders did work inside large chrome vats. Within the cloisters, wooden olive presses sat dormant. Dozens of oak barrels littered the property, and some were dismantled into piles of wood. A towering mechanical crane perched over the roof of the abbey. Jacoby strained his neck to take it all in, but soon the unusual production site was behind them and the fence with the open gate to the villa lie ahead.

They progressed slowly up hill and onto the property. Bruna waived from a knoll and Bill cranked the throttle as the faded motorini suffered under their weight and urgency. But they made it up to the ridge, on a flat grove behind the villa, well-kept and planted with potted fruit trees and large plants. Wild flowers grew out of the grass and around the edge of a swept, slate patio from where two wooden chairs looked over the grounds below and the rolling hills beyond.

The two men stepped off the motorbike; Bruna took Bill's hand and told him to come. "Vieni," she said.

Jacoby trailed well behind as Bruna led Bill through a meadow toward a cluster of umbrella pines. Within the shadows of the tall trees lay a mausoleum of stone. Jacoby stayed back, behind the pines, as Bruna and Bill slowly approached the burial chamber. Bruna pointed and Bill collapsed to his knees. He put his face in his hands, bowed to the ground and wept without restraint.

Jacoby retreated to the patio, and Bruna joined him shortly after. They sat in silence, staring at the land, which eventually - through the somber ambiance and empathetic distraction - came into focus for Jacoby. He removed the photo from his wallet and handed it to the elderly woman.

"Qui è qui?" he asked if 'here is here,' pointing at the yard just off the patio.

Bruna squinted at the photo, looked up at the property and back again to the picture.

"Si," she said nodding. "Questa è la sorella."

Bill quietly approached, smiling shyly, his eyes red and glossy, his shoulders square.

"Now that was a good cry," he said. "I needed that. Grazie, senora."

Bruna nodded. "Prego."

"Sorella means sister, right?" Jacoby asked Bill.

"That's correct."

"Then that's her," Jacoby said, pointing at the picture Bruna held.

She extended the picture to Bill, but he shook his head.

"Non è mio," he said and motioned to Jacoby. "È suo."

Bruna stood up and asked how. "Come?"

Bill explained how it was found in a box of Jacoby's mother's belongings, in America.

Bruna put a hand on her heart. "Dobbiamo dire la signora!"

"Lo so!" Bill confirmed the immediate need to tell Filippo's mother. "Ma, Dov'è lei?"

"Nella città," Bruna said, a little hesitantly. "In un palazzo segreto."

"Come?" Bill asked.

"La signora ha un posto a Firenze, un posto che nessuno conosce, tranne il gatto."

"Il gatto?"

Bill looked dumbfounded; Jacoby began to worry. This was getting weird.

"Si. Quando va a Firenze, dice, 'vado a vedere il gatto.'"

Bruna wiped her hands together two times in a quiet clap, as if there was nothing more to say.

Bill turned to Jacoby. "All we know is that Fillipo's mother is in Florence in a secret palace marked by a marble cat."

"A cat!" Jacoby gasped, suddenly back in touch with his stake in the matter. "Oh. Yeah. That shouldn't be too hard to find."

Bill asked Bruna when she would return to the estate.

"Non lo so," she said sadly. "È molto vecchia, ma forte, ma molto vecchia. Rimarrà a Firenze fino alla morte. Credo."

Bill turned to Jacoby. "She's very old but in decent health, but we'll have to find her in Florence, by the cat, because she's not coming back here."

Chapter 15

After a harried return to the village, full of bounces and sharp turns and whipping wind, Bill parked the motorini in an alley behind the hotel and quickly dashed off, leaving Jacoby, still sitting on the warm, pinging vehicle, unsure as to what to do until Bill returned, a bashful look highlighted by a sheepish grin.

"I'm terribly sorry, dear Jacoby. I seem to be losing my mind somewhat."

"Why don't we regroup, slow it down a little," Jacoby offered, feeling overwhelmed, as well, but a little more pragmatic than his bouncing new friend.

"Fine idea," Bill said, gusting a flamboyant huff. "Fine idea."

"I've got to get my phone from the store there," Jacoby said, pointing toward the newsstand. "To get in touch with my fiancée."

"Your fiancée?" Bill declared. "I've done all the talking so far, haven't I?"

"Not a problem," Jacoby responded with his hands up. "You probably didn't see this day coming."

"Did you?"

"I had hopes, but you know how that goes."

Bill smiled. "Well, let's, as you suggest, slow it down before rushing into town. Why don't you do what you need to do here in the village, go home, rest up and return for dinner this evening with me at the hotel. Around eight? We can get to know each other better, and I can introduce you to our cucina tipica."

· · ·

Jacoby appreciated that Claire wasn't obsessive about texting. He couldn't imagine the burden of being constantly connected to others through steady sharing of mostly useless information. It was one of the agreements that kept them together and sane to date, though he was kind of anxious to hear from her now, but he couldn't decide if he should let her in on the story of the villa and the reality of the picture. It still seemed a bit too fantastic to share, and he just didn't sense any role for Claire in the adventure.

He picked up his phone from the news kiosk and waited on the corner for it to power on, only to find a bunch of New York City weather updates from an app he forgot to uninstall, a message from his former work friend which began PLEASE READ THIS, which Jacoby deleted, assuming it was another pathetic attempt at a belated apology. There was a single message from his fiancée who had been gone for two whole days to unspecific locations with an unreliable wing-man:

Hi babe. All is well. Dolores a loon. Back day after tomorrow. XO.

He tapped out a return text to Claire of similar tone and shape then stood on the corner feeling genuine enthusiasm about the day's events. Just connecting with such a sweet man as Bill - and aiding him in an act of closure - felt empowering. It was luck and happenstance, but he had been a part of it, and now he was on an adventure of sorts, in Italy, off to find a marble cat in Florence that marked where distant family might await. A lightness came over him: a sense of purpose and peace that he had not experienced in a very long time, but had been coming for him since setting foot in Italy.

Uplifted and optimistic, Jacoby kicked down the narrow street, thinking happy thoughts but leery, always leery, of being too optimistic. Pragmatism was as much a part of him as his brown hair and eyes, so he battled his fledgling sense of deliverance with recognition that this hiding matriarch, pushing a century of life, may never be found or be willing to recognize his story. He had used the photo as kind of a crutch, of something to put some faith in, a mystery to pursue that had more value in its unknown than known. But now the known seemed of potential, yet Jacoby could not reconcile its reality or prevent himself from dabbling in its import. Was he in line for an inheritance of a castle and acres of land? No. No way. He would not do that to himself. Someone who understands profound disappointment and loss does not set themselves up for such things. He took pride in his pragmatism, despite his desperation. At this point of his life, it was day-to-day, a work-in-progress approach. He did not need the fantastic; simplicity is what he sought.

Privilege had never been part of Jacoby's identity - beyond the obvious tenets of race and gender and health and class - but it's hard to feel lucky without a mother, or a stable childhood and adolescence. A mercurial father. He never even had a best friend. Deep down, he felt robbed, and held on to a belief that redemption for his suffering would someday arrive. It was a faith he once put into his serendipitous meeting with Claire, but he knew that he'd been wrong about that. He wouldn't make the same mistake again, so, as he walked down the narrow street in the cool shadows, he dedicated himself to couching his expectations in appropriate skepticism and an appreciation for what it had already accomplished, and the immediate and irrepressible sense of place he enjoyed in Italy, which included this charming, essentially hidden village, a place that somehow already felt like home. He'd even made a new friend.

As he whisked past a minuscule alley, a familiar melody interrupted his thoughts. Jacoby stopped and returned to the opening, a sliver of cobblestone barely wide enough to fit a couple holding hands. The music drew him toward yellow light at the alley's end. The sound increased with each step and soon it was unmistakably what Jacoby suspected from the first: Pearl Jam. Pearl Jam???

Staggered by the dichotomy, he followed the music toward the light. At the end of the alley, the doors and windows were open to an artisan's workshop. Inside, a burly and bearded young man, showing only a sleeveless t-shirt under a thick apron, sat on a stool and stretched leather around the form of a shoe under blaring light from uncovered bulbs that dangled from the ceiling. The music came from a small speaker next to a cellular phone on the wooden counter.

Jacoby cleared his throat. The young man looked up, quizzically at first, until a face of recognition formed. He pointed towards the town square.

"Il negozio è vicino alla piazza. Dietro al forno."

Jacoby understood the sense of directions being provided, assuming the store that sold the workshop's product was near the piazza and that the artisan thought he was interested in shoes.

"No. No," Jacoby said, touching his earlobe. "The music. La musica."

The young man's face lit up. "Pearl Jam. Dagli Stati Uniti. Buono, no?"

"Lo so," Jacoby nodded, tapping his chest. "Sono americano."

The young man's face lit up. "Lo sai Pearl Jam?"

"Si," Jacoby said. "Io. Io sono..." he tried to come up with the word for musician, but it got stuck on his tongue. He strummed a mock guitar instead.

"Ah!" the young man exclaimed, smacking his chest with both hands. "Aspetta!"

He hurried to the back of the shop, banged some things around then returned with a worn and dusty acoustic guitar with plastic strings and corroded knobs.

"Ti piace Pearl Jam? Conosci loro canzoni alla chitarra?"

The young man's eyes blossomed as he shook his hands together in prayer.

Pearl Jam's first album *Ten* had come out when Jacoby was ten years old. And though he didn't discover the album or the band until a few years later, the coincidence always struck him as meaningful, especially after he took up guitar in junior high and the first band he joined, in high school, covered a lot of 90's grunge, especially tunes from Pearl Jam's first four albums. After that, Jacoby's tastes changed and he effectively lost track of the band, but he fondly remembered their early work and remained aware of their perseverance and continued relevance.

Jacoby sat on a stool and began to tune the terribly out of tune guitar, a Giannini that needed the bridge tightened and the pegs lubed, new strings, as well. Not to mention a solid dusting. Even in horrible shape, the guitar had a decent tone, due to being well-built. It felt so good in Jacoby's hands, like a secret place he had lost and rediscovered. An old lover. His mind skirted back to his many hours over many years practicing guitar alone in his bedroom and then his days as a fledgling guitarist in his very first band.

"Piace Nirvana?" Jacoby asked.

"No," the young man said with a grimace and a vigorous shake of his large head.

"Soundgarden?"

"No."

"Alice in Chains?"

"No."

"Only Pearl Jam?"

"Only Pearl Jam. Number one. The best."

He held out his left forearm to proudly show the band's emblem emblazoned in dark blue ink. He looked like a little boy in that moment, and even more so when Jacoby tested the tone of the strings with the opening lick to "Alive."

The young man patted the work counter in front of him, his face aglow with exultation. Jacoby stopped after one, slightly sloppy, turn through the riff.

"No, no, no," the young man implored, spinning a front finger round and round. "Vai. Vai. Vai."

Jacoby played the refrain a few times over until, right in time, the young man began to sing the opening lines of the song. Jacoby was stunned. Not that he knew the English words but that he sang them in such perfect pitch, an Eddie Vedder sound-alike in dead-on baritone.

They made it through two rollicking verse and chorus sections before Jacoby stopped abruptly at the musical interlude. He rarely played guitar solos and his wrist began to ache, his fingertips burn, from lack of practice. The young man swayed for a few more moments, as if the music were still in his ears. He looked up, flushed with his chest rising and falling in rhythm.

"Do you speak English?" Jacoby asked. "Parli inglese?"

"No," the young man said with a shaking finger. "Only Pearl Jam."

Jacoby smiled, held out his hand and introduced himself as 'Jake.'

"Giovanni," the young man responded.

Giovanni motioned toward the guitar for more, but Jacoby begged off, shaking his hands, muttering "practice."

"Ah," Giovanni sighed. "Capsico."

"Conosci Bill, l'americano?" Jacoby asked.

"Si! Naturalmente," Giovanni said. "Siete amici?

"Si," Jacoby said, warmed by the confirmation of his new friendship.

"Domani parlerò con lui," Giovanni declared. "Prendi la chitarra e fai pratica."

Jacoby held the guitar up and motioned toward the door.

"Si," Giovanni confirmed. "Vai. Pratica. Ci vediamo presto. Parlerò con Bill domani."

Jacoby nodded. He understood the imperative from Giovanni, to take the guitar and practice. Only Pearl Jam. Giovanni would speak of their new arrangement with Bill. Jacoby walked out of the shop with a guitar over his shoulder, back down the alley and through the village, up the hill toward home, unobservant of the rose colored twilight awash on the plush surroundings, thinking only of how wonderful it was to have new friends, and to be in a band again.

•　　　•　　　•

At the barn, Jacoby brought the guitar to the shed out back, on a knoll beyond the thick hedge, and rummaged through the utilitarian detritus in the last remnants of light gathered in the shed. The structure was old, no door or lights, with listing wooden walls spotted with knot holes. The tin roof corroded along the edges. It smelled of dust and rotting wood. Half of the available floor space was littered with rounds cut from oak and birch trees. On a thick and wide stump sat an iron wedge for splitting lumber. A rubber-handled ax leaned against the stump. A few pieces of wood had been split, but most remained whole. On a rusted set of metal shelves, tools were scattered along with various cans without labels.

Jacoby shook and sniffed the cans he could lift, until he found one with a viscous smell of oil. Through a long, narrow straw attached to the nozzle, he released a sample of lubricant onto the floor of wood chips and sawdust. Sitting on the wood stump, with the guitar between his knees, he carefully dabbed a small portion into the guitar's metal tuning pegs, turning them gently to nudge fluid movement. He tuned the guitar some more and played a few notes. His left fingertips stung from the pressure. He knew he needed new strings and to recondition his wrists and forearms and fingertips for playing. Since leaving the band and moving to New York, Jacoby hardly played. He sold his ESP electric, handmade in Japan with a wooden neck, for a much needed $2,000, but he kept his Yamaha acoustic, less valuable and more personal, having been a gift from his father. But it stayed mostly in its case in a corner, coming out for a periodic walk down memory lane but never true practice. Jacoby figured that he was finished with music and that nostalgia was a deterrent to moving on, like keeping in touch with an old lover after breaking up. But the feel of the guitar in his hands and the feeling of playing, with someone else no less, had his passion for music resurfacing fast.

Just outside the barn, on impulse, he leaned the guitar against a wheelbarrow and went back inside. The ax felt formidable in his hands as he used the flat edge to tap the pointed wedge into a piece of oak. Once secure, he drew back the ax, using the flat side to smash into the wedge. It was heavier than he imagined. The wedge only sunk in a few inches as the ax sent vibrations through his hands and arms and neck. He pulled back the ax again and, raising it higher this time over his shoulder, delivered a blow that split the wood into two pieces. Pores opened along his forehead as his breath instantly increased. The idea of a workout occurred, splitting wood until dark, but that would have to wait for another time. He had dinner plans at the hotel with Bill.

Chapter 16

The village was dark when Jacoby arrived. Between a Smart car and a three-wheeled Ape, he parked in an angled spot across from the hotel, facing the piazza. There were no other vehicles and no people around. Everything was closed. Serene. The church bell rang eight times before Jacoby took an easy breath and pushed the buzzer beside the hotel's front door.

Bill quickly answered, dressed nicely in a tailored oxford shirt, slacks, and suede loafers, a starched white apron around his waist. "Please, come in," he said with a slightly decorous bow.

The foyer was lit from a lone light in the sitting area. Light from the dining area in back illuminated the hallway. The front desk was dark except for a desktop monitor that blinked with a Dell logo.

All the tables in the dining room were covered in white tablecloth without settings, except for one in the middle where two places were set with patterned ceramic bowls over matching plates at either end of a table that could seat six but only had chairs at each end. The light from dangling fixtures had been adjusted to just less than bright. Atrium windows at the far end held a reflection of the room.

"Care for a cocktail?" Bill asked, already walking towards the small bar. Jacoby hadn't noticed it in the morning, a cozy, dark corner made of oak, fronted by three stools. Bill lifted the counter and stepped behind the bar. Jacoby sat on a stool.

"What do you recommend?"

"The house special is a Negroni."

Jacoby looked around the empty 'house.'

"Fillipo and I had one together every night, both here and in Rome. I do love them, but I refuse to drink alone. Well, I refuse to drink a Negroni alone, that is."

"I'm here for you," Jacoby joked, patting his heart with mock-sentimentality.

Bill smiled and whisked two long cocktail glasses from below the bar and added some ice. Bottles of gin, Campari, and sweet vermouth were tossed in the glass and given a quick spin with a long spoon. Orange peel was sliced off and used as garnish. Bill presented the translucent ruby cocktail with a nod.

"To a magnificent day," Bill toasted.

The men touched glasses and drank. It both smelled and tasted a bit medicinal to Jacoby at first, before the gin shot through, balanced by the sweet vermouth, to create a fine, heady balance.

"Yikes," Jacoby said. "That's pretty good."

"The perfect apertivo," Bill declared, closing his eyes to savor the pleasure and sensory memory. "Now, if you'll excuse me, I have a little work to do in the kitchen in preparation of our supper."

"Can I help?"

"No. No, but thank you. Enjoy your cocktail and forgive my absence."

Bill took his drink and hurried across the room and through the kitchen door. Jacoby sat in the quiet and surveyed his surroundings. He loved the ambiance of bars and dining rooms. The ceilings and floors and walls. Stone and brick and wood. The bottles and glasses and tables set for guests. He found wine racks beautiful, and Bill had a cool one carved into the stone wall, crisscrossed and filled with hundreds of bottles. The room soon smelled of onions, and Jacoby relaxed on the barstool like it was a hammock.

•   •   •

They started with a spring minestrone, generous with pieces of artichoke, asparagus, and carrots in a broth of pureed onions and leeks with a snap of garlic. Torn basil and spinach added to the texture and perfume. On the side was a charred piece of country bread rubbed with tomato. Bill had grown all the ingredients in the garden out back, except the asparagus, which he found wild on the side of the road.

"I was wondering what you were looking for," Jacoby commented on the asparagus.

"Oh, you've seen me?"

"A few times."

"I forage every morning, first thing," Bill said. "And again in the afternoon, if there's time."

"Just for asparagus?"

"Oh, no. There's all sorts of wonders growing wild out here. Mushrooms and spring onions. Leeks. Garlic. Frutti di Bosco - fruits of the woods. And, of course, the greatest prize of all, the exotic tartufo."

"Truffle."

"Very good," Bill said with a nod. "Have you had the pleasure?"

"A few times now."

"Well, you are very lucky. They are my absolute favorite, but they are becoming harder and harder to find, especially around here."

"Maybe I could help?"

Bill smiled. "I have some young cacciatori on retainer, but they are far more interested in the beasts who eat the tartufo than the tartufo itself - not that I can blame them for that since cinghiale are magnificent, especially when well fed on something most people can't find or afford."

"I've seen them."

Bill's chin rose. "Cinghiale?"

"No," Jacoby said, disappointed in disappointing his new friend. "The cacciatori. They hunt in the hills near the property where we live, even though they're not supposed to be up there."

"Where is it precisely that you live?"

"In a barn behind a villa in the hills, just off the road that leads to

Florence."

"Ah," Bill smiled. "The high rent district."

"If you say so."

"I do," Bill said, matter of fact, "But please - and forgive me for getting around so late to this - tell me what has brought you here for one year. Are you some sort of heritage hunter?

Jacoby laughed out loud and nearly choked before being able to speak.

·　　·　　·

Over fresh fettuccine with fava beans and grated Pecorino cheese, Jacoby told Bill his story and the story of him and Claire and their primary reasons for being in Italy. Bill was a terrific listener, tending to their needs at the table while remaining focused on Jacoby's narrative.

"Fired for homophobia, eh?" he mused, rubbing his beard. "A sign of progress."

"Yeah, but," Jacoby protested. "It was a joke..."

"Oh, I know," Bill interrupted. "Your innocence is obvious, but it's just that I grew up gay in the 50s and 60s in East Texas. I was called 'cocksucker' and "faggot' more than I was called Bill, and while I hate to see anyone treated unfairly, there's a sense of redemption knowing that kind of language, and the brutality that usually comes with it, is no longer as acceptable and that gay people and their advocates can be entitled to justice, on occasion, not to mention the same sense of absurdity and overreaction that others have been entitled to for so long."

"I guess," Jacoby muttered, feeling both wronged and foolish for his self-pity.

Bill refilled their wine glasses with a round, violet blend that Jacoby recognized from Paolo's collection. With a raised glass and no precursor, he said, "And here we are."

·　　·　　·

The wine-soaked main course was a rabbit loin wrapped in

pancetta served over fluffy polenta dotted with chopped green olives. Bill and Jacoby ate and drank and spoke of their looming adventure into Florence proper, in search of a matriarch holed up in a palace marked by a cat statue. They laughed at their dim prospects, which were soothed by the magnificent meal and flowing wine.

Bill offered a glimmer of hope. He knew a native son, a famous restaurateur and unofficial Florentine historian, who might be able to help them and could certainly provide a decent meal. At least they had a plan, and prospects for a solid lunch.

"Let's say we somehow find Fillipo's mother," Jacoby broached, swirling his wine and spinning his own skepticism. "What do we tell her?"

"We don't tell her anything," Bill countered. "We show her the picture. She will either recognize it or not."

"Yeah, but then what? Won't she want answers? Won't she want to know how this strange American found a picture of her daughter in a dusty box in Massachusetts?"

Bill rubbed his chin, pulled down his bearded cheeks. His eyes were glassy, and Jacoby could tell he had kept Bill up too late, accepted too much of his hospitality. It had been a long day, especially for Bill. They sat in silence for a few minutes; Jacoby got up to clear the plates and would not take no for an answer.

"Wait," Bill said. "I have an idea."

Jacoby ignored Bill, piling up the plates and platters, ferrying them through the kitchen door. The open space was bright and spotless as an operating room, of white tiled walls and floors, of stainless steel counters and metal racks. The cooking equipment was modest yet functional, well-maintained. Jacoby washed the dishes above an industrial sink then dried them by hand.

Back in the dining room, Bill had filled the bulb of two long-stemmed glasses with clear grappa.

"Now," Bill pronounced. "Can I share my idea?"

"Sure," Jacoby answered. "Go ahead."

Both men sipped the grappa.

"In the morning," Bill announced, "we shall go see the butcher."

"Um. OK. Why?"

"This is not America, where butchers are hidden in the back of grocery stores. Here, they are men of honor. Revered. Respected by the whole community. They are like mayors. And historians. They know everything. And this particular butcher has been around for many, many years. If anyone knows what happened to the missing daughter, what circumstances surrounded her disappearance, he will."

"Sounds good to me," Jacoby said. He finished the grappa and stood to leave, too quickly, though; he swayed a bit and had to hold the back of the chair to keep from stumbling.

Bill laughed. "Looks like we stayed up too late making our plans. Good thing we're in a hotel. I should be able to find you a room. Come with me and I'll make you up a bed."

"No. No. No," Jacoby refused. "Do you have a blanket? I'll sleep on the couch in the front room."

"That we can do," Bill said with a nod. "We must be well-rested for our adventure."

Chapter 17

Light began to slip through the shuttered front window around six a.m., but Jacoby didn't notice until Bill opened the wooden blinders fully to the piazza around 8:00. Jacoby rubbed his eyes and slipped from the cashmere blanket Bill had told him came from a nearby goat farm. Jacoby stood, stretched and rubbed the so-soft blanket on his face before beginning to fold it into squares.

"Buongiorno," Bill, bathed in morning light, greeted him.

"Buongiorno."

"Dormi bene?"

"Si."

Jacoby had slept well.

"I thought we'd go to the cafe for a cappuccino," Bill said. "Before we pay our visit to the butcher."

"Works for me," Jacoby said, recognizing the importance of having made peace with Nicoletta.

•   •   •

The sun had risen over the hills and spread orange light on the piazza and its surroundings. The stores were open and shoppers came and went into the small shops like bees browsing flowers. Three little boys kicked a soccer ball around. A group of old men in tweed suits and caps sat around the statue and fed the pigeons. As Bill and Jacoby passed, the old men tipped their caps and nodded, their old eyes shaded from the rising sun.

"Does it ever rain here?" Jacoby asked.

Bill laughed. "Wait until the rainy season. You'll forget you ever asked that question."

"When's that?"

"After the harvest, late in Autumn. It will start raining one day and not stop until winter's nearly over."

"Sounds depressing."

"Oh, it can be."

Jacoby could sense the dread in Bill's tone. What an especially lonely time it must be for a widower. He thought of his father and the burden of being left alone. He then wondered if he would be alone come harvest time or where he'd even be. It was all so uncertain, but it was morning, and the sun shined upon him and his new friend as they crossed to the piazza's far corner in search of a simple pleasure in a cup of cappuccino.

Adjacent to the cafe's far side, right up on the piazza's surface, a mud-caked jeep was parked askance. The top was off, a shotgun aimed at the sky rested on the passenger seat. Jacoby recognized the jeep from the passing on the dirt road by the barn. He remembered Paolo's anger. A short-haired border collie, with a black spotted coat, sat shivering in the back seat. Jacoby approached with a fist out, offering his scent.

"Better not," Bill said. "That's a good dog, but mistreated. You never know what might set him off."

The dog whimpered as Jacoby pulled back and followed Bill into the cafe. The small front room had a polished curved bar along the far wall. Behind was a large mirror fronted with bottles of Italian liqueurs and wines. An industrial espresso machine took up much of the available space, its aroma filling the room with a scent of bitter roast beans circulated by a ceiling fan. The counter under the bar had pastries behind glass. The rest of the room was filled with cafe bric-a-brac, drinks and snacks and boxed varieties of cakes and chocolate.

From the back room, Nicoletta appeared through the riotous clamor of masculine conversation, her hands full with cups and small plates. She hurried to the bar and blew the bangs from her eyes. Bill cleared his throat.

"Oh! Ciao. Ciao," Nicoletta called, wiping her hands on the apron over her hips. "Prego."

She motioned to the bar, which she scurried behind, dumped the plates and cups in a small sink and began to put the espresso machine into action, banging and twisting and pulling. Steam rose along with fresh aroma.

Bill leaned into the bar; Jacoby sidled up next to him.

"Due cappucino, signorina," Bill asked cordially.

"Si. Si. Pronto," Nicoletta answered over her shoulder. "Due minuti." She threw her head towards the backroom and said with mock-formality. "I cacciatori sono qui." She made a harrumph with her shoulders that Jacoby found charming. She checked over her shoulder and gave him a quick smile.

"Ciao, americano," she said.

"Ciao, Nicoletta," he answered.

She wore a hooded blue sweatshirt from Aeropostale along with factory-torn jeans. While Jacoby didn't necessarily appreciate American fashion aimed at teens, he was pleased to see a familiar style and to know not every woman in Italy dressed to the nines on every occasion. He began to feel self-conscious of his own ruffle-clothed, mussed-hair appearance. His mouth tasted sour. He felt sticky under his arms.

Nicoletta ferried four espressos in two hands to the back. Bill followed. Before crossing into the back room, he waved Jacoby over. The table in the center of the room held four men in camouflage gear. They were wild-haired, unshaven, and relatively young. A bottle of grappa and four shot glasses was on the table in front of them. Two shotguns rested on the next table, muzzles pointed at the far wall.

Bill approached the man with his back to the room, who did all the talking in a boisterous voice, cracked by fatigue and informed by alcohol. Bill put a hand on the man's shoulder, and he turned quickly with his chair, holding his arms out wide in the new found silence.

"Ah, Mr. Bill!! Come stai?"

The man had chestnut brown hair turned into curly locks that dangled on his forehead and neck. He sat tall in the chair and crossed his arms over a broad chest, throwing his head back in mock-contempt.

"Sto bene, grazie," Bill said. "Qualunque fortuna ieri notte?"

"No," the hunter said. "Niente."

Bill took a deep breath, stared at the floor for a moment.

"Va bene," he said with a nod. "In bocca al lupo stasera."

He turned to leave but the hunter grabbed his arm.

"Chi è questo?" the hunter asked with curious detachment, raising his chin and eyes towards Jacoby. "Il tuo nuovo pezzo di culo?"

Jacoby sensed the crudeness in the comment. The other men laughed, and Bill joined in good nature, though Jacoby could tell Bill couldn't stand the hunter and his friends but knew how to handle himself in hostile company.

"No. No. Solo un amico. Sfortunatamente per me, preferisce la compagnia delle donne."

The hunters all nodded at Jacoby. The leader filled their glasses with grappa and raised his own to the sky. The others followed.

"Ficha!" the curly-haired hunter said, looking at Jacoby.

"Ficha!" The others repeated in concert.

They drank together then slammed their glasses on the table and saluted Jacoby with thumbs up and wolfish grins.

Jacoby returned a self-conscious thumb-up. Bill caught him by the arm on his way back into the bar room.

"What was that all about?" Jacoby asked, bemused, as they approached the bar where two cappuccinos awaited.

"They were toasting to the fig, ficha."

Nicoletta shook her head as she wiped the counter.

"A fig?" Jacoby asked.

"Why, yes," Bill said, "but in their vernacular, they are referring to the vagina."

"Nice," Jacoby said, offended and amused, recognizing that men were morons all over the world.

"Not my tribe," Bill said, adding sugar to his foam-topped coffee. He grew quiet for a moment; Jacoby sensed his distress. Nicoletta put two pastries in front of them on a plate and walked away but not before patting the hand of Bill and offering a wan smile.

"What were you talking to the hunter about?" Jacoby asked. "Truffles?"

"Yes, but also cinghiale. The village sagra is at the end of the month, and every year I make a wild boar ragu - it's actually my grandmother's recipe from East Texas - and everyone loves it. Say it's the best they've ever had, which is something. I'm getting worried that this year I won't have anything to cook, which would be a shame since it's really the only day that I feel like a true part of the village."

"What's a sagra?"

"A festival. People have them all over, especially in Spring and Fall, seasons of bounty. Ours is right here in the piazza, every year, the day after the city of Florence fetes their patron saint, St. John the Baptist, on the 24th of June."

"Sounds like fun."

"Oh, it is. I do hope you'll join me. In fact, I could really use your help that day - it's a lot of work. If we have any work to do, that is."

"So, you pay the hunter a fee whether he catches the cinghiale or finds truffles or not?"

"Yep."

"You trust him?"

Bill shrugged. He tore a piece of pastry off and put it in his mouth, where he allowed it to dissolve before washing it down with a sip of cappuccino.

"I trust her," he said, nodding at Nicoletta who was on another journey to tend to the back room party.

"So?"

"They're married."

"No."

"It breaks my heart, too. Poor thing. Met her down in Naples a few years ago, brought her up here. She must have been desperately poor.

This is his family's business, but she does all the work."

"How do you know you can trust her?"

"Well, I'm not certain, of course, but we have a special bond, if you will, as stranieri."

"Strangers?"

"That is correct, though I as an American, a gay one at that, am far more strange."

Jacoby took his pastry off the plate and motioned for Bill to follow him out the door.

"What is it?" Bill asked once they arrived outside.

Jacoby approached the jeep and started feeding small pieces of pastry to the dog, who gobbled them up with sloppy vigor.

"I don't think the hunter is being straight with you."

"And why's that?"

"They've been hunting up in the hills where we live. I saw them one morning, a few days ago, coming back down the hill with a huge cinghiale strapped to the hood."

Bill looked distressed. Betrayed. "I suspected as much," he said, staring at the end of his nose. "But I had no proof."

"Now you do," Jacoby stated.

"They will call you a liar."

"Look at the hood. And the grill."

Bill walked over to inspect. Among the mud were clear traces of blood.

"Well, there you have it," Bill sighed.

"What are you going to do?"

"Stay here," Bill told Jacoby before walking into the cafe.

Jacoby continued to feed the hound until the pastry was gone. He petted the neglected dog behind the ears and along its dirt-caked breast bone as tightness filled his own chest; adrenalin coursed through his veins, making his head spin. He regretted telling Bill, though he was also glad that he did. He hated fucking bullies, and these pricks were bullying and cheating a man three times their age, a man somewhat displaced and deserving great respect. The firearm loomed in the front seat of the jeep. He didn't know if he should hide it or take up arms. He thought of grabbing the dog and escaping once Bill came out. If Bill came out.

Bill came out a moment later and walked straight across the piazza. The dog barked as Jacoby left its side to sidle up to Bill on his way. They were past the statue, more than halfway across the piazza. Bill stopped. He looked back at the cafe. The hunters had come outside to stand in front of their jeep to glare but not speak. The dog was silenced, as were the men. Bill stared them down and then addressed Jacoby.

"What happened in there?" Jacoby asked.

"I got my retainer money back."

"How?"

"When I made a deal with the hunter and his cohorts, I insisted on a little insurance be held by an intermediary, in case of malfeasance or misrepresentation."

"And who was that?"

"Why, Nicoletta, of course."

"And she had no problem giving you the money back?"

"Not at all."

"Won't she get in trouble?"

"I made the deal with her separately, before I agreed to her husband's terms. She simply siphoned off the money and held it for safe keeping. The man knows nothing about his own business. I didn't even have to ask for it. I went to the back to tell her asshole of a husband that we were no longer in business together and, afterward, I came to the bar and she handed me the money. Not a word was exchanged. Smart girl."

"Wow," Jacoby said. "Pretty smart on your end, too."

"You don't mess with Texas, son, not even in Tuscany."

Both men laughed, though not with mirth.

"By the way," Bill said, filling Jacoby's hand with a fistful of Euros. "Take this."

"What? Why?" Jacoby asked, somewhat stunned, holding the money like it was contraband.

"Found money."

"What?"

"It's a custom in Italy not to keep found money, to give it to someone else so as to avoid bad luck."

"This isn't found money - it's yours."

"Well, yes, technically that's correct, but to me it feels found. I don't want it. I'm giving it to you."

"Am I supposed to give it to someone else? Is that how it works?"

"Absolutely not. It's yours and yours alone. Be generous with it, though."

Jacoby felt staggered and touched by such an odd and generous gesture. He smiled and shrugged at Bill, stuck the money in his front pocket, wondering how much it actually was.

"Come on," Bill said. "Maybe you can spend some at the butcher."

Chapter 18

The butcher shop was across the one lane road that topped the piazza. The two men walked through plastic slats, into a pristine, odorless room where cuts of meat garnished with rosemary and thyme glistened under the protective glass of a long, marble-topped counter. From the ceiling, shanks of prosciutto and cylinders of cheese dangled. Bottles of wine and condiments were shelved on the walls. In the corner, a large rotisserie oven was dormant. No one was there.

"This, my friend, is an antique macelleria," Bill said with his hands out to his sides. "Established the century before last. Still owned and operated by the same family. I find that very inspiring."

"The meats' pretty good, too," Jacoby added.

"You've had?"

"Our landlord had me over for dinner the night we arrived. Served a mixed roast from the village butcher. I felt like rubbing it on my chest."

"Oooohh," Bill said, his lips forming a o. "That does sound good."

"Ohhh!" The butcher's bellow added to the odd chorus as he barreled through swinging doors centered behind the counter. He was fair-haired and rosy cheeked, well-fed and vibrant despite a slight limp and a stoop to his shoulders. "Come stai, Johnny?"

"Buongiorno, Lorenzo," Bill responded, smiling and bowing his head with fond reverence.

"Vieni," the butcher said and disappeared back through the swinging doors.

Bill led Jacoby by the arm around the counter and into the back room. The white room was well lit, with a large table in the center flanked by a wooden block draped with mallets and enormous carving knives. The tiled walls and floor sparkled. Behind a glass door of a meat closet, massive carcasses—bone white and blood red—hung from hooks. There was still no odor.

"Salsiccia," the butcher said, motioning toward the table where ceramic bowls were filled with ground pork and pancetta, surrounded by mason jars full of seasonings. Beside a sullied meat grinder was a sausage-stuffing device, with an opaque casing hanging flaccid off the tip. The butcher sat in a wooden chair next to the sausage making apparatus and measured by hand equal portions of salt, pepper, and fennel seed, which he sprinkled over the ground meats and began to gently mix with his fingers.

"Think he's done this before?" Bill asked rhetorically of Jacoby.

"Once or twice."

The butcher lifted his head from his task. "Chi è questo? Un altro Johnny?"

"Si," Bill said. "Da New York. Lui è qui per, forse, un anno."

The butcher made a grand smirk, as if impressed.

"Bravo, Johnny," he said to Jacoby and went back to his work.

Bill explained that the butcher calls all Americans "Johnny" since that is how they referred to the Allied soldiers of American descent who aided the British in the liberation of Florence from The Nazis during World War II. In preparation for the attack, they had set up in the hills south of Florence, including this village, for many months. The butcher was just a boy then. To Jacoby, it seemed, that he was still a boy.

The butcher got up from the table and hung a flaccid sausage casing from his crotch and shook his pelvis as a goofy smile bounced around his face.

"Lovely, Lorenzo," Bill commented. "Bravo."

Without washing or even wiping off his hands, the butcher went to a windowsill where baguettes were stacked in a basket. He ripped one in half and returned to the table to tear off smaller pieces and slather them with the sausage filling.

"Qui," he said, handing a piece each to Bill and Jacoby. "Sushi di Toscana," the butcher toasted to the offering of raw meat.

Bill and Jacoby exchanged hesitant looks as the butcher gobbled his own slice of pork tartare, waiting to be joined by his guests. Jacoby's stomach jumped, objecting to the offer that his head had to overrule, not wanting to offend the man they came to see on important business.

Jacoby took a reluctant bite and fought off thoughts of his former colleague back in New York who got trichinosis simply from eating under-cooked pork. What he had in his mouth hadn't been cooked at all. The paste covered his tongue and teeth, alerting his taste buds to the seasonings, especially the fennel seed. The meat had a mild, pleasant flavor. The bread was a blessing. He kept a calm countenance, nodding at the butcher as if they were sharing a familiar and tasty snack. Jacoby swallowed the last bite and quickly circled his mouth with his tongue and pushed it across his teeth to squeegee off the odd sensation that permeated.

He looked over at Bill who was still holding his piece of raw breakfast pate, which he quickly handed to Jacoby with a wan smile and a sly wink before addressing the butcher in rapid conversation regarding the missing heiress.

Jacoby held the second offering at his side, thinking about a way to discretely ditch it, until Bill and the butcher stopped speaking to study him and his odd pause from breakfast. Jacoby smiled and dug into his encore offering of "Sushi di Toscana" as the two other men continued to speak at length in a way that he couldn't understand but could tell was of great value to their purpose and, hopefully, worth the sacrifice of risking death from food poisoning in the back of an antique butcher shop.

●　　　●　　　●

"What'd he say? What'd he say?" Jacoby begged, hot on the heels of Bill who had bounded out of the butcher shop and across the narrow street and into the piazza after offering profuse thanks to the old butcher, including a firm grasp of two sausage-smeared hands and a fat kiss for each rosy cheek.

"You won't believe this," Bill said over his shoulder without slowing down. "My head is spinning."

They passed the corner news kiosk and were soon upon the hotel, where Bill stopped abruptly. He waited patiently for the church bells to bong nine times and then resumed his enthusiasm.

"We have to find her."

"Who?"

"She has to hear this."

"Who? Fillipo's mother?"

"Yes, it's almost too fantastic to believe, but the butcher knows the whole story."

"What story?"

"About her daughter and the American."

"What about them?"

"She fell in love with an American lieutenant. He was from Ithaca, New York. The butcher remembered precisely because it's Greek."

A shiver ran through Jacoby from the fantastic story coming to light. It had been smoke, really, to him, even as things began to come somewhat together, but now there were enough pieces in place to provide a picture of reality. An actual connection was being made. Something might literally come of it, all the waiting and wondering, always belied by skepticism. But now, the enthusiasm was vital, real, he could feel it thread through his blood and breath.

"That's where my mother was from. Ithaca," he said quickly. "My father was at Cornell, for college, right, in Ithaca, and my mother was from the town. She grew up there. That's where they met. Holy shit."

"Well that makes sense then, doesn't it?" Bill said more than asked. "Because that's where they would have gone when she left Italy with the American after the war. Back home."

"So, what are we thinking here - that the woman in the picture is my grandmother?"

"Seems possible, if not probable."

Bill's face looked boosted by collagen, and Jacoby felt warmed by the discovery of information rooted in logic not magical thinking. There was currency in the words "grandmother" coming out of his mouth; he could feel it on his lips. He needed to know more.

"So what happened with them?" Jacoby begged. "You know, like what was their deal? Did the butcher know?"

"He most certainly did," Bill declared with relish. "They were the talk of the village. The beautiful heiress and the dashing American. Her family, of course, was not to know any of it, as they would absolutely not approve of her involved with a soldier, much less an American one, so they stole away together one night, never to be heard from again."

"What?" Jacoby asked. "That's it?"

Bill nodded, but Jacoby was annoyed by the abrupt ending.

"And they never found out? They never asked around, investigated? I mean, like, why didn't they ask the butcher or anyone else?"

"Because, my dear sweet boy," Bill said, "This is Italy, and the nobilità do not speak to the butcher or the other common people. The answer was right in front of their nose, but they never bothered to open their mouths to simply ask."

Jacoby felt sick. "How awful," was all he could think to say.

"Yes," Bill agreed. "It is awful. It destroyed them, really. The husband, Fillipo's father, left shortly after, and Fillipo himself left for Rome as soon as he was old enough, so the poor mother has been living essentially alone in misery for half a century."

He thought of his father but still had to ask, "How could someone be so miserable and live that long?"

Bill laughed without humor. "This is Italy. Mothers embrace the pain brought by their children. They practically live for it."

Chapter 19

Bill sent Jacoby home to clean up and dress properly for a day "in town." Despite the sad reminder of his father's suffering and knowledge that his great grandmother shared the same fate, he felt uplifted by the news. He had a family, or at least he had had a family in Italy. And they were of the nobilità. It didn't bother him that they had fallen on hard times. Seemed like a family trait, and - who knows - maybe he could redeem them all. And that was his fate. Regardless, he felt the kind of steady confidence associated with his better days, periods in his life of fortitude and comfort, when his one-man band was tight.

Jacoby moved about the barn efficiently and returned to the village square an hour later in a crisp, white oxford over indigo stretch denim from an East Village designer famous for outfitting fashionable rock stars. With his hair parted and tight on the sides and fresh skin under his clothes, he felt very, very clean. And very alive. Things were happening for him, good things. It seemed like a blessing.

"Ready young man?" Bill asked after climbing into the front seat of the car idling in front of the hotel. "To find your great granny?"

Jacoby revved the car's engine and set the wheels into motion with a chirp.

The drive was quick and quiet, a straight shot down the hill into Florence proper past the low-slung ramparts of apartment buildings and retail offerings before the trees rose as the river grew near. Jacoby followed a tour bus up the winding road to Piazza Michelangelo. He parked in the nearly empty lot and got out. Bill followed, looking around curiously while admiring the view.

"And how do we get to town from here?" Bill asked.

"You've never been up here before?"

"Why, no," Bill said. "I'm not a tour bus."

He smiled and followed Jacoby down the switchback path to the San Niccolo Tower, from where Bill took the lead through the namesake neighborhood and across the River Arno towards the heart of Florence. They initially followed a similar route that Dolores had led, on the narrow sidewalk of a busy street, curving toward the city center, but after Piazza Santa Croce, they turned in the other direction to take quiet lanes spotted with bicyclists and pedestrians and the occasional compact car, towards the outskirts of what would still be within the once high walls that surrounded the city.

They strolled in silence on ancient streets - Bill's hands clasped behind his back; Jacoby's tucked into the front pockets of his pants - past cracked facades and tiny storefronts and fruit stands with cats asleep in wicker baskets. At an open air market, Bill browsed antiques while Jacoby came upon a ruffled man selling musical supplies out of a crate. He found a pack of metal guitar strings.

"What are those for?" Bill asked.

"The shoemaker's guitar," Jacoby said, feeling a pang of belonging.

"Ah, you've met Giovanni," Bill sighed. "He's a true artisan, fourth generation. His shoes are exquisite, though I recognize his passion lies elsewhere."

"How do you know him?"

"I tend to find more companionship with the village's younger generation than their parents or even my own contemporaries."

"He's definitely passionate about American music."

"You know what else he is passionate about?"

"What?"

Bill looked playfully in both directions.

"Nicoletta," he whispered.

Jacoby's mouth opened in a pleasing gesture of surprise.

"Yes," Bill confirmed. "And she feels the same way. They are in love. I pretend to pay her to clean rooms at the hotel, and young Giovanni sneaks around back, where they rendezvous on the terrace."

"Do they, you know, get a room?"

"No!" Bill laughed. "That's what I would do, my God, but they seem happy to stay under the cover of trellis and kiss. He reads her poetry. Sings her songs. It's incredibly romantic, and no one knows, besides me, and now you."

Jacoby turned the key to lock his lips, enjoying the thrill and empowerment of being privy to a juicy secret. Bill nodded and continued down the road with Jacoby in tow, happy to follow along.

Bill stopped suddenly and put his hands on top of Jacoby's shoulders. "My dear boy, you are Italian. You just have to be."

"What do you mean?"

"The Americans I encounter here are so obvious in their pacing, their need to do everything and know everything, right here and right now. God, I used to give tours in Rome, but I just couldn't continue, despite the good pay, the great pay, really, because it was non-stop, with their dog-eared tour books and endless questions and people constantly on my heels, rushing not walking, practically tearing at the city with their eyes and their feet and their need to photograph everything and buy everything. It was too much. Too much to bear. Though I do miss the money."

Bill removed his hands from Jacoby's shoulders, realizing he had been shaking him a bit during his rant. "But you, my boy," he said slowly, "are right in time here among the Italians. Happy to follow the road to where it takes you, not asking damn questions every step along the way."

Jacoby swarmed with pride and a sense of validation. And though he appreciated the words from Bill, they were not entirely revelatory. He'd felt since adolescence that he existed at a clip that was somewhat tempered as compared to everyone else. He didn't indulge in the excesses that so defined American youth and even adulthood. He didn't dream of some pie in the sky, fantastic future. He didn't fetish celebrity. Or wealth. He simply went along at his own pace and enjoyed what he could in the process. This approach never felt so satisfying, or shared, as it did since arriving in Italy.

"Thanks," he said to Bill with a straight face. "But, sorry, I'm dying a little here now. Where are we going again?"

Bill did a little hop. "To have lunch with a Renaissance man, and see if he knows about our cat."

• • •

Their destination was in the Sant'Ambrogio section of the city. The neighborhood's namesake church announced noon with a dozen bongs from its bell tower as Bill and Jacoby turned a corner into a pocket zone dominated by the "Cibrèo" brand, including a ristorante, trattoria, and cafe. A small side-street split the franchises and ended on the cross street that they walked, toward alfresco tables on either side of the street. It looked like a gourmet bazaar. Bill searched the crowded tables and the street clustered with pedestrians. A lone man in a linen suit with a fedora low on his head sat on a chair in the middle of it all, reading a newspaper and smoking a pipe.

Jacoby smelled something pungent and bright that awakened his stomach, though it was hard to tell from where it came since aromas were emanating from kitchens in nearly every direction. A waiter walked by with a flat bread on a plate covered in a vegetable ragout. Another crossed, going from the trattoria to the cafe, with a chrome shaker and two martini glasses with a big green olive nested above each stem. Many people at the outdoor tables took salads bright with assorted vegetables or bowls filled with grains or pasta. Every table had carafes or bottles of wine and bottles of water. Many had packs of cigarettes, and Jacoby wanted to smoke, after he ate and drank. Claire crossed his mind, but the thought was quickly dashed by Bill's hand on his forearm, after he had consulted with a waiter, leading him through the crowd and down the small street away from the beautiful scene.

"I thought we were going to have lunch?" Jacoby yelped.

"We will. We will," Bill responded. "But first we must find Fabio!"

They walked quickly toward an open air market, just down the road, under a slanted and corrugated steel roof. The stalls were piled with fruits and vegetables of enormous size and color. There were peppers as big as forearms and lemons like fists, apples and plums and figs, baskets of great berries with flesh ready to burst. A table top was covered with thick-stemmed mushrooms with huge brown caps. Other counters had white rounds of fresh Pecorino and golden wheels of aged Parmesan. Mongers of meat and fish displayed their goods. Buyers haggled with vendors in quick, impassioned exchanges. Bill cut through the crowd and walked directly up to a man in checkered pants and a chef's coat, arguing with a farmer over a crate of artichokes. The chef was large, with wild gray hair and a wild gray beard around his mouth and off his chin. He looked to Jacoby like an anachronistic, poet-philosopher type visited upon Florence from a previous century. He was head and shoulders above the other market goers and a figure of great animation, his hands flailing and his voice booming through the open air under the slanted roof as if he were debating an important civic matter as opposed to the fate of a bushel of artichokes. The passionate man stopped speaking abruptly upon noticing Bill, his hands rising up like a Baptist preacher recognizing the return of a prodigal son. Bill returned the gesture and the men hugged and kissed each other on both cheeks numerous times over.

"Caro amico. Caro amico," Fabio finally said to Bill after the elongated physical greeting, his fingers on both hands pinched and raised. "Dove sei stato?"

Bill and Fabio had a charismatic conversation in full animation that Jacoby could not follow beyond its good will and eventual apologies from Fabio which Bill did his best to refuse. It was fun for Jacoby to watch: two men putting on an impromptu play in broad daylight. Eventually, Jacoby was called over and introduced. Fabio put a hand on the back of Jacoby's head in an endearing if not somewhat startling gesture and said in broken English, leaning down close to Jacoby's face, "I see you tonight, at the theater!" He then broke abruptly away from Bill and Jacoby to argue once again with the artichoke vendor.

Bill led Jacoby through the maze of food stands toward the market's back corner where they stopped at a chrome street cart with a sandwich board in front that read "Lampredotto."

"Ready for the most incredible sandwich in all of Florence?" Bill asked.

"Yep," Jacoby said. "What is it?"

"Lampredotto," Bill answered, pointing toward the sandwich board. "Rolled tripe, stewed to perfection, served on bread that's been dipped in broth."

"Isn't tripe stomach or intestine or something?"

"Stomach lining, from the cow's fourth stomach, to be precise."

"That's good," Jacoby quipped, "because I won't go near the first three stomachs."

Jokes aside, Jacoby felt a bit queasy in his only stomach, considering for breakfast he had filled it with raw sausage, which hadn't yet revolted but still kept Jacoby on guard, but Bill was upon the stand owner ordering away and returning quickly with two glasses of Chianti in plastic cups, which they drank and refilled once the sandwiches were ready.

The glass of wine up front helped prep Jacoby's gastro-tolerance. Plus, he was eager for a meal. The aroma out of the stand was pungent; the sandwich warm in his hand, of tomato infused broth and hearty filling tucked between the bread. The taste was super savory to the bite, ample aromatics and a soft texture from the holy trinity of bread and filling and broth. The smell entered Jacoby's nose as a vinegary-tomato flavor filled his mouth and excited his palate. The fruity red wine washed it down nicely. He nodded at Bill who smiled upon gauging the approval. Both men went back to work on their lunch.

About 3/4 of the way through the sandwich, Bill abruptly wrapped his up in wax paper and napkin and tossed it in a garbage can. Jacoby followed suit, recognizing that at a certain point one's stomach might realize that it is being filled with stomach in what could be considered a moment of meta-stomach, which changes everything.

Jacoby burped, and felt funny for a moment before finishing off his wine and following after Bill who was on his way away from the market down an empty, narrow lane. They walked in shadows down curved streets and straight alleys before coming up from behind on Piazza Santa Croce and its namesake basilica. Along the way, Bill explained to Jacoby that Fabio was too busy to accommodate them for lunch, as all of his tables were full and he was tasked with creating his famous artichoke flan for Florence's most famous entertainer, who happened to be his wife. And that his wife would be performing that evening at their supper club located in a theater across from the restaurants, and that he and Bill were cordially invited for dinner and then the show. Afterward, they would join Fabio and his wife, who knows the Floria-Zanobini family, to discuss the whereabouts of their missing cat. In the meantime, they had half a day to spend in the city of Florence, which would begin at Santa Croce, with a quote from Dante recited by Jacoby.

Chapter 20

"Do not be afraid; our fate cannot be taken from us; it is a gift," Jacoby quoted while looking up at the enormous statue of Dante erected on the steps in front of the basilica.

"Very impressive," Bill said.

"My father was a classicist."

"Was?"

"He died last year."

"How?"

"From what had been killing him for as long as I can remember," Jacoby said, still staring up at the statue, thinking of his father's final days. "He repeated that line over and over while in hospice."

"Perhaps he was seeking comfort," Bill suggested.

Jacoby turned his eyes to Bill and could feel his kindness, his shared sense of suffering.

"I think he was comforting me, or, at least, trying to."

"Are you a believer in fate, Jacoby?"

"I believe in something," he said. "I'm just not sure what it is."

"Well," Bill said, "Let's call it fate and see what it has in store for us today. Shall we?"

"Sounds good," Jacoby agreed.

They climbed the steps and entered into the majestic church of some 700 years with the white marble facade trimmed in green and pink. Inside was cool and quiet, of diffuse light, not interrupted by tourists on this day. Surrounding the long nave bordered by high columns, individual chapels held the tombs of famous Florentines, like Michelangelo, Machiavelli, and Galileo. Jacoby circled the room and searched for names he recognized in the tombs while Bill admired the frescoes by Giotto and Gaddi. After the limestone relief at the nave's far end, they walked into the fresh air, under loggias that led to the cloisters. They soon exited and found themselves on the piazza, at the far end of the steps, opposite where the statue of Dante stood.

"This way," Bill said.

They walked away from the church on a straight road lined with panino shops and gelato stands and craft stores through a quiet neighborhood tucked beside the River Arno, which Jacoby could smell at high tide with the help of a slight breeze. The riposa was coming, and shutters were closing in the apartments above the street, though most of the stores stayed open. Groups of tourists gathered in the narrow crossing behind the enormous Uffizi Gallery that blocked the blue sky from view.

A small incline aside the museum led them to a corner of Piazza della Signoria, a vast and elegant square lined with palaces and eateries with outdoor seating under umbrellas and boutiques with shining storefronts. Overlooked by a massive tower above the facade of Palazzo Vecchio, throngs gathered in the clogged corner where a woman played a cello and tourists gaped at street performers and took pictures in front of the collection of statues in open air or under a loggia. Jacoby felt the power of collective awe, as if the stones of the buildings and the square had absorbed the history and radiated it out to those who passed, as if the statues could talk and tell the bloody and magnificent story of what had transpired here so many centuries ago, how light had been brought to the Dark Ages and the modern cradle of civilization was born. Right fucking there. Jacoby felt overwhelmed by the history.

Bill took Jacoby's arm and ferried him through the swarming tourists beyond the Palazzo Vecchio and its crenelated tower to a quieter corner of the piazza where a well-heeled hotel was located between two men's clothiers.

The lobby had faded pink marble floors, pastel walls and columns of plaster. Lots of dark wood trim. Bill directed Jacoby toward a leather-bound seating area as he walked toward the lovely concierge in a tailored navy blue suit who sat with perfect posture behind a mahogany desk. She smiled with extraordinary warmth and twisted her head from side to side as Bill spoke for merely a minute. Then she nodded formally and removed something from the desk drawer which she handed to Bill with another nod and the words "Prego" formed by her lips.

Bill returned and handed Jacoby what looked like a credit card in a Mylar sheath.

"What's this?"

"A pass to the museum, my boy."

"What museum?"

"The museum," Bill said without pomp. "The Galleria dell'Uffizi. It's right down the road and houses arguably the world's greatest collection of art."

"You're not coming?"

"I've been through so many times, there's nothing more for me to discover. Besides, it's quite a slog, 45 halls in all, and I could use a rest." Bill motioned with his head toward a leather chair.

"So, you're just going to wait here for me?"

"Yes. The owner of this hotel is an old friend of Fillipo's. You're holding the establishment's sole pass for the museum, so don't lose it. It will grant your free entry and spare you the hideous line."

Jacoby felt like a young American. "Sweet," he said.

"Indeed," Bill agreed. "Go straight past the line to the entrance where there is a guard, but no line. Show them the pass."

"Then what?"

"Enjoy the museum. Take your time. Meet me back here where we will take an apertivo in preparation for our supper and evening at the theater."

"Sweet," is all Jacoby could come up with.

Bill smiled. "Yes, it is. Now go."

•　　　•　　　•

Jacoby slipped through the crowds and through the gateway to the Uffizi's entrance, fronted by a carnival of vendors and street performers and a line that snaked out of sight behind the museum. Basking in privilege, Jacoby presented his pass on the ground floor and entered without interruption. "Prego" was becoming his favorite Italian word.

The vast entrance area was crowded but not cluttered. Still, Jacoby didn't know where to begin. As he looked around for direction, he heard a tour guide with an English accent instruct a group of a dozen pale tourists, who had just passed through arduous security, to follow her up a wide staircase to the second floor. Jacoby followed her blonde bob from a few steps behind the group's tail end before leaving them on the 2nd floor landing.

Jacoby liked museums, though he often felt overwhelmed by their volume, especially since he wasn't particularly interested in the craft or knowledgeable about art history beyond the handful of household names that most educated people knew. What he liked most about museums was the ambiance, the serenity of being surrounded by what people have created. Affected posturing aside, he liked the polite manner in which most people behaved in museums, humbled by the skill and passion and dedication of their fellow man, struck silent by an inability to put language to their impressions. No douche bags allowed. Jacoby visited the museums of Boston and New York pretty often and always left, vowing to return more frequently, with a sense of life affirmed.

Atop the landing of the second floor stairwell in the Uffizi Gallery, Jacoby wandered in the only direction the long, austere corridor would allow, stepping into each silent hall to admire the works of art and seek familiarity of their source, trying to remember new names, too. He wasn't ardent in his observations, moving quickly from picture to picture. The Renaissance art was wildly impressive but a bit redundant in style and motif. A lot of baby Jesus in the house.

After spending what felt like a lifetime with the work of Botticelli, followed up directly by a visit with Leonardo, Jacoby found himself tired mentally with some pain in his legs from the unforgiving marble floors. He studied a map and realized he'd only covered a fraction of the museum's offerings. Cutting out would suit him fine, but he worried about disappointing Bill, so he decided to carry on, maybe after a quick short cut.

He bypassed the rest of the corridor and the short hall which followed. Turning a corner toward the last long stretch of the second floor, he noticed the English tour guide and her group well ahead of him and entering a hall. Jacoby assumed she was only hitting the highlights and decided to follow her lead into a hall that featured the only painting by Michelangelo left in Florence. Jacoby acquired this fact by eavesdropping on the tour, which inspired him to not only follow the tour's path but tether himself anonymously within earshot. He stayed in back and kept his head low, only looking up on occasion to register the blond bob.

The rest of Jacoby's museum visit went by quickly and informatively, with visits on the first floor to halls dedicated to Tiziano, Raffaello, Andrea del Sarto, and Caravaggio, the latter having created Jacoby's favorite painting of the day - one of Bacchus, the god of wine, bathed in light and depicted in incredible detail, holding a goblet of ruby nectar.

When the tour group returned to the ground floor, Jacoby moved quietly away, not noticing the shade thrown at him from the tour guide. He thought of himself as clever, but he mostly thought about how impressive the tour was, not being only about the minute details of each work but as much, if not more, about the artists themselves, their lives as artists and their lives as men of flesh and blood. Jacoby hated hero worship and appreciated the respect artists deserved for perseverance throughout their imperfect art and their imperfect lives. He loathed the idea that successful artists were somehow touched by the hand of god, and that their success was predetermined. The tour guide was great at humanizing these men in their lifetimes which made them all the more real, all the more impressive. Jacoby suspected the guide was not just an art historian but an artist as well. He should have thanked her before running off.

·　　·　　·

Twilight sifted slowly down in rose bursts on the Piazza Signoria as the sky faded from blue into orange beyond facades of palaces now cast in shadows. Regal Florentine couples in elegant attire walked slowly, hands relaxed, observing their sacred city at this magic hour. Jacoby hurried to the hotel, anxious to find Bill and share his experience at the museum. This town was making him giddy.

Bill sat still as a statue on a leather chair, his eyes closed, palms down on each thigh. Jacoby thought of the Lincoln Memorial and roused Bill to make sure he wasn't in a sort-of-memorial pose of his own.

"Oh, hello Jacoby," he said without pause seconds after opening his eyes. "How was the galleria?"

"It was amazing, thanks. Really amazing."

"Wonderful," Bill said, rising to his feet. "Let's return the pass to the concierge and discuss over a glass of Prosecco out front, to begin our evening."

Chapter 21

A covered, open-air gazebo of wooden floors and metal frame was positioned in front of the hotel, an annex of sorts, above the piazza's ground and open to the public. They sat a table by the far end, facing the piazza. A bowl of mixed nuts seasoned with salt and rosemary was placed in front of them, along with a bowl of cured black olives. They ordered Proseccos and waited in the kind light for their sparkling wine to arrive as pedestrians on feet and on bikes flitted past.

With glasses of Prosecco in hand, the two men toasted to each other's health and took sips that would begin a night that would last until the next morning. Unaware of such forthcoming events, Jacoby told Bill of his afternoon in the museum.

"You certainly hit all the right salons," Bill commented with an impressed expression. "And acquired some important knowledge as well."

"Yeah, well," Jacoby said with a coy slant to his eyes, "I tagged along on a tour given in English. The guide was amazing. Kinda cute, too."

Bill's look faded into consternation. His eyes lowered as he asked Jacoby if he'd, at least, offered the guide a tip. He had not, and felt ashamed of himself for being so fucking tacky. He felt the "found" money in his pocket and realized he should have shared some with the amazing tour guide with the blond bob, a style easy to follow around a museum and also easy to spot crossing a piazza on a bicycle at twilight.

She peddled through the piazza from the direction of the Uffizi and past the hotel. Jacoby stood, raised a hand, and opened his mouth to say something, but her loveliness silenced him. He simply stared, but before she could pass out of sight, and away forever, he waived his hand to catch her attention. She turned her head in his direction, then turned away before snapping back with a jolt, skidding her bike to a stop. Jacoby sat down.

"Did you enjoy your tour?" she called sarcastically from twenty yards away, adding a little public shame to Jacoby's already unnerved status. A bolt of courage struck him - the kind of confidence he possessed in his better days. He stood and waved the woman over with charming persuasion. She paused. He raised his glass of Prosecco. She smiled, got off her bike and walked over to lean it against the railing. She put her hands on her hips and looked up at Jacoby with playful incredulity.

He reached for his wallet. "I know it's really bad manners at this point, but can I offer you a tip for the tour? It was so amazing. I was just telling my friend here this very second, I swear, when, when you passed by."

She looked at Bill. He nodded cordially. She returned the gesture and returned her ambivalent glare to Jacoby.

"I thought you were offering me a glass of Prosecco."

"Are your eyes green?" he asked.

She looked startled and did not respond. She was more lovely than Jacoby first realized from the back of a tour group, behind a dozen heads, trying not to make eye contact. Her skin was white and tight as crisp apple flesh, little cat's eyes evident as she squinted at Jacoby's non sequitur, her red mouth open, ligaments extended in her neck above firm shoulders and a firm frame under a silk, beige blouse.

"Would you like that instead?" Jacoby asked when she didn't respond. "Prosecco, I mean."

"Why, yes. Yes, I would. There's few things I prefer more than a glass of Prosecco."

"Please," Jacoby said, overwhelmed with relief and a sense of fledgling magic, gesturing around the gazebo to the entrance. She walked her bike to a nearby street sign and locked it around the post. She walked to the gazebo with her head high, her patterned skirt swinging from side to side. Jacoby's heart ticked in 4/4 rhythm.

He pulled over a chair from a vacant table and stood waiting for her to arrive. She ignored his welcoming smile and put out her hand toward Bill. "Helen Dempsey," she said.

Bill stood and took her hand. "Bill Guion."

They exchanged warm smiles after parting hands. Helen crossed her fit arms and sized-up Jacoby, burrowing into his brown eyes with her green lasers.

"And who are you, my interloper?"

"Jacoby Pines."

Helen relaxed her arms down and turned her head in a curious tilt. "What an interesting name, especially for an American, you seem to be all Steve Johnsons and Tom Browns."

"I'm all Jacoby Pines."

Helen sat down. Bill and Jacoby followed suit, the latter signaling the waitress for another glass of Prosecco.

Jacoby crossed a leg and tried to act relaxed. "So, Helen Dempsey, where in England are you from?"

"Melbourne," she answered without pause.

Bill coughed on some suds; Jacoby churned with embarrassment, pinpricks zipping across his forehead.

The third glass of Prosecco arrived as a reprieve. Helen raised her glass to both men and took a sip.

"Don't worry, Jacoby Pines," she said, putting her glass on the table and patting his knee. "Most Americans I meet don't even recognize the correction."

"Well," he said with a shrug. "I've got that going for me."

"And, to be fair, I've spent quite a bit of time in England, starting with university."

"That's what must have thrown me," Jacoby said with a small, staccato nod and a knowing smirk. "The conflation of accents."

"Was it now?" Helen asked, continuing the ruse.

Jacoby continued to nod.

"And where in America are you from?" she asked.

"Toronto," he answered dead-pan.

"Very clever," she said and turned to Bill. "He's a clever one, isn't he?"

"He's a magnificent young man," Bill announced with utmost confidence.

"Are you two related?"

"No."

"Are you traveling mates?"

"No."

"Boyfriend and boyfriend?"

"No."

"Then what precisely are you doing?"

"We're looking for a marble cat."

"A marble cat?"

"Yes. A marble cat."

"This I have to hear," Helen declared and took a sip of Prosecco.

Over another round of apertivos, Bill explained the story of Jacoby's photograph and its connection to Fillipo and the reclusive matriarch hiding about somewhere in Florence in a palazzo marked by a marble cat, and the appointment that evening to have dinner and a show and seek knowledge of said cat. By the story's end, Helen had decided it was a fantastic tale. She also agreed, upon Bill's charming persuasion and to Jacoby's delight, to join them for dinner.

Chapter 22

The sky was black above the city streets that were lit by the soft glow of small lights. Night fell with a cool touch and a hush. It felt like an impressionist painting to Jacoby. Pedestrian traffic dwindled, and wandering tourists lowered their voices in reverence to the ambiance that resembled that of an open-air church. There was no odor, and the streets felt swept and hosed down.

Helen held Bill's arm as they walked. Jacoby, on Bill's other flank, felt excluded and wanted in on the small gesture of intimacy.

Upon Sant'Ambrogio, small crowds of young locals gathered outside of cafes, talking and acting and smoking like young locals do, their voices bouncing freely off the walls of their territory. Bill and Jacoby and Helen passed by silently.

Around the corner towards the auspices of Cibrèo, chatter and the rattle of active restaurants filled the small area with dinner music. Jacoby smelled roasted potatoes and lemon. The outside tables were full. At the T in the road, in front of a marquee, a cluster of people gathered.

"Stay here," Bill said then cut through the crowd.

Jacoby and Helen stood for a moment in awkward silence.

"Have you ever been here before?" Jacoby asked.

"No, but I'm certainly aware of all this," she said, looking around and motioning with her hand. "It's a bit too fancy for me, I'm afraid, but I have heard great things about the theater. I've been meaning to join."

"Join?"

"Yes, it's a supper club of sorts. You pay a fee to join and then come for, I believe, lunch or dinner for an additional price. All very reasonable. The meals are buffet style, you know, as they do in the States. Supper comes with a show most nights."

"How cool."

"Not very Italian at all, really, and I've heard that Maria Cassi is fantastic."

"She's performing tonight."

"Really?"

"She's Fabio's wife, right?"

"You know Fabio Picchi?"

"I just met him today, but Bill, I guess, knows him really well. They invited us. They're the ones supposed to help us find out about the marble cat."

"My god," Helen laughed. "What a gas."

"I'll say," Jacoby teased.

"No you wouldn't," Helen disagreed. "You'd say something American, like, like 'That's freaking awesome, man.'"

"I've never said that in my life," Jacoby declared with a look mock-seriousness and slight indignation

"Have I offended you?" Helen asked, trying to maintain a serious face.

"Fucking A right, you have."

Helen slapped him on the arm and held Jacoby's eye. A whistle interrupted their flirtation. Bill waived them over. They followed him through the crowd and into the theater. A black-haired young man in a fine-threaded shirt showed them into the entry foyer, which was a crowded commissary / flea-market, stuffed with jarred and vacuum-sealed food products, dry goods, books, compact discs, clothes, home supplies. It looked like a bon vivant's fire sale.

Down the long wooden counter, by the register, a woman handed them three pens and three forms to be filled out with innocuous, occasionally quirky, personal information and returned in exchange for a green membership card. Helen reached into her bag. Bill held up a hand.

"These are all compliments of Mr. Fabio," Bill stated with a bit of pomp.

"Mr. Fabulous is more like it," Helen declared.

Jacoby smiled at her; she smiled back.

Following the black-haired, young man again, they pivoted away from the counter, down a short, wide hall adored with cushioned chairs and glass tables. It looked like a sitting room in a fine home or a private clubhouse. Beyond was a vestibule of sorts, adorned with large, wooden boxes with spigots at the bottom, set on a table that also held wine glasses, water glasses, bottles of sparkling water and a spout for flat. Through red velvet curtains to the table's right, entry was gained to a large, wood-adorned room with a high ceiling and communal tables among the wide pillars. The right side of the room, half the width, was mostly of glass that partitioned the seating area from an active kitchen manned by chefs of mixed background and gender. A rotisserie turned, and a wood burning oven raged with orange flames. The far end of the room featured a stage cloaked in a burgundy curtain.

They were brought to a table for two aside the glass partition, center stage for the show in the kitchen.

"I'm sorry," the man said in broken English, "Fabio tell me to set a table of two."

"Yes," Bill said. "I'm sorry about that. We've seemed to have picked up a third on the way."

Helen blushed and rubbed her thin arm.

"We can sit somewhere else," Jacoby said quickly. "No problem. Anywhere's fine."

"No. No. No," the man said, pinching his dimpled chin. "Wait."

He began to move the chairs away from a nearby four top. Jacoby helped him. They carried the table, careful not to move the settings, next to the partition. They exchanged it with the table for two, reset the chairs, and shook hands.

"Gianluca," the man said.

"Jacoby."

"Piacere."

"Piacere mio."

Gianluca motioned toward the table. "Help yourself to the wine outside, from the box. We open the doors now and soon the food will be ready. The show is later. After the dinner."

Gianluca walked out of the room but not before opening the curtains. A breeze swept into the room. Voices came from the front of the theater. Bill and Jacoby sat at the ends with Helen in the middle.

"And here we are," said Bill.

Jacoby flattened his lips and raised his eyebrows, trying to think of something clever to say.

"Shall we have some wine from the box?" Helen suggested.

"Great idea," Bill confirmed.

Jacoby jumped up. In the vestibule, he filled a carafe with red wine and returned with it in one hand, the stems of three inverted wine glasses in the other. People sat themselves at the communal tables. Chairs squeaked against the worn wooden floors. Chefs handed platters of food from the kitchen to serving staff through a retractable window in the partition. It smelled of vegetables and spice and roasted meats.

At their table by the kitchen, Jacoby poured three glasses of wine, which were soon held in the air by three hands.

"To what should we toast?" Bill asked.

No one seemed to know.

"Ficha," Jacoby abruptly declared.

Bill burst out laughing.

"To a fig?" Helen questioned, now smiling along with good nature, aware of a joke at hand but not sure what it was. "You're toasting to a fig?"

Bill leaned over and whispered in her ear the meaning of the toast and its inspiration to Jacoby.

"Oh, how awful," she said with a hand over her smile. "You're fast becoming a typical Italian man, and you've only been here how long?"

"One week."

"And you're staying for how long?"

Jacoby knew then that Helen was attracted to him, as well.

"I don't know," he said. "Maybe a year."

"A year?" Helen gasped and blushed. "I thought you were just one of those tourists chasing after their ancestry while on holiday."

"It's a little more complicated than that," Jacoby admitted, trying to appear mysterious as opposed to deceitful (not to mention pathetic).

"Do tell."

Fuck. The hot surge of dishonesty coursed through his veins. He opened his mouth, unsure what words would come out, when the partition behind him slid open and a chef leaned into the room and yelled with exaggerated theatrics: "La prima corso è pronto, un misto di verdure d'Elba!!!!"

Everyone seemed to stand at once and advance on the buffet tables, now prepared for an onslaught.

"Let's see if they have Gurguglioni," Bill teased, rising from his chair.

"What exactly is that?" Helen asked, also rising.

"Spicy potato and greens, indigenous to the island of Elba."

"I'll go," Jacoby volunteered. "I'll get enough for all of us."

"I'm coming, too," Helen said.

"Fair enough," Bill said, sitting back down. "I'll make sure the wine is safe for consumption."

Jacoby and Helen joined the small scuffle, among Italians not familiar with buffet etiquette. Jacoby was bumped out of place, twice, by a stocky woman twice his age; he exchanged smirking glances with Helen during their slow advance. By the time they reached the table, most every platter had been picked over. They salvaged some carrots sautéed with thyme and returned with their pithy offerings.

Bill awaited, upright and pleased. Full plates of potatoes and green beans in front of each spot. "Gurguglione, my friends."

"How'd you get that?" Jacoby asked.

"Gianluca brought them for us," he said. "We're in the seats reserved for guests of honor. We, therefore, don't need to risk our safety in that scrum."

"Oh, thank god," Helen blurted.

Jacoby rubbed his arm where he was sure a bruise would rise. They chinked wine glasses and began. The gurgulione was full of flavor and bite. The soft potatoes and crisp greens were coated in a bright sauce with a spicy twang. This kind of dish reminded Jacoby of the things he could survive on, temporarily, as a vegetarian. It also reminded him that he was famished, his hots for Helen having distracted him from his appetite.

Before they could finish their first plates, Gianluca arrived with three small ramekins filled with an off-white, flan-like concoction.

"These are from the maestro, from the street across in the kitchen of Cibrèo."

"Let me guess," Bill said. "Fabio's sformato di carciofo."

Gianluca smiled, bowed his head then walked away. Jacoby knew by the smell and his earlier encounter with Fabio in the market that "carciofo" meant artichoke. He made a vow to learn Italian language through food, to become kitchen fluent, which might be the perfect type of fluency.

"The carciofo part I understand, of course," Helen said, her eyes wide and curious. "But what's a sformato?"

"Traditionally, in cucina tipica, it's a timbale, egg-based, almost like a fluffy frittata, but Fabio's are more like a savory flan, lighter and infused with flavor of the primary ingredient, which, in this case, is carciofo."

They dug their spoons into the gelatinous surface and came away with mouthfuls of rapture. "My, my," Bill said, wiping a napkin on his mouth.

"Is that your way of saying 'holy fucking shit'?" Helen asked, leaning in for discretion, her eyes bulging and her shoulders raised.

"Yes," Bill said. "It is."

They laughed then spooned down the sformato to the last schmear. Their spotless ramekins were replaced with three bowls of tiny clams in a pungent broth, followed by a platter of whole roasted anchovies just removed from the wood burning oven, dressed and handed to Jacoby directly through the opened partition.

"Grazie," he said to the chef.

The chef smiled and went back to his happy work on full display. They continued to receive supplemented plates not available to the rest of the room, including small, turkey meatballs in a light tomato sauce, fried pieces of rabbit, and roasted zucchini stuffed with ground pork. They ate as if they were participants in a show, not speaking of anything else except the food but mostly enjoying the silence of their experience and washing it all down with carafes of wine.

The final course was roasted chicken pieces with sausage, potatoes, cloves of garlic and caramelized onions. Gianluca brought their food on a platter along with a bottle of Vino Nobile di Montepulciano, a robust red among the best of Tuscany's celebrated wines. It tasted to Jacoby like tongue music.

There was nowhere else in the world Jacoby wished to be. This was his Grand Canyon. His Hawaii. Mount Everest or Disney World. His paradise was a theater-cafeteria-commissary, sharing a table with two people he hardly knew but liked immensely, full of possibilities, in a room full of shamelessly happy people. Everyone: Those working and those eating. It was all so magical. So alive. And there was still a show to come.

After sharing plates of flourless chocolate cake, strawberry crumb cake (topped with fresh whipped cream), and a lemon tart (also topped with fresh whipped cream), an announcement was made in Italian by Gianluca. Everyone brought their plates and cutlery to a dishwasher by an open vestibule in the corner by the kitchen. After the tables were cleared, people began moving their chairs toward the stage as staff pulled the tables to a far corner. Jacoby and Helen and Bill were led by Gianluca to three padded seats in the very front of the stage. Jacoby felt so flattered and blessed and full, so immersed in the pleasures at hand, he'd forgotten all about the mission to find the marble cat.

Chapter 23

Just before show time, Fabio joined them in a seat on the very end of the front row, next to Bill who was next to Helen. The curtain opened and a small woman with shorn hair and doe eyes walked out to great applause. She wore a striped men's suit and a bowler hat, a slight Vaudeville comedic aesthetic, complete with suspenders for stretching, and a thin layer of white make-up. She spent a few minutes, in an exaggerated fashion, warming up her limbs and, especially, her face, making contortions with every available muscle and sticking out her tongue. Jacoby feared some sort of high-brow mime act, but the crowd seemed to recognize this as a silly preamble, smiling and laughing along, not yet fully invested in the act of Maria Cassi.

She suddenly stopped moving and began to speak, a theatrical passage soon interrupted by her own interpretation. All in Italian. People laughed and clapped and rocked back and forth from hysterics. Jacoby couldn't understand a word, so fast and out of context, though he could clearly sense, through voicing and posturing, that she was shifting back and forth between dispirit characters, male and female, young and old. Jacoby pulled the program wedged under his hamstring and tried to translate the title in the meager light: La Mia Vita con Uomini...e altri animale.

He tapped Helen's leg and pointed at the title. She leaned over and whispered through breath scented with food and wine and a bit of fatigue: My life with men and other animals.

She gave him a knowing look, acknowledging the evergreen subject matter. Jacoby smirked and, playfully, looked away, up at the stage a few feet away, where Ms. Maria Cassi would alone act out her story with men and other animals over the course of a non-stop 90 minutes, which seemed like a combination aerobics class for physical comedians and a lecture from a professor and a play inhabited by a rotating cast of characters, all through the portal of one small, indefatigable, astonishingly-talented woman. The crowd followed every word, every move, laughing loud or nodding along, listening intently to the deeper passages. Bill and Helen, like everyone else, were enthralled. Jacoby was excluded from such intimacy, but he could - thanks to the performer's pathos and talent - follow along. It reminded him of the time, on a date, he went to a Prince concert and was blown away - even though he was never a fan, before or after - of Prince's music. It was performance which transcended the immediate medium, a feat, according to Jacoby, only capable of genius.

Fatigue started to set in at a certain point, and Jacoby felt a sense of relief as the climax seemed at hand, a grand finale of sorts of physicality and verbiage and humor which ended abruptly in a triumphant pose that inspired a standing ovation that lasted five minutes, though the star never returned from the small room she entered directly off stage after the first two minutes of the highest praise a performer can receive. Fabio, before following Maria into the room, smacked Bill's leg and motioned with his hand to stay, which they did as the room cleared out in an orderly fashion.

As staff rearranged the room, stacking the tables and chairs in an out of the way corner, Bill and Helen and Jacoby stood out of the way themselves, near the room's far side, where the former two raved about the show, it's brilliance and energy and the impossible use of one's face and body as such a versatile instrument. Jacoby listened, trying to confirm his language-less understanding of the show's theme, which he was able to do easily enough through the effusive praise of his two companions, which ended abruptly when a collective bathroom break was needed.

They returned to find a large, country table set by Gianluca and other staff, dead-center near the back of the cavernous room. Places weren't formalized, but cloth napkins, wine glasses, silverware and small ceramic plates were clustered together in the table's center. When all was in order, Gianluca motioned for the lingering trio to sit, with word that Fabio and Maria would join them shortly.

Helen and Jacoby sat together on the side with its back to the kitchen; Bill assumed a seat on the left flank. They kept quiet, anxious almost, as if waiting on royalty, and it did kind of feel like they were in the castle of a king and queen who lorded over the little kingdom of the arts.

"By the way," Helen broached sotto-voce to Bill, "just how do you know them?"

"Oh," Bill laughed. "I met Fabio in Rome 20 years ago. I hosted a dinner in his honor at the university where I worked to celebrate and promote the release of his first book on cooking and Florentine culture. Filippo made sure his newspaper covered the event thoroughly, and with great enthusiasm, and, well, not surprisingly, we've been friends ever since and have had many, many exquisite meals and adventures together."

"How wonderful," Helen declared, her voice echoing around the room. "When's the last time you saw each other?"

Bill grew wistful but didn't have a chance to answer as the door near the stage swung open and Maria Cassi descended the stairs, fresh-faced, dressed in comfortable clothes with a towel around her neck, buttressing her wet hair. Fabio followed in Bohemian attire, a head taller and a barrel wider than his wife but equal compliments to each other, the former at the moment the more animated actor.

"Non è vero! Impossibile!" she proclaimed, her eyes wide on Bill. "Non è vero! Incredibile!"

Bill blushed and shucked as the mesmerizing Maria waltzed her way across the room, dancing with her own poses until she stopped in front of Bill to mime extraordinary delight, with her hands raised to the sides of her face. They embraced. Fabio followed with kisses on Bill's cheeks and big pats on his back. Bill introduced Jacoby and Helen to Maria, and then Helen to Fabio.

"Sit. Sit," Fabio said. "Sit."

They sat, and Bill took to his own theatrical skill to cordially and emphatically thank their two hosts, in Italian, for a magical evening. Maria and Fabio waved him away, but Helen chimed in to continue the praise, of both the food and the performance, gesturing frequently toward the confines of the magnificent room as well. Jacoby smiled along and nodded like a solid sideman should.

Gianluca appeared with a plate of food for Maria, a carefully partitioned offering of vegetables and chicken from earlier. He also brought bread and a bottle of glistering olive oil. Fabio made a request of Gianluca, who nodded and left the room, returning a minute later with a bottle of red wine stuffed in each back pocket and a wooden platter stacked with hunks of crumbled Parmesan cheese. The wine was popped and poured; the eating devices dispersed. Fabio motioned for Gianluca to join them, so he took a seat next to Jacoby. When they chinked glasses, Jacoby noticed Gianluca's simple, silver wedding band, reminding him - momentarily - of his moral duplicity in action.

The pungent yet buttery aroma of the cheese made Jacoby's still-full stomach rustle to life. As Maria took her dinner with a knife and fork, the others helped themselves with eager fingers to pieces of hard cheese, pale gold with crystallized specs on the surface. Helen moaned as Jacoby broached the explosive surface with his teeth, both soft and crunchy, releasing a flood of flavor that shot into his jowls and sent a gust of ventilation from his nose. The guests looked at each other as if they'd experienced a miracle.

Convinced of the collective amazement, Fabio raised his wine glass and made a long toast in Italian.

"And here we are," Bill reiterated the abridged sentiment in English to Jacoby.

Fabio addressed Helen, shifting his wild-eyed glance on occasion to the other guests, and began a discourse on the philosophy that he and Maria had, for the restaurants and the theater and the city of

Florence, one that Gianluca translated in quick whisper for Jacoby. The philosophy revolved around the belief that the table is the best place to share humanity, and that the stage is itself, another table. He went on and on, as Maria finished her plate and joined them in enjoying the cheese, though Jacoby got the picture soon enough and indicated to Gianluca that the translation could end. Gianluca smiled and helped himself to some cheese.

When finished, Fabio leaned back and enjoyed a healthy sip of wine from his glass, which he returned to the table with his memory jogged. "Ah, Maria!" He began, rattling off a request that included enough recognizable words for Jacoby to know that he was asking about their marble cat. Bill suggested that Jacoby show her the picture, which he produced from his wallet and was passed, hand by hand, around the table to Maria.

She put a hand over her mouth and widened her eyes. She sat like that for a moment, thinking, it appeared. Or distraught. Everyone watched her intently, and even Gianluca, with no skin in the game, seemed to shudder with anticipation next to Jacoby.

Fabio said something to Gianluca, who explained to Jacoby in a whisper that Maria had known the Floria-Zanobini's while growing up, having been a Florentine of many generations and of a social class that was not of the aristocracy but close enough for intimate knowledge and occasional contact, unlike Fabio, who was an absolute product of the middle class and, therefore, never got within a mile of the nobilità.

Maria put the photo on the table and began to rub her face, as if trying to conjure the information from her flesh, where so much wisdom could be culled. But, alas, she eventually broke into a saddened shake of her head. She'd lived in this small city her whole life; and knew this family the entire time, yet she knew nothing of a palazzo marked by a marble cat. She couldn't even think of anyone to ask. She handed the picture to Bill, who kept it in his hand, not wanting to recognize the failure of returning it to Jacoby without having gleaned even a bit of information from their day dedicated to such pursuit. No eye contact was made, and a sad silence followed, quickly broken by Gianluca who rose abruptly and walked out of the room, a gesture which struck everyone as odd, perhaps bad mannered, but also indicative of the evening's end. Fabio yelled a request to him that smacked of closure.

Bill yawned. Helen stood, slowly, the fatigue of a long evening after the long day of a tour guide evident in her hands inverted on the small of her back and the lock of limp hair draped alongside one eye. Jacoby sat still, savoring the remaining flavor in his mouth, resigned to an end, at least for now, of their unlikely adventure. They could always go back to the villa, seek Bruna's help. Or they could just let it all go, though he liked the hope it had inspired in Bill, and the distraction it had provided for himself. My god, he wouldn't be where he was in that very moment, relocated from New York to Florence, had it not been for the picture. He thought of Claire and acknowledged the return tomorrow from her trip, ambivalent about what that would mean or how it would feel to be in her company again.

The hosts refused the guests' attempt to help with the cleanup. With arms locked and shoulders touching, the group walked out of the theater and into the welcoming area, mustering energy and good will to paint a positive élan onto their lovely evening, full of food and performance and company that had ended in disappointment but still made for a damn good night. Gianluca was behind the counter, bundling parting gifts, in three separate bags, of signed copies of Fabio's latest book along with compact disc collections of Maria's songs. The guests thanked their hosts graciously with hugs and kisses, and accepted the gifts from Gianluca, who walked them to the front door, which he unlocked. Gianluca shook the hand of Bill and Helen, respectively, but leaned in to buss Jacoby on his left cheek and then whisper something incredible and mysterious in his ear.

Chapter 24

The threesome - two somber and fatigued; one internally effusive with the sparkling energy of a fresh bit of promising news - walked in silence away from the theater. When they arrived at the Piazza Sant'Ambrogio, Jacoby pulled his company up the stairs of the namesake church, under the light above the wooden door of the basilica's simple plaster facade.

"What are you doing?" Bill asked with impatience as Jacoby dove into his gift bag to pull out Fabio's book.

"Do you plan to have a read-a-long right here and now?" Helen asked.

Jacoby ignored them and began rifling through the pages. He pulled out a piece of inserted paper.

"Here," he shoved it at Bill, as if he couldn't stand to hold the paper in his hands.

"Piazzetta d'Ombre," he read. "The tiny piazza of shadows."

"What of it?" Helen asked.

"Do you know it?" Jacoby asked.

"I do, yes," Helen said with a rush. "It's beyond tiny, not really even a piazzetta at all, more like an alcove, right in the city center, so easy to miss, but there's an obscure fresco, nearly ruined by flood waters, that is reportedly the work of Tiziano. I take tours there, on occasion, of serious art students whom I task with deciding if the rumors are true or not."

"So, what of it?" Bill asked Jacoby. "Who tipped you off? And why?"

"Gianluca," Jacoby gushed. "He told me to look in the book, to find our cat."

"How would he know this?" Bill asked.

Jacoby shrugged. "He whispered it to me before we left."

"I thought he was asking you out on a date," Helen quipped.

"I'm pretty sure he's married," Jacoby said, thinking of his ringed finger.

"Why was he being so secretive?" Helen asked. "Why not just come right out and tell us?"

Jacoby had no idea.

"Have you ever noticed a marble cat while there?" Bill asked Helen.

"No," she answered. "I haven't, but I'm entirely focused on the fresco, not really looking for anything else."

"Do you know how to get there from here?"

"Of course," she declared. "It's tucked away behind Piazza della Repubblica."

"Let's go."

•　　　•　　　•

They walked quickly through the abandoned quarter under a midnight moon casting a veil of fine light on the silent streets. Helen and Jacoby riffed a *Da Vinci Code* routine, turning inanimate and innocuous items into secret clues marking the address of an ancient heiress.

"Wait. Wait!" Helen would exclaim. "Surely that crooked cobblestone means something!"

Jacoby thudded walls in certain spots, waiting for them to open to a secret entrance.

Bill was amused; and Jacoby was impressed by Helen's sense of humor and good nature. She'd also, once outside, shaken off any fatigue evident in the theater after the show, as if the deep night provided her with an endless source of energy and inspiration, something Jacoby recognized in himself. He often, when unaccompanied, would abandon bars or music venues when the after-hours mood became maudlin or rancorous, and walk home in the small hours of night, taking the long route, timing his trip to approach home as the sun crested the horizon. He most liked to watch sunrise from Beacon Hill in Boston or the Brooklyn Bridge in New York.

Piazza della Repubblica, grand and regal, was empty save for the dormant carousel stationed slightly off the piazza's center. Helen petted a sleeping blue stallion. Dim light spread from signs of the shuttered cafes that book-ended the wider flanks of the majestic piazza. Bill pointed out Il Gubbio Rosso, the famous cafe where he and Fillipo would visit whenever they came into town. The sky above the expanse swarmed with stars; a crisp breeze lifted the bangs off of Jacoby's forehead and tangled Helen's skirt.

"This way," Helen instructed, hugging herself against the slight chill.

They walked out of the vast piazza onto a narrow street lined with news kiosks under an arched loggia. A quick turn down an unmarked alley, followed by a second turn, under a low archway, led them to the tiny piazza, like a secret garden with a fountain in the middle and darkened windows within neglected facades. The air was still and musty. A lone street lamp cast a yellow pallor. Bill washed his hands and face with the running fountain water and took a long drink. The ground seemed to pulse and Jacoby detected a nearby beat of music though he focused on his eyes and their search for a marble cat. Helen stood in front of the fresco, its image hidden by shadows.

They walked silently around the tiny piazza. Wild grass and mint grew through the shifted surface. A rusty bicycle leaned into a corner. The fountain was dull and unlit. An orange feral cat hissed and ran out under the archway. Helen followed.

Jacoby put his hand on Bill's forearm. "Do you hear that?"

"I'm afraid some of my hearing has gone," Bill admitted.

"It's music."

"From where?"

Jacoby turned toward the far corner and walked to the shadows.

"Found it!" Helen's voice interrupted from the alley beyond the archway. "Our kitten is out here!!"

Bill and Jacoby hurried out to find Helen. She pointed toward a small ledge, across the alley, barely noticeable from the angle, where a little statue of a white cat seemed to be looking across the alley into windows high above the archway.

"No wonder I never noticed it," she said. "It's not in the piazzetta at all, only marking its entrance."

Bill leaned against the far wall and studied the building under the cat's gaze.

"I bet this whole structure is a rather unorthodox palace. Intentionally obscure."

"Why?" Jacoby asked.

"I'm guessing, and this wouldn't be unusual, that this is where the family hid during times of strife and bloodshed here in Florence, which were often. It was probably more a fortress than a palace."

"How do they get in?"

"There would be a secret corridor somewhere nearby, a block or so from here, maybe more."

The term 'secret corridor' gave Jacoby a thrilling shiver.

"Like the Vasari Corridor, from Pitti Palace over the Ponte Vecchio to the building where the Uffizi is now housed," Helen said.

"Exactly," Bill confirmed, "though I don't imagine this one is quite as elaborate, or as well decorated, as the corridor employed by the Medicis."

"There has to be a door somewhere," said Helen.

"How do we find it?" Jacoby asked.

"Not a clue," Bill sighed.

His look of dejection and fatigue saddened Jacoby.

"Maybe they know in the club?" he suggested.

"What club?" Helen asked.

"Over here," Jacoby said, walking briskly under the archway and through the piazzetta, towards its far corner where the thump of the music grew stronger under each approaching step. He stopped in front of a door, large and of dull metal, sealed tight with no light emanating. He put his ear against it. "There's music from inside, club music."

Helen put her ear to the door.

"He's right," Helen declared, impressed. "How did you ever hear that?"

Jacoby pulled on an ear lobe. "I'm a musician. Good ears."

"The boy is a sensory superhero," Bill announced, suddenly revived. "I imagine he's fantastic in bed."

Helen gasped and giggled, covered her mouth with both hands. Jacoby felt a jolt of embarrassment like he hadn't experienced since adolescence. "Bill!" he cried.

"Oh, don't be a puritan, Jacoby," Bill scolded with good nature. "It's so American."

Jacoby and Helen consulted each other like parents unsure of what to do with an unruly child. Bill investigated the door.

"I'm guessing this is the back," he said, unable to find any method of entry or announcement. "The front must be on the other side."

He walked off at a brisk clip; Helen and Jacoby followed. They turned left out of the archway and made another quick left onto the first available alley that was not far away but previously hidden in shadows and night. The dark alley had a small red light at the dead end. They walked slowly, Helen holding Bill's arm, Jacoby right on their heels. House music in the narrow chamber echoed off the wall, its beats bouncing around the threesome approaching the red light. It was a neon rooster, alone on a wide, two-panel wooden door. The word "Sriracha" was hand-written in red ink on a small white piece of paper tacked below the glowing insignia.

"A secret club!" Helen announced. "How exciting. Shall we go in?"

"Of course we shall," Bill said, charged. He looked for a bell or a ringer.

Helen and Jacoby exchanged another look of amused concern as Bill continued to attempt entry. Finally, he tried the doors, and they separated easily. "Allora," he announced like a magician presenting a trick. "And here we are."

Chapter 25

Dim light and a thump of music through the walls welcomed them under a low, cracked ceiling of stone and a floor of packed dirt. A nicked bar with a backdrop of crumbling brick strung with exposed white bulbs lined the left side of the room. The bartender was built, with a head so white and shaved clean that it resembled alabaster and gym muscles packed into a stretched black t-shirt with the sleeves turned up. There were no stools in front of the bar and no one in the room except the bartender, who looked curiously upon the new visitors to his parlor. The music pulsed from somewhere beyond the room's far wall.

Bill strode to the bar and ordered three Negronis. The bartender stared curiously at him for a moment, looked over Helen and Jacoby, his eyes lingering for an extra beat on Helen's face before giving Jacoby a full body scan. When he went to work on the drinks, Helen and Jacoby sidled up next to Bill.

"Do you still have that money?" Bill asked Jacoby with hushed urgency.

"The found money?"

"Yes."

"Yes."

"Give me some."

"What?"

"Give me some," Bill repeated.

"I thought it would be bad luck?"

"Just give it to me," Bill hissed.

Jacoby went into his wallet and removed some of the stash he had been given by Bill earlier in the morning that seemed so long ago because it was so long ago. While handing over the Euros, Jacoby felt a pang of wonder at what an extraordinary day he was having. And it appeared far from over. He gave Bill 40 Euros; Bill put it on the bar next to where the drinks appeared.

"Oh, Negroni!" Helen cheered. "We've reached the Holy Trinity of Italian liquors: Prosecco, red wine, and now Negroni. Always the sign of a good day."

They raised their long cocktail glasses in concert and chinked to acknowledge their very good day.

"There will be no toasting to ficha here," Bill said with a coy smile. "Present company excluded."

"Why not?" Helen asked. "I so want to have part of my anatomy objectified."

"You'll see."

A copper-colored and gorgeous woman, six feet tall in a sheer, curve-hugging dress, sauntered in from the back room to the bar on three-inch heels. The bartender fixed her a tall glass of ice water without request. She drank the water, blew the bartender a kiss and disappeared back from where she came.

"Not what you think," Bill said, leaning into the bar, checking out the room.

"I don't know," Helen said, "it seems your no-ficha theory just got squashed by that magnificent specimen there."

"Maybe it was wishful thinking," Jacoby added, which cracked up the two heterosexuals.

"No, no," Bill countered. "That person you just saw is very much a man, by ways of Brazil, I imagine."

"Wow," Jacoby coughed. "That's one hot man."

"I guess," Bill said, "if you like your men to look like women, which I don't."

"So, you're saying," Helen queried, "that this is a club for transsexuals?"

"Oh, I'm sure there's plenty of conventional gay men back there, too."

"Wait a minute," Jacoby interrupted. "Does this mean Gianluca is gay? I mean, he's the one who knew about the cat, which is, or has to be, like, a sign for the club, right?"

"No wonder he was so secretive about it all," Helen added.

"But he wore a wedding ring, and, I don't know, and no offense, but he seemed so straight."

"Yes," Helen continued. "He had his eyes on my chest most of the evening, like a good Italian heterosexual."

Jacoby savored the thought of Helen's lovely little jugs nestled nicely in her blouse.

"He's not gay," Bill said assuredly.

"Right," Helen scoffed. "He just prefers clubs filled with gay men. Very common."

Two openly gay young men came from the back, sloppy and flamboyant, talking loudly. They spilled themselves over the bar, ordered drinks and kept on their banter.

Bill leaned toward Helen and Jacoby, speaking in a professorial tone. "The reality is that anal sex feels good, at least for men. All men, not just gay men. It has primarily to do with the prostate and its location just below the anus. Straight Italian men seem to be well aware of this, even if it remains a mystery to the men of America and the rest of the Anglo-Saxon puritan world."

"Kanye knows," Jacoby referenced, apropos of nothing, according to his company, who looked at him like he was having a different conversation altogether. "You know, Kanye West, with his old girlfriend and the Twitter feud about booty play...Never mind," he said, sensing instantly his cultural drift into another universe, one which his companions were thankfully, for their sake, unaware.

Helen shot him a look of mock disdain; Jacoby countered with a blatant, wide-eyed gawk at her breasts. She gasped and punched his shoulder, hard, as Bill continued his lecture on anal intercourse and

Italian straight men. "In Rome, it was rampant. There was so many Brazilian trannies in a neighborhood near the Termini station they had a union of sorts, with political influence on the fringe left."

"Why trannies?" Jacoby asked. "From Brazil?"

"You saw that person at the bar. He or she was beautiful. Who would you, as a straight man, rather have sex with - the Brazilian beauty we just saw or one of these two gentlemen?" He motioned toward the two men, now mauling each other against a wall in an act of sloppy man-on-man lust.

"Gotcha," Jacoby concurred.

"OK," said Helen. "We've confirmed a heterosexual proclivity for exotic women with South American penises. Excellent. I guess without that fact we wouldn't be here, after all, but we did come here for a reason. No?"

"We did," Bill said, reinvigorated once again. A smattering of club goers had wandered in from the back, including a boyish man of Arabic decent wearing a cardigan over a t-shirt, khaki shorts and baseball cap with the brim back. He was alone, sipping Prosecco through a straw, staring at Bill.

"Give me the money," Bill said under his breath to Jacoby.

"How much?"

"All of it."

"What? I thought you said it was found..."

"Just shut up and give me the damn money," Bill said, now holding Jacoby's arm with some force and speaking with a sense of urgency.

"OK. OK," Jacoby said, producing his wallet and all of its contents.

Bill shoved the money in his pocket and approached the boyish man at the bar. They chatted amiably for a few moments and then walked into the club and out of sight.

"Think we should follow him?" Helen asked. "Keep an eye."

"I don't know. Let's give it some time. See what happens."

"Another drink then?" Helen asked, reaching into her small satchel to produce some cash. "It's about time I contributed to the party."

"Got enough in there to spot me a Brazilian tranny?"

"Afraid not."

"A Negroni it is," Jacoby said, feeling expansive and charming. "And then we have to dance."

•　　•　　•

The back rooms were dark and cavernous, each pulsing with light and deafening sound of EDM that Jacoby didn't care for since it had relentless beats but no soul. Men, mostly young and stylish, spotted with oddities, danced with abandon and made out like horny teenagers. In the shadows, tucked against the crumbling stone, some had sex. Jacoby took Helen by the hand and led her down the labyrinth of corridors away from the EDM into a subterranean world of a different theme, one of 70's New York nightlife, where the light increased, somewhat, along with the sense of communal revelry, fueled by a disco soundtrack and a crowded but not too crowded dance floor filled with trannies, sailors, men in three-piece-suits, men dressed casually and one dressed as a baby complete with a cloth diaper, binky and braids. Balloons swirled. The DJ on an iMac in a Hounds Tooth suit spoke in German and programmed tunes from the American disco songbook. Helen and Jacoby danced for hours. They danced together and they danced with others, everyone - seemingly - wanting to share the floor with the heterosexuals who had tumbled with good nature down their secret rabbit hole. Jacoby felt high, expanded by life but softened and smoothed at the same time. He had not a negative thought. Not a wrinkle of doubt. He sweated through his shirt then took it off. Helen, whom he was dancing with at the time, shouted "Lucky" in his ear and then sauntered off to dance with a diva drag queen masquerading as Cher.

At a makeshift bar in a neighboring room, Jacoby passed on pills of Molly but took shots of tequila with a crew of hunky sailors on leave from the dance floor. The boyish looking fellow that had escorted Bill into the club stumbled in, a halo of powder around one nostril and his pupils bloomed like morning glories. Jacoby tried to speak to him, inquiring about Bill, but the boy couldn't speak. He leaned against the wall and began to nod off.

Jacoby put on his shirt and found Helen doing a pogo dance with a six-foot tranny whose head and heels were simultaneously threatened by the low ceiling and the floor of shifted stone.

"We should find Bill!" Jacoby yelled to the still-bouncing Helen.

"What time is it?"

"No clue!"

Helen stopped dancing and walked off with her arm inside of Jacoby's as if they were on a proper date and she was ready to be escorted home. She wiggled her fingers in the air above her shoulder as a goodbye to the room.

On the ground floor, which was mostly abandoned and silent, they found Bill asleep on a chair in the corner of an empty room. Jacoby shook his leg, and his eyes popped open.

"Oh, hello, Jacoby. Helen. What time is it?"

There were no nearby windows, yet the mood suggested night was over.

"I think it's morning," Jacoby said, "or close to it."

They walked out of the caverns and down corridors, past a few party casualties splayed along the floor. The big, bald bartender was in the front room, standing by the entrance, encouraging those leaving to do so quietly. The alley was dark and cool, a fake dawn glowing in the sliver of available sky. They stopped beneath the marble cat where more light penetrated.

"Do we have any money left?" Jacoby asked Bill.

"No, we do not."

"Well spent?"

"Absolutely."

They smiled, a bit awkwardly, at each other until Jacoby gave Bill a reassuring shove on the shoulder.

"And did you two have fun?" Bill asked.

"Only the best time ever," Helen answered matter-of-fact.

"Glad to hear it."

"And did we find anything out about the doorway to the secret corridor of our hidden palace?" Helen asked.

"Not a thing," Bill answered.

"We're not Da Vinci Code types now, are we?"

"Hey," Jacoby playfully interjected. "We found the cat!"

"Well, there's that," Helen acknowledged.

"And here we are," Bill said.

They stood there for a moment until Helen broke the silence.

"I really should be getting home. Thankfully, I haven't any tours today; otherwise, I'd be an absolute wreck."

"Come on," Jacoby said. "We'll walk you to your bike."

On this walk, unlike the night before, Helen sidled up to Jacoby, and though she didn't hold his arm as she had held Bill's on their way to dinner, the bond between them was evident in grazed shoulders and playful rapport. Bill strolled a few steps behind, saying nothing.

Light began to appear in soft bursts on the empty streets, though darkness still prevailed. Helen hugged herself against the swirling breezes still cold with nighttime. Jacoby put his arm around her shoulder; she looped a hand to his far hip. They walked in each other's warmth without speaking.

Piazza Signoria was empty. Bill wandered off when they arrived at Helen's bike. She unlocked it and wiped the moisture off the seat, and then abruptly faced Jacoby with the bike between them, her chin tilted and her eyes up, only a few inches under his.

"So, you're going to be here for a year, you say?"

Jacoby's stomach soured, and his stank breath festered as his mouth went dry, though Helen seemed oblivious to his consternation and only recognized his nod.

"In that case," she continued, "we should find time for a proper date, though I'd be happy to go dancing with the Brazilian trannies again some time as well."

She smiled with warmth and confidence, spinning Jacoby's moral compass, draining him of whatever energy he had left. He lost sensation in his feet and struggled to find his footing.

"Are you alright?" Helen asked, a concerned hand below her throat, an amused wink on her lips.

"Yeah, yeah," Jacoby said, gathering himself. "It's just that...it's just."

Helen's hand fell and her face went flat. "Oh," she said. "I thought for a second there that my charming offer had nearly swept you off your feet."

A pigeon fluttered down, and the front gate of a store across the piazza squealed open. Spots of light began to appear and flickers of day gathered in the sky high above the facades.

"It's just that," Jacoby tried, again, to kick start his explanation, which somehow had to balance reality with a need to convey genuine interest. "It's just..."

"Oh, stop," Helen implored. "My god, if you utter the word 'complicated' I'm going to slaughter you right here."

Jacoby saw the opening for humor. He opened his mouth as if to speak the unspeakable word and then held it in mock-pause. Helen smacked him on the forearm and faked a countenance of contrition.

"It's not like, over the past 12 hours or so, that I haven't imagined what it would be like to kiss you or wake up next to you on a lazy morning or to introduce you to my expat friends and my Italian friends or show you some of my favorite places in Florence or take a drive on the magical road between Montepulciano and Montalcino or anything like that at all."

"Good thing," Jacoby answered.

"Oh, Jacoby," Helen said in a playfully affected voice. "We could have had such a damned good time together."

"Yes," he answered, right on cue. "Isn't it pretty to think so?"

Helen clapped her hands and held them in prayer position. "Don't tell me that's your favorite novel, too."

"It's not," he said, "but I do love that line. I'm more of a Fitzgerald man, myself."

"I wish you were more of a dolt, you know? It'd be easier to hop on my bike and ride away."

"Trust me," he said. "I'm worse than a dolt. I'm a hot mess."

A street sweeper roared into the piazza to make its rounds. Bill nudged his head out from a nearby alley. Helen pinched Jacoby's chin like a piece of fruit.

"Well, Mr. Hot Mess," she said, climbing on her bike, "if you find yourself free of the messy part, your hot self can always find me at the museum."

"How poetic," Jacoby said.

Helen smirked, pecked him hard on the lips and rode off. A taxi warbled into the cobbled piazza and crossed in front of Helen just as she flitted out of sight. The sting from her kiss faded from Jacoby's mouth as the sun threatened to topple the hills to the east of the city.

Chapter 26

In the fledgling light, Bill and Jacoby walked the awakening streets, now busy with deliveries and the first cafes opening. Outside a bakery, a man loaded crates of fresh bread into the hatchback of a car. Bill offered him some coins, but the kind man refused payment and handed over a loaf of warm semolina. They ate in silence as they approached the river, a sheen of silver spread across its pacific surface cut by a single rower sculling at a decent clip. Bill looked particularly fatigued, so Jacoby offered to make the climb alone up to Piazza Michelangelo to retrieve the car and return down the hill.

"Thank you, Jacoby," Bill said. "I will watch the sunrise from here."

Jacoby crossed the empty Ponte Vecchio, past its jewelry shops of mixed configurations. He wandered through sleepy San Niccolo and breathed the morning air deep through his nose as he trudged up the dewy paths towards the piazza and tried to resist the reconciliation that was long overdue. He was lost. The pursuit of the heiress/relative had been fun, a distraction and adventure that served its purpose beyond what Jacoby could have realistically predicted. It had helped settle him in the village and familiarize with town, but now he was decidedly unsettled and about to return to the barn in the hills with a fiancée he would never marry, though he'd have to stay with Claire for the time being because he still had nowhere else to go. No real idea of what he wanted beyond the sense of place and pleasure he enjoyed in Italy. The idea of having to return to America crept over the edges of his fortress walls. Back home, he'd have to attempt to reinvent himself in a setting that provided no inspiration, no purpose. And very few options.

He reached the top of the climb and turned around to face the east just as the sun fully rose above the mountains. And the city below, its terracotta domes and stone towers and silver river, were flooded with gold in an instant that took Jacoby's breath and made him vow to never leave. He felt, for the first time in his life, what it was like to be home, to be in love with a place. He would have to stay. The city had just told him so. His job was to figure out a realistic way to make it happen.

•   •   •

Bill snoozed gently in the passenger seat as Jacoby, fast becoming an expert, navigated the city and its ramparts and the small roads that led the way to Antella. He liked driving people around; even though it could be or seem subservient, he didn't mind. He was often the designated driver in high school, shuttling around boozed up classmates. Someone had to do the driving in life, and it got them places. He liked going places. And having a role. Maybe he could be a driver and guide for English-speaking tourists in Italy, take them all over the central peninsula. Maybe Claire could help. Or even Bill. Maybe he could be a waiter or tend bar in one of Fabio's restaurants. Or he could help Paolo with his olives and Paolo's friends with their grapes. His scrambled mind was working on a plan to stay in Italy, not as a sort-of-spouse or sidekick, but as his own person, on his own volition. He had some money of his own, a small inheritance from his father and his own savings stashed for the potential rainy season that would follow his split from Claire. But even in his sleep-deprived fantasy fever, Jacoby knew that a split from Claire was neither imminent nor wise. He loved and respected her enough to allow them to function as an engaged couple for as long as it took. Jacoby didn't mind being a 'kept' man of sorts. This was the situation that he found himself, and he would deal accordingly, his morals intact. His eyes on the prize.

Jacoby parked the car outside the hotel and turned off the ignition. Bill woke on cue and extended his hand to Jacoby.

"Thank you, young man," he said, shaking Jacoby's warm hand. "That was an evening unlike I've had in some time."

Jacoby looked over the piazza. "And here we are."

"Indeed," Bill agreed. "And I have no idea what to do next."

"We could go back, in the daylight, and try to find the door."

"We'll never find it," Bill said, looking resigned and exhausted. "It really, truly, could be anywhere in that vicinity. And how would we even know? It's not like the 100-year old woman goes out often, if at all. She's probably cared for by a staff who we'd have no way of even recognizing. They surely just come and go like pedestrians."

"So what are you saying?"

"I'm saying that this is not the movies, Jacoby. We don't get to extend our improbable narratives or construct our happy endings."

"Yes, I know," Jacoby said, thinking again of the Hemingway line. "But isn't it pretty to think so?"

"Indeed it is," Bill sighed. "And now I must go to sleep, for a long time. Come and call on me soon? I'll have to meet this fiancée of yours at some point."

Jacoby nodded. Bill climbed out and hobbled to the hotel door. Jacoby remembered as the door closed that Bill held the picture, but he didn't want to disturb him or even leave the car. It seemed appropriate that Bill have it anyway; he was in love with her brother. Jacoby started the ignition and drove the winding hill up to the barn, feeling forlorn and so tired.

•　　　•　　　•

Paolo waived from his ladder in the olive grove and climbed down. Jacoby dreaded a stilted conversation in broken English, but Paolo approached with purpose. He held up a hand.

"Wait. Wait," he said. "I have something for you."

Jacoby sat on a metal chair on the terrace behind the barn as Paolo hurried down the steps beneath the branches of the plunging fig tree, onto the terrace and through the gate of the giant fence. The screen door to the villa creaked and slammed. Jacoby felt fidgety and defeated, so close to the bed he so desperately needed to crawl into and slumber, yet resigned to a cold, iron chair still wet with morning dew. Flying insects were curious about his odor; he flipped at them and picked at his cuticles and then – from somewhere deep in his conscience – he remembered what Bill had just said about meeting his fiancée.

Sprung by a jolt of panic, he scurried for the car and yanked his phone from the glove compartment. He sat sideways on the passenger seat with his feet out of the door, waiting for the damn phone to power on in a breathless moment of panic. A string of texts pinged and appeared in a slew of verbiage. Jacoby read furiously, fearing his lack of accountability over the past 24 hours had been inexcusable. He fucked up. Again. And Claire would probably have his ass, again, and rightly so. How would he possibly explain to her where he'd been? She knew nothing of his recent adventuring. His seeking a family secret; his night of emotional infidelity. All this after his meltdown at the butcher's restaurant. He'd become a shitty fiancé, even more so than before. He was entering the realm of being a serious burden. This couldn't happen.

But the texts from Claire were soft. Curious but not overly concerned. The delicious breath of reprieve filled Jacoby's lungs, matched by a rush of fondness for Claire. He loved the fact that she respected his resistance to over-connectivity. She was so unlike the significant others of almost everyone else he knew, engaged in a form of stalking that bordered on - or crossed well into - the realm of pathology. Claire was cool. She got Jacoby, and he felt ashamed for not appreciating what he had in her. Maybe they would survive the year in Italy. And maybe he could even convince her to stay. He didn't need some ridiculous mission to find long lost family. He had a beautiful and successful fiancée who provided what the photograph could not: security and love among all the splendor of Italy. He shut the car door and walked to the barn feeling foolish along with a surge of emotion for the woman who essentially gave him life as he knew it in that moment. She was his only family; and she would be home soon, texting when close so Jacoby could open the gate, sometime around lunch. Jacoby needed some sleep before then. His mental and emotional faculties were in disarray. His thought process a blizzard. Claire couldn't see him that way. He went upstairs, yanked off his clothes, used the bathroom, brushed his teeth, and crawled into bed, forgetting all about Paolo and whatever he had for him.

Chapter 27

He dreamed of Claire as an older woman, still desirable and smoothed around the edges. Her hair was shorter and less vivid, resting on her shoulders, and she had one of those streaks of gray, like a bolt of lightning, that started at the hairline above her right eye. Jacoby loved that look in women, something about the confidence it exuded. In his dream, they lived in a country house in a country of unclear origin. It felt Nordic, with rivers and dales and woods beyond the expanse of their property. They wore warm, comfortable clothes, sipping from steaming cups, as they sat reading in separate chairs in a white living room with vaulted ceilings, large windows and high bookshelves. He slept so well.

Jacoby woke from the vibration of his phone. Claire was on the access road, he assumed, being chauffeured by Dolores. While cleaning up quickly and dressing in fresh clothes, he thought of taking the cousins into the village, proving how he'd been busy acclimating himself to the new surroundings. He'd have to avoid Bill in order to keep his recent whereabouts a secret. He decided not to tell the cousins his stupid story of the hidden picture and its dead end. There was no need for another addition to his failures.

With some solid rest, fresh clothes and breath, Jacoby stepped out of the barn and down the slope to the gate. When he heard a car rumble to a stop, he pushed the button and let the gate swing open.

The beige Audi lurched past and up the track to a flat spot beside the Jetta. Claire got out of the driver's side, and Jacoby felt side-swiped by doubt. Where was Dolores?

Claire pushed aviator sunglasses beyond her hairline and stretched her long arms high over her head. She wore designer jeans and a short-sleeve, cashmere sweater the color of goldenrod. She looked so beautiful, so empowered, tan and well-rested, he should have known to be afraid, but instead, he just puzzled over her arriving alone, operating a manual transmission sports car with relative ease.

"Hey," Jacoby called, high-kneeing up the incline of the drive.

"Oh, hey, Babe," Claire responded, a little confused by his whereabouts. "Did you lose the remote?"

"No. No," Jacoby said. "I just thought to come down and open the gate for you manually. You know, like opening a door."

"Oh," Claire said. She looked around the property like it was her first time there.

Jacoby arrived in front of Claire, and they stared at each other in silence, before Claire offered an awkward and exaggerated "Hi," and smiled without showing any teeth. She reached into the car for her purse and closed the door.

"Where's Dolores?"

"Long story."

Jacoby rolled his eyes. "Hey – now we're like a two-car family." He tapped the trunk of the Audi. "I get this one."

Claire smiled and gusted some air out of her nose. Jacoby sensed her unease.

"I'll grab your bags," he said, approaching the trunk.

"Leave them for now," she said quickly and began to walk inside. "I've got something in my purse for you. Something yummy."

Jacoby followed like a good dog, curious about the yummy treat as a yummy treat, but he also interpreted the treat as a sign that things were OK with Claire. He assured himself that his unsettled feeling was due to lack of sleep after a very long night.

Inside the barn, Claire put a giant bistecca on the kitchen counter. It was vacuum-sealed in clear plastic. Jacoby picked it up and measured the heft of a bright red and boneless slab of strip. His stomach interrupted with a reminder of hunger.

"Damn," he said. "Where's this from? La Maremma? I should have gone. So how was it, anyway? Find any joints good enough for Alistair Haxby?"

"I'll tell you'll all about it after a shower. The steak is sealed, so you can put in the freezer if you want. Save it for another time."

"Alright," Jacoby shrugged, drawing the steak in one hand back over his right shoulder, as if it were a football. "Go deep."

Claire ignored the gag and spiraled up the staircase to the lofted bedroom. The shower went on instantly as Jacoby's hunger returned. A magnificent idea was born: Steak and eggs!

Relieved and hungry, he sliced the meat out of the seal and patted it dry with paper towels. After a coating of olive oil, he seasoned it heavily with coarse salt and black pepper. He cranked up a burner and topped it with a cast iron pan, barely big enough to hold the steak that he seared on each side, the sizzling sound obscuring that from above, of drawers being opened and closed. With the steak resting on a cutting board, Jacoby whipped up some eggs and scrambled them in the pan that held the steak drippings. The steak sliced smooth against the bias without spilling any juice, all the flavor settled into meat more rare than medium, crusted in a seared and seasoned exterior.

The shower stopped running. Jacoby plated two thick slices of meat next to the eggs and had a seat at the small table in the front room. The aroma filled his nose and his hand trembled slightly as he cut a bite-size piece and began to chew rapidly as the meat melted in his mouth and destroyed him with its distinct flavor.

Tears fell down Jacoby's face as he continued to chew enough to swallow safely. The salt from the tears entering his mouth brightened the flavor, making it more clear what was happening even before Claire began to descend the stairs in the same clothes she wore before, a suitcase thumping beside her.

"Mommy," Jacoby said quietly to himself and pushed his plate away. He'd never felt so alone.

The clunking of the suitcase on each stair felt like a death knell.

Claire left the suitcase by the stairs and took a seat next to Jacoby who wiped away any sign of tears.

"I didn't go to La Maremma," she said quietly.

"I know," Jacoby answered, looking down at his discarded plate.

"How?"

"The steak is from the butcher in Panzano."

"How'd you know that?"

"Sage."

"What?"

Jacoby looked at Claire. "Sage. The cows he gets his meat from are fed on enough sage that there's a hint of its flavor in the meat. I knew it that night at the restaurant but never got a chance to tell you."

"You're incredible."

"And you're a slut."

Claire sprung from her seat, shocked and furious.

"How dare you!"

Jacoby stood for battle. "You said you were going to La Maremma."

"I was!"

"How the fuck did you end up in Panzano for three days and not tell me if you weren't holed up with that butcher?"

The betrayal Jacoby felt was sickening, but he also sensed a strain of relief, of absolution. He knew something like this was coming. Or, at least, he feared it would, and maybe he hoped it would. And now it had arrived.

"It was Dolores, you fucking asshole!"

"What was Dolores?"

"She was the one fucking the butcher. We stopped in for lunch so I could finish my interview - you know, the one you ruined with your pathetic dash - and Dolores got him boozed up and took him to bed, where they, essentially stayed for days. She refused to accompany me to La Maremma, and I didn't want to go alone."

"And you just forgot to mention any of this? You could have called or texted. I would have gone down to get you."

"I didn't want you to do that," Claire said quietly and sat back down.

"Why not?"

"Because I needed some time to think."

"About what?"

"About us."

"What about us?"

The panic button for being broken up with went off inside Jacoby and caused him to be sickened in a different way as Claire took a breath through her nose and jetted it out of her mouth. This was worse than betrayal: It was rejection.

"I don't want to be here."

"Where?"

"In Italy. Working for boring old Alistair Haxby. With you."

Jacoby fought off the sting and responded deftly, somehow steady enough to be witty. He sat back down.

"What did Alistair Haxby ever do to you?"

Claire laughed and took Jacoby's hand.

"I'm sorry, baby, but this was a mistake. I've known it nearly since we arrived. I sensed it before we left. I've been on edge for so long, and I'm sorry to have been so stupid and so difficult at times. My life is in New York. I love it there. It's where I belong right now. Among people my own age, with the same passions. When you lost your job, I didn't know what to do. I felt like I was losing you, so I came here to save you, to save us. I know you. I knew you'd love it here. The pacing and the beauty. Of course, the food. I overlooked that fact that I'd only love it for a while. For me, at this point in my life, it's just a place to visit. A few weeks, tops, and my few weeks are up. Our time, I'm afraid, is up, as well."

"So, you're un-proposing to me now?"

"I guess."

"What if I said no?"

"Would you?"

"No."

Jacoby stared at dust motes in front of the kitchen window and let the wave of emotions manifest. As painful as this was, not to mention how massively inconvenient, he knew it was right. The undeniable beauty of the truth obvious among all the complications and hurt. All the frightening uncertainties. All the other doubts and fears. He clenched and released his fists, and then faced his former fiancée.

"So, what are you going to do?"

"I'm going back to New York."

"When?"

"I don't know. I just can't quit on Alistair Haxby. I need to talk with Mum first and make it all on the up and up, so I'll be here for a few more weeks, at least."

Jacoby looked at the suitcase and into Claire's eyes.

"You can stay here."

Claire rubbed Jacoby's thighs lovingly and wiped a tear from her eye.

"I think I'll be better off at Dolores' for the time being. This is hard enough."

They sat in the silence for a minute, looking elsewhere, letting the separation settle.

"Sorry I called you a slut."

"Sorry I ruined your steak and eggs."

"Oh, I'll be eating those."

They laughed together. Truth and relief lightened the mood. Jacoby stood to help Claire with her suitcase, but she held up a hand. "I've got it."

She dragged the bag to the door and stopped. "I'll need to return for the car at some point, take it back to Nice when I fly out. You'll also need to figure out what you're going to do. The rent here is paid through June, but there's no way Haxby's will pay anymore once I turn in my resignation, which will have to be by month's end. Can you deal with Paolo?"

Jacoby nodded.

"You have the return plane ticket which is open-ended as far as the date goes."

"I know."

"Just take it to a travel agent to arrange your flight."

Jacoby nodded.

"And you'll have to let me know when you're leaving so we can work things out in New York with your stuff and all. You should probably get home before I do. I don't want to have to be there to watch you move out. I don't think I could stand that."

Jacoby shrugged. "Good thing I don't have much."

Claire creased a smile that was heavy with sympathy and sorrow. Tears poured from one eye.

"Do you need some money to get by for a while?" she asked, sniffing.

"No," Jacoby said. "I'll be fine."

"Maybe in New York I could help you find work."

"Thanks, but I'm not staying in New York."

"Where will you go?" Claire asked quickly, the enormity of her decision finally landing.

Jacoby looked her in the eye without seeking sympathy. "I don't know," he said.

Claire walked over quickly, fighting back more tears. They hugged for a long while. Her tears wet his back as Jacoby breathed in the apple smell of her hair and knew he was delving even deeper into the world of suffering and loss.

Chapter 28

Claire stayed too long, assuring Jacoby she would help him in any way she could. Her guilt was of little comfort to Jacoby. And after she finally left, he sat for a long while in the silence of the barn, in the same spot he had been for the breakup. He eventually got up and walked around, taking in the new surroundings, getting used to them as his alone, getting used to his life alone. It didn't feel so unfamiliar, and his somber mood and concern for his future was positively informed by a sense of relief, and a thread of optimism. He was clearheaded. He'd felt depression before, and that was brought on by events more emotionally jarring than his disengagement from Claire. And that previous blow of being fired was compounded by not having effectively dealt with the loss of his father and what that loss represented. This was different. He would not succumb to sadness. No singing the blues. There was no severance pay and/or a sympathetic partner either. He'd have to act alone; and he'd have to act now. Figuring out what to do was going to be the hard part. He thought of his favorite line from his favorite movie, *The Shawshank Redemption*: "Get busy living, or get busy dying." It was corny, he knew, but so fucking what? It was truth.

Jacoby stored the unfinished steak in the fridge and tidied up, opening up windows and the front doors to light and breeze as he cleaned and rearranged. Then he shut them all tight. With the barn doors shut and curtains drawn over the kitchen windows, the front room was dark and cool. Jacoby curled up on the couch like a cat and went to sleep.

He did not have any dreams that he remembered, but he woke up in the small hours of the next morning with sweat soaked clothes. He lumbered upstairs, stripped and slept a few more hours under the covers until the light of dawn crept around the edges of the balcony doors. Jacoby opened the doors to the new day but nothing was waiting for him. He knew panic could set in if he didn't get busy. Seeking something to keep his hands and mind active, Jacoby went for the shed to retrieve his borrowed guitar.

The new guitar strings had made it through the all night affair in Florence, tucked into the back pocket of Jacoby's pants and then tossed in the back seat of the car once he had reached the parking lot in Piazza Michelangelo. Under the carport of the barn, Jacoby retrieved the guitar strings from the Jetta and was fondly reminded of Helen, but he dashed the idea of finding her at the museum. Romance was not an option at the moment.

Back in the barn, in the sunlit room on the side of the ground floor, he changed the strings, tuned the guitar and noodled for a few minutes before beginning his familiar warm up routine of pentatonic scales in various keys up and down the neck, followed by a chord progression he used to play for hours on end in his room as a lonely teen with dreams of his guitar as a ticket to a better place. Finally, he got around to the handful of Pearl Jam songs that he knew, working his way through them slowly, imagining himself as the accompanist to Giovanni's vocals. Jacoby played until hunger interrupted at lunch time and his fingertips and wrist begged for rest.

He reheated the leftover steak in a pan and ate it with vigor and no lingering bitterness over its presence in the previous day's events. He could feel the strength from the protein and iron. He was happy from his work on the guitar, high from mental exertion and soul exercise, but he knew he had no more playing in him that day. He read from his novel for a while after lunch and took a short nap.

In the middle of the afternoon, he went out to the shed and began to chop and stack the piles of wood cylinders until the sun began to set and a chill clung to his sweaty upper body. After a shower, he drove to the nearby groceria and picked up some provisions, including bread and wine and eggs and cheese. He made a gigantic cheese-steak sandwich with the remaining meat, soft Pecorino, and a loaf of semolina. He cut the sandwich into four sections, wrapping three in foil and washing down one with the familiar red wine he had purchased in an unmarked bottle.

After dinner, he smoked one cigarette from a pack Claire had left in the glove compartment of the car. Then he read some more and played Dylan's *Love and Theft* until it was time to go to bed, the bawdy, rancorous "Lonesome Day Blues" stuck in his head and serenading him into a deep and fitful sleep as he commiserated with the lyrics, "Today has been a sad and lonesome day..."

$$\bullet \qquad \bullet \qquad \bullet$$

He followed the routine the next day, working on his guitar in the morning after breakfast, eating lunch and napping at midday, then spending the afternoon in the shed chopping and stacking wood. At dusk, he would walk up beyond the property and sit on a rock to watch the sun sink in the west and draw a curtain over the sunken city. He drank wine with dinner and smoked one cigarette afterward, before reading with music on until it was time for bed.

He grew strong and content. Purposeful and confident. Ideas began to form. And when there was no more wood to cut and his fingertips grew thick with protective callouses of a working musician, he walked down to the village in the middle of another sunny afternoon and rang the buzzer at the hotel.

There was no answer. Jacoby checked the cafe. Nicoletta shrugged and communicated through excessive body language and 100 untranslatable words that she hadn't seen Bill around much at all of late. He wondered, based on her exasperation, if she had missed a rendezvous or two with Giovanni on account of Bill's recent absence. He hoped she didn't blame him.

The piazza was empty at the end of afternoon riposa. The only open business was the cafe. Jacoby sat beside the statue and sought inspiration. The door of the pasticerria, across the piazza, a few storefronts down from the hotel, opened and two women in matching polyester dresses and hairnets walked onto the sidewalk to survey the surroundings, smoke cigarettes, and signal their return to the business of serving pastries and gelato. The sun hung high above the piazza, the heat gathering in the hollow of the village and especially within its inner confines of stone and cement and plaster.

Jacoby walked into the pasticerria, nodded at the women behind the counter and asked for a glass of water, which he sipped while deciphering the vast array of flavors and vibrant colors within the cooler that held stainless steel tins of gelato. He settled on a medium cup that allowed for his choice of two different flavors: pistacchio (pistachio) and straccinella (vanilla with chocolate chips). He took his cup back to the piazza and sat in the shade of the statue. The creamy texture and vivid flavors filled his mouth with song and a pleasure equal in its visceral decadence to sex. He actually found himself a little bit aroused, so he crossed a leg and kept his thoughts on the gelato to avoid any association with the most peculiar perversion.

People began to reappear after their midday rest, and some young boys showed up with a soccer ball. They played a pickup game in the corner of the piazza, against a wall on the cafe's far side. Their voices sounded like angels singing, and Jacoby wandered over to watch. When a loose ball came his way, he flipped it into the air with a foot and juggled the ball successfully a dozen times before losing control. The boys cheered "Bravo," and Jacoby joined them in a pickup game, astonished at their ball skills and passing and elusiveness. This was their sport, and they pretty much ran circles around him.

Nicoletta came out the side door to smoke a cigarette and watch. She sat at a small table tucked against the wall of the cafe and assessed Jacoby's skills with a smirk of mild admiration before calling them all inside where she poured the boys regular-sized glasses of water and playfully gave Jacoby a carafe full which she adorned with a straw. They all laughed as Jacoby sucked in some much needed hydration.

After the break, they played some more, until shadows covered their small annex of the piazza and a savory aroma arrived on the breeze brought by dusk.

A female voice bellowed, and the boys stopped playing instantly. They waved goodbye to Jacoby and ran away. Jacoby returned to the cafe to wash up and take more water. There were a few customers in the back, lingering over newspapers. No sign of the hunters, which Jacoby appreciated. At the bar, now having a cold beer, Jacoby inquired about the aroma by touching his nose and sniffing the air, rubbing his belly.

"Ah," Nicolletta recognized. "Oggi è venerdì, la giornata per i ceci al forno."

Jacoby couldn't put the sentence together. He got 'today' and 'Friday' but the rest left him lost, though the words were somewhat familiar.

"Il forno," she said, pointing to the road out of the piazza. "Il posto per pane."

She grabbed a roll of ciabatta from under the counter and held it up. "Pane."

"Si," Jacoby said. "Pane. Bread. Capisco." He felt stupid but not ashamed, and he was inspired to piece the next part of the puzzle together on his own. He recalled signs above shops marked "Forno" and matched it with Paolo's reference to his outdoor oven using the same name. "Bakery," he said. "Il forno è il posto per pane."

"Bravo," Nicoletta said with only a hint of sarcasm at his ability to recognize a bakery as a place for bread. She smiled, which encouraged Jacoby to continue.

"Ma, che cosa ceci?"

Nicoletta held up her hands. "Troppo difficile," she confessed, too difficult to explain, which - at least - Jacoby understand. "Ha fame?" she asked, rubbing her belly.

Jacoby knew both the Italian phrase and international signal for hunger.

"Si," he said.

"Vai," Nicoletta instructed him to go, flapping her hand upward, toward the door and down the street where the young boys had run. "Segue tuo naso," she said, touching her nose.

Jacoby smiled and followed his nose toward a savory smell which grew stronger as he left the piazza and walked a one-lane road over a bridge that spanned one of the many narrow creeks that rippled down from the hills and eventually fed into the River Arno.

A small line extended out the door of an ancient storefront. Jacoby stood behind a woman in her 80s, dressed impeccably and holding a designer handbag across her bosom. She gave Jacoby a strange look. Locals soon lined up behind him. The blinds were drawn over the storefront's windows. The line moved silently forward as each patron left with an aluminum tin covered in foil or a sealed ovenware dish and a paper sleeve filled with bread. Jacoby could figure out the contents of the sleeve, but the product in the tins or dishes had him puzzled and desperately curious to identify the aroma since it was now so profound yet unidentifiable. He could feel the warmth from inside the shop inspired by the cooking; he smelled something nutty, accompanied by smaller aspects of flavor, like rosemary, other aromatics and, was it, lemon? He had to know; he had to eat.

Upon the doorway, Jacoby peered over heads of old Italians, afraid to speak but desperate for knowledge. He was also very hungry, as the soccer game had kicked in a metabolism raised by the daily workouts with the ax and wood. The room was sparse and shaded with a glass counter and metal baskets of bread varieties displayed in the window. Women in white hats manned the counter; a man in an apron around his waist hurried through the swinging kitchen door in back, filling orders called by the women in the white hats. It was busy, but not frantic. The women smiled kindly at the guests but didn't chat as they might normally. This was all business, Italian style.

Behind the counter, on a crude jet print, a sign in stylish font read "Ceci" across the top and "Venerdì" across the bottom. OK. Jacoby put together that Friday was the day for "Ceci." All he had left to figure out was the latter.

Feeling slightly unnerved but determined, Jacoby found himself in front of a woman at the counter who looked upon him with curious eyes as he was probably the only person she served all day who was unfamiliar. He summoned his charm and courage, clasped his hands in front of his heart and said "Ciao."

"Ciao," the woman said back, tilting her head in expectation of more conversation.

Jacoby tried to swallow through his dry mouth. "Mi dispiace. Sono Americano. Che cosa ceci?"

The woman laughed and told the whole store that they had an americano with them who wanted to know what 'ceci' was. Everyone laughed. Someone clapped him kindly on the back. The woman in front of him turned and patted him on the cheek. Jacoby looked around and registered many kind smiles. Almost everyone was older than him, most of the senior variety. He liked that. He liked older people. He held up his hands, smiled and said. "Mi dispiace. Ho fame."

Everyone seemed to fall over themselves refusing his apology and recognizing his hunger. The explanations of 'ceci' came from so many sources with such enthusiasm that Jacoby could not understand at all. Finally, the man in the apron whistled, and the room went silent. He waved Jacoby over and handed him a tin mounded with small, round objects the color of caramel, specked in seasonings and glistening with oil. They had been cooked, almost braised, as the tender outer shell separated in places. Jacoby still wasn't sure what he was looking at.

"Prendi," the man said, motioning with his hand toward the food.

Jacoby took one and popped it into his mouth. Warm and flavorful, bright with lemon and oil, toothy but soft, it melted in his mouth and vanished down his throat. "Ah," Jacoby declared that he now knew what had lured him down the street and into the bakery. "Io so! Io so!" he declared with his hands raised like a true Italian.

The room waited his answer.

"Chickpeas!" he blurted.

Everyone cheered as if he had delivered news of utmost importance. Jacoby shook hands and felt touches on his arm and shoulder. The man wrapped the tin tightly in aluminum foil with pantomimed instructions to, before eating, swirl with oil and sprinkle with salt.

Jacoby nodded and reached for his wallet, but the man refused payment. Jacoby thanked everyone behind the counter and left the happy room through a crowd of smiles and touches and well-wishes, his hunger temporarily replaced by a tremendous sense of good will and camaraderie. He walked in the slanted sunlight back toward to piazza, feeling invincible, committed to carefully carrying his tray of food all the way home.

By the time he got to the piazza, the smell was overwhelming him, and the warm tin became uncomfortable in his hand. He would eat alfresco, right there in the piazza. Most stores were now shut, and the public space was empty except for pigeons and doves on eaves and swallows circling high in anticipation of the evening's cool. Jacoby sat on the shady side of the statue and pulled the foil from the tin. A fresh aroma arose and made the pores on his face open along with his nostrils. Using chunks of bread as a makeshift spoon, he scooped up some chickpeas and ferried them to his mouth, losing a few along the way but relishing those that arrived. He chewed slowly, pausing to breathe, then chew again. His eyes were closed; he didn't see Nicoletta approaching with her face screwed up in disdain.

"Che stai facendo?" she asked what he was doing, her intensity belied by familiarity.

Jacoby smiled and pointed at his nose and then the chickpeas.

Nicoletta pinched her right fingers together and shook them in disappointment. "Bravo," she said with maximum sarcasm before changing her tone to a didactic one. "Ma non mangiate qui, così."

Jacoby gleaned that she didn't approve of the manner in which and where he took his dinner. Italians did not eat in public spaces, and even the street food he had with Bill was taken in a manner of slight dignity, standing still, eating slowly, sipping wine. You'd never see an Italian walking the streets, slurping down a slice of pizza or chomping on a sandwich. Jacoby got that custom, appreciated it, but didn't see much of an option at that point, a warm tin of chickpeas on his lap and the only instrument available being a large square of what seemed like a crisp version of focaccia, dimpled and seasoned with large grains of salt. He shrugged without shame at his lack of decorum.

Nicoletta pinched her lips and shook her head. "Vieni qui," she ordered Jacoby to come with her and walked off toward the cafe where she turned the corner to the annex, lifted the gate that covered the side door. Jacoby covered his food and followed.

"La," she directed him to sit at the small table tucked along the side of the building. Jacoby sat down in the cool shade and listened to doves coo from eaves across the side street until Nicoletta returned with a table setting of a bowl, fork, napkin and a goblet. She set them in place and returned inside for a bottle of oil, a small ramekin of salt and a bottle of wine with a cork in the top. She set them in front of Jacoby and motioned for him to proceed, as if on his own.

Jacoby swirled some feint green oil over the chickpeas, then anointed with a large pinch of salt. His hostess nodded and brought the oil and salt back inside. Upon return, she shuttered the gate and pulled the cork from the bottle of red. Jacoby assumed it came from behind the bar as one used to serve those who ordered by the glass.

"Buon appetito, Americano," she declared, clapped her hands twice and began to walk away.

"Aspetta," Jacoby asked her to wait. He couldn't find the words to invite her company, so he motioned toward the food and the table setting.

"Non grazie, americano," she said, smiling with anticipation. "Ho un appuntamento."

Jacoby gathered that she had plans. He thought of Giovanni and where they must be meeting in Bill's absence. Maybe in his workshop. How sexy.

"Ma," Jacoby muttered, gesturing toward the table setting.

"Lascia," she said. "Per domani."

Jacoby nodded, happy to understand that she wanted him to leave the things for tomorrow and how unlikely that would happen in America.

"Ciao," she said and hurried off.

"Ciao," Jacoby called before tucking into his plate of oven-baked chickpeas that tasted as flavorful as anything he'd ever eaten, washing the legumes and bread down with the local red wine as he sat in the cool shadows of his own private dining terrace on a Friday night in a silent village as twilight settled upon him in what felt like the most important place in all of the world.

Chapter 29

Jacoby clanged Paolo's bell. It rang his ears and set the big dog to barking for a minute before it settled down with a muffled growl. Jacoby waited on the terrace on his side of the gate. It was still morning, and Jacoby feared he may have woken his elderly neighbor/landlord. But Jacoby had been up for hours and couldn't wait any longer to show Paolo what he'd done in the shed and to make a request that could have a major bearing on his future, at least his immediate one.

In the lemony light, insects circled and settled, mostly on the fruit from the fig tree which had grown heavy over recent days. Some of the fruit had fallen from bent branches strewn with large green leaves. Jacoby walked over near the staircase and easily separated a fat fig from its stem. It felt firm yet plump in his hand, heavier than expected. He bit off the bottom half, and it exploded in his mouth, shocking him somewhat and sending juice and pulp from between his lips. He jumped back to avoid staining his shirt, aware all along of that sweet flavor coursing around his tongue and teeth. The magnificent texture felt wholly unique, and he was reminded of its sexual connotation though he still assumed that the salutation of the crude hunters was inspired by color alone.

Jacoby reached for another fig and ate this one with more care. Jacoby thought of figs wrapped in prosciutto later that day and throughout the summer, and harvesting the excess fruit into fig jam which he would store in mason jars on a shelf in the kitchen to be enjoyed throughout autumn and the rainy season, which would come after the harvest that now seemed so romantic. If only he'd be able to stay.

The screen door slammed. "Ha-lo?" Paolo's voice came from behind the fence. "Ja-co-bey?"

Jacoby tried to shake the nerves from his skeleton.

"Yes. Si, Paolo. It's me."

Paolo opened the gate, a cloth napkin still tucked into the open neck of his cotton work shirt.

"I'm sorry to bother your breakfast," Jacoby said, carefully, feeling the nerves of a looming proposal rising.

"No. No," Paolo demurred, pulling the napkin free and stuffing it in his pants pocket. "It is O.K."

"I wanted to show you something," Jacoby said. "If you have the time, a few minutes."

Paolo looked pleasantly surprised and motioned with his hand for Jacoby to proceed. They walked around the barn, past the carport above the driveway, and up the slope toward the shed. Paolo showed signs of fatigue in labored breath and a supportive hand on one thigh as he climbed the steady incline. Jacoby found hope in this, thinking he could really be of use around the property.

Upon entering the shed, Paolo held a hand to his beating heart as his eyes adjusted to the shade. Dust motes swam in the light that splintered through cracks in the wall boards. The room smelled of wood and sap. The work area was neatly organized along one wall, on and below a shelf loaded with tools and supplies against which the ax leaned. The wood was chopped and neatly stacked nearly to the ceiling around the perimeter of three sides. Jacoby didn't know exactly how much it was, but he assumed it would be enough to get Paolo through the upcoming winter and maybe the next.

"Very, very good," Paolo said. "Thank you so much."

"My pleasure," Jacoby answered, picking up the ax, showing how comfortably he could handle it.

"I must use some wood for the forno to pay you with misto arrosto and pizza."

"Actually," Jacoby broached, sensing an opening, squeezing the ax handle. "I'd like to discuss something a little more, uh, formal than that."

Paolo looked puzzled. "More formal?"

Jacoby feared that Paolo thought he was hitting him up for cash or something. "No. No. It's nothing to be worried about, it's just…"

Paolo held up a hand. "Listen. Let us go to the villa and talk slowly with caffè."

Jacoby smirked and nodded. He leaned the ax against the wall just beside the doorway and motioned for Paolo to exit first, which he did, leading down past the carport but around the front of the villa this time, where Paolo showed off his small arbor of lemon trees potted in enormous ceramic basins and hosting lemons already the size of baseballs. Beyond the citrus orchard lie supplies for collecting olives, including nets and ladders and a three-wheel "Ape" with a bed in back to transport the fruit to be cold pressed into extra-virgin oil.

They entered through a gate on the opposite side of the barn where, on the villa's back terrace, the dog gave Jacoby a vigorous sniff and Paolo motioned toward the large wooden table under the umbrella. Paolo hobbled into the house as Jacoby petted the dog under its chin while rehearsing his pitch.

Paolo returned with a platter holding an antique espresso maker, a bowl of sugar, and two demitasse cups with tiny spoons. He poured for both and then sweetened his own cup. Jacoby followed. The coffee was bitter and strong, balanced by the sugar.

"So," Jacoby said. "I have to tell you that Claire, mia fidanzata, has left."

The words felt foreign to Jacoby's ears. Paolo was the first person he had told, and the reality of it jarred Jacoby, spinning him somewhat, but he kept on as Paolo's expression didn't seem to register the import of the news. "She's not coming back."

"Oh," Paolo said. "She is gone. Not on a trip."

"Yes."

"Oh."

"She had to go back to New York," Jacoby lied. "For an important job."

"OK."

"The thing is that it was her job, the one here that paid our expenses, including our rent on the barn."

"Oh."

Jacoby creased a smile and thought to wait a moment before suggesting his solution, but Paolo spoke first.

"But, but the contract is made in your name."

Jacoby hadn't thought of that, but he didn't let on.

"I understand," he said, "but I can't afford to stay here alone."

"What do you do?" Paolo asked, exasperation on his face and in his voice. "About the money that is owe on the first of next month?"

"That's what I wanted to talk to you about," Jacoby said. "Maybe I could stay here and help you."

"But how?"

"With the property," Jacoby said, his sense of hope draining out of him as he spoke. "Like, with the wood and the trees. Harvesting the olives."

"Instead of the money?"

"Instead of the money."

Paolo was silent. Jacoby's heart sank, and the tendrils of panic wiggled upward from his stomach which now burned with sour coffee and pending defeat.

"Maybe not all of the rent, but some of it," Jacoby offered.

He always sucked at negotiating, though he never hated himself for it until now. Paolo held up his hand as if to stop the flood of nonsense.

"Look, Ja-co-bey," Paolo said with resignation, and some sympathy. "I am sorry for this what happen to you. The work with the property is kind, and maybe a good idea, and maybe possible until la stagione, the season, but there is maybe, most likely, no season this year."

"Why not?" Jacoby asked, bolstered by reference to 'possibility' in Paolo's response. Why was he up in his trees every day if not to prepare for the harvest?

"This is difficult to say" Paolo said slowly. "But there is a woman, a very old woman who own the fattoria, the farm, where the people from all the commune bring the olives, the grape, the frutta per produzione."

"I know," Jacoby interrupted.

Paolo looked puzzled. "How?"

"Long story," Jacoby said.

Paolo smiled kindly. "OK, so you know this woman. Do you know she is now dead?"

Jacoby felt a gaping hole in the pit of his stomach. Oh, no. It couldn't be. It couldn't. It could. This explained Bill's absence from the village. Two stars colliding. The heiress is dead; and Bill knows. Jacoby was certain of this, though he wasn't sure why. Paolo continued.

"And the property of the woman is now the property of the province because she no, she no pay her tax for many, many year."

"Oh, no," Jacoby said out loud.

"So," Paolo continued, unaware of the depth of Jacoby's sorrow and his fleeting dreams, "there is, most probably, no season this year for oil and wine, the other prodotti. I have enough to last, but still it is something we all in the commune like very much. Something we will try to save if we can, but I do not know."

Jacoby's chin fell to his chest, and he finally stopped petting the dog. Under the table, he rubbed the shed fur from his fingers and stood up to leave.

"So, what do we do about the barn?" Paolo asked. "Your rent."

"I don't know," Jacoby said. "Can I tell you in a few days?"

Paolo sighed. "Yes. But, please, tell me very soon what you will do."

Jacoby nodded and walked away, but before he got to the gate,

Paolo called out.

"Oh, aspetta! Wait. There is this something for you. That I tell you before."

He hurried into the house and returned with an envelope adorned with an automated international postage seal and the familiar letterhead of a Manhattan law firm.

Chapter 30

Jacoby hurried into the barn and closed the doors tight. He flipped the letter from New York onto the small table and sat on the couch, rubbing his face and wishing away the truth he had just been told. Regret and what-ifs ran through his mind, a desire to have acted sooner with more determination, and he felt the sickness of such thoughts rushing toward him. He paced the room, reconciling the fact that his last living relative had died and died bankrupt. The shuttered estate symbolized his life. And any mystery or majesty, any belief in fate being a gift, was now dead, too. He so wished that he could have met the woman, just once, though there was a prevailing sense that it would have been a disappointment anyway. It always seemed to work like that. We trick ourselves into believing something better is coming, but it never does. At least not for Jacoby. He had done what he was supposed to do: behave, show respect, get educated, work hard, play fair, live right. And what did he have to show for it? Fuck the American dream.

The envelope on the table was further proof of his fatalistic mindset. A letter came quarterly from the law firm Claire's mother had asked to take up his wrongful termination suit. At first, the legal possibilities had given him hope. In a large conference room overlooking Madison Square Park, he sat with a junior partner at the firm, a sharp young woman with great confidence, to whom he shared every detail of his career in PR right up to his firing. The testimony was recorded, but the lawyer also took notes at times. She nodded throughout and showed great empathy for Jacoby's situation. She asked smart questions and made no promises of victory in court or even a settlement, but Jacoby sensed her confidence. One of the forms he filled out even asked for bank information for transfer of potential payment once the suit was resolved. This particularly made Jacoby hopeful: the glorious windfall of cash that fills the dreams of every desperate person.

But after a few quarters passed, marked by what looked like form letters stating the case was still pending, Jacoby recognized this legal avenue was nothing more than a favor-for-a-friend arrangement with very little chance of results. Some big shot Manhattan law firm had done a favor for Claire's mother, taken up the case of her pathetic son-in-law-to-be, assigned to a young lawyer, some quid-pro-quo bullshit that Jacoby would never be privy to any effect beyond a letter every three months stating that the case was still pending and being pursued with utmost consideration. Jacoby assumed now, with his personal ties to the firm officially severed, that this would be his last letter and the matter, like his short-lived career, would be finished for good.

Jacoby grew fatalistic and morose. What would he do? He'd been entertaining this notion of finality since arriving in Italy, but now he was out of threads and pipes and all the other metaphors of hope that kept the ugly truth at bay. He started to sweat. His heart beat inside his chest and rattled at his ribs as his breath grew short. He had to get to a bank to confirm his savings and access the internet to send out queries for work back in the States. Any work. He had to find new hope. He needed a plan, but no plan - not even another unrealistic one - occurred to him.

The only thing he could think to do at the moment was to get out of the barn. He grabbed the car keys and dashed to the Passat. He did not know where he was going, but he knew that he had to get the hell out of the house and into the bright world to avoid the demons that gathered in dark spaces. He had to get busy.

He drove quickly into the village and parked in front of the hotel.

Bill did not answer the buzzer, which added to Jacoby's anxiety. He got back in the car and drove the other way out of town. He tried to find the Floria-Zanobini estate, to take a final look, to confirm its existence, to find solace somehow, but he got lost on the twisted and wood-banked back roads. After an hour of hapless navigating, he happened onto a service road that fed into a traffic circle laden with signs for major destinations. Harried cars and commercial trucks edged a shattered Jacoby to an on-ramp of the Autostrada with signs marked for Rome. He traveled south at a high speed without any desire to enter a teeming and strange city, but the rapid escape felt good, so he continued driving in the same direction, his mind solely focused on the road ahead, both hands firmly on the steering wheel.

At a point 30 kilometers south, a sign indicated an exit for another highway with Montepulciano as one of its destinations. Jacoby remembered the drive Helen had mentioned that she wanted to take him on, from Montepulciano to Montalcino, and Jacoby was familiar with those towns from the famous wine each produced. And there was a spectacular drive that connected them? A positive thought popped into Jacoby's head: a final encounter with the extraordinary privilege that was so everyday in Italy, the beauty of the land that produced such incredible food and wine, available to all.

Jacoby exited the highway and followed signs for Montepulciano. After a long and winding drive, through various resorts and rustic hamlets, up and over and down and around the grape-lined hillsides, he arrived atop the high hill, home to a walled-in city. He entered on foot through a portal that once could be closed to keep out enemies. Within the walls, replete with narrow streets and more wine shops than one could visit in a year, Jacoby wandered for an hour in the ancient ambiance before finding himself back at the gate through which he had entered. He felt relaxed and took pleasure in his desire for food.

A narrow road, dead west out of Montepulciano, had signs marked for Pienza. Once beyond the lofted auspices, the Val d'Orcia began in a swooning landscape of low hills of yellow hay and verdant fields. The road careened over undulating land, the breadth of sky and light seeming endless. In the distance, ancient monasteries and farmhouses were framed in shadows and bordered by mighty Cypress trees. The light seemed to shimmer, as if alive, and Jacoby knew this was the part of the drive that Helen, as an artist, must have coveted. It felt surreal, as if in a painting made with manufactured colors as opposed to real ones in real life. It was so beautiful, it almost pained Jacoby. He had to stop.

The lofted, tiny village of Pienza had one main corridor of enotecas, churches, gift shops and purveyors of the local specialty, Pecorino cheese, where rounds of various interpretations were on ample display. In a shaded osteria at the end of town, Jacoby couldn't decide between two pastas, a plate of pici with porcini or pappardelle with wild rabbit ragu, so he ordered both, taking the mushroom plate first, followed by the gamy second course, both washed down with separate, massive goblets of Vino Nobile, which he swirled and sipped with great delight. He bummed a cigarette from a country waitress and sat on the wall behind the village proper, blowing smoke at the resplendent valley that shook with quiet beauty.

The road to Montalcino was interrupted at times by industrial byways, severing the central peninsula with access to populated arteries like nearby Siena, but it was still a pleasure to drive and behold, full of rolling fields, broken by gullies, dotted with grazing animals, before the topography dramatically changed in the foothills near Jacoby's final destination.

The steep drive up to Montalcino was spectacular and a little scary, its sharp increase in altitude tugging at Jacoby's breath, popping his ears. It felt, in some ways, like God's driveway, climbing toward the heavens on a narrow, twisting two-lane bordered by endless vineyards on slanted hills draped in the abundant light which allowed this area to grow the formidable grapes that are pressed and oak-aged into Brunello di Montalcino, the indisputable granddaddy of Italian red wines. Jacoby decided to buy a case.

He parked near a fortress on the edge of town, outside the medieval walls, with a sign marking its history and also current status as a wine bar. Jacoby vowed to pay a visit before leaving. Within the ancient walls, he was anxious to work off his two-plates-of-pasta lunch with an eye towards an afternoon snack or even an early dinner. The undulating village of quaint shops and narrow streets lent itself to exertion, and Jacoby found himself breathing heavy and sweaty around the neck by the time he walked the circumference of the quiet town, the elevation obvious in sweeping views and thin air. Upon the town's peak, bordered by an arbor of oak, he approached a handsome church welcoming a small parade of locals as the bells rang five times. Jacoby recognized in that moment that it was Saturday, a fact previously unconsidered by him as he'd simply lost track of the days at some point. He followed the procession through the opened doors manned by a nodding priest in full cloak and cap. Once inside, Jacoby sat alone, tucked in the shadows of the far aisle of the furthest pew, admiring the ornate relief at the front of the church, under lofted ceilings and stained glass dedications. Jacoby kept his head low in an attempt to seem more pious and less threatening as a young stranger poorly dressed for church.

The service was in Latin, full of bellow and pageantry, smoke and chalices, worship and chant. Jacoby breathed steadily with his eyes closed and soon drifted off to sleep, chin on chest, arms crossed, fully aware of his surroundings yet removed from reality, as he flew like a wide-winged bird over the open land the surrounded Montalcino, following the roads that split the vineyards and groves, leading to villages and farmhouses and abbeys, all dressed in yellow sunshine under a pristine blue blanket. A bell clanged in the church service, and it broke Jacoby from his dream of flying. There was no one within three rows of him, so he slipped from the pew and through heavy curtains and out the enormous front door. The air had cooled a bit and white light began to gather in the sky as small birds swarmed and chattered in the oaks.

Feeling refreshed and uplifted, Jacoby walked back through the town as merchants and neighbors gathered on a Saturday evening. Jacoby smelled food, but he wasn't particularly hungry for dinner, so he padded past the osterias that smelled of game and aromatics and earth, back down out of the gates to the fortress beyond where he parked. Tourists wandered the courtyard beneath the massive stone walls, reading history from plaques and studying the ancient weapons of warfare. Jacoby entered into a darkened corridor and followed signs for the enoteca, which was open and airy, full of wood and light, homage to one of the world's greatest wines on display everywhere, in still life and in real life. Jacoby sat at a counter and studied the racks of bottles, some antiques and some ready to be enjoyed. All of them from the immediate vicinity. It felt like a museum that was partially interactive.

From a handsome man about his age, Jacoby ordered a plate of Pecorino in three varieties and a goblet of 2007 Brunello from a producer called Il Poggione. He sipped and swirled the marvelous wine, deep yet floral, complex yet accessible, taking little bites of cheese, some soft and studded with tiny black truffles or unadorned but dripped with local honey; some aged and dappled in syrupy vinegar. When it was over, Jacoby felt a thread of sadness which he hoped to dash through the purchase of a case of the very wine he'd just drank. The man smiled and explained in very good English that they only sold wines by the glass or single bottles at the fortezza, but, if Jacoby wanted, he could show him how to get to the producer to buy in quantity directly.

"Yes, please," Jacoby said.

The man smiled and walked to the room's far end. He paused in the doorway and motioned for Jacoby to follow. They took a staircase, darkened and cool, up three flights of stone stairs to a metal door that opened to a walkway at the top of the fortezza's walls that overlooked splendor beyond any artist's or even photographer's ability to capture. Jacoby instantly thought in this breathtaking moment that he had indeed, after all, paid a visit to God's house. Who else could have such a view?

In every direction, the countryside spread in a perfect patchwork of green fields and fields sown with red poppies; arbors of oak and birch; farmhouses marked by Cypress trees and umbrella pines; rows of ancient vines; shimmering olive groves; humble lanes connecting quaint villages. The light, like in all of Italy, seemed unfiltered but particularly so here, high above the lands that were so visible, so vibrant that one could see details on the surface of the earth from just below the clouds.

They were so high in the June sky that it was chilly, but Jacoby didn't move. He was afraid that a break from his status would shatter the illusion and that all this in front of him would disappear, as if in a dream.

"There's where you go," the man said, pointing down a lane that wended toward a village in the distance. "To Sant'Antimo. Follow signs for the abbey there; in the square, very small, across from Trattoria Il Pozzo, there is the business for Il Poggione. Just tell them what you would like. Tell them that Antonino send you."

"I will," Jacoby said. "Thanks."

He returned to look over God's front yard, but Antonino interrupted. "I am sorry, I know that the view is incredible, but the business will close soon, so if you want the wine, you must go now. I can call and ask for someone to wait."

Jacoby turned from the view and stuck out his hand. "Thank you."

"Of course," Antonino said, shaking Jacoby's hand like an old friend.

Chapter 31

Jacoby drove back down God's driveway toward the country ramparts of Montalcino, working the clutch on the steep decline, feeling tension in his calf from the steady pedal work. Before the roads flattened, he followed a sign for Sant'Antimo and hummed down the rural road in the champagne twilight, overwhelmed by an emotional cocktail of contentment and wonder.

The village was even smaller than he'd imagined, and finding the square proved as simple as one turn. He wished he had desire for a meal at the trattoria, but vowed to return at some point, but he knew not when or how. He parked in front of a string of low-slung, stone buildings and found the door marked for Il Poggione. He knocked. An older man answered but did not speak; he had a hangdog visage, an unlit cigarette dangling from his mouth, and a tweed hat low on his forehead. He motioned to an administrative area where a case of wine waited on a desk.

Jacoby gave the man his credit card, which he ran through a hand device that cranked out a receipt. The man gave Jacoby the card and the receipt, then held open the front door. Jacoby picked up the case of wine, exchanged a nod with the tired man, returned to his car and placed the wine carefully in his trunk. And just like that, in the time it would have taken to get a hot dog on the streets of New York, Jacoby had acquired, for a very reasonable price, a case of one of the world's finest wines.

As he headed home on now familiar roads, Jacoby felt like an American-Italian, a distinction he determined that was wholly unique - a reverse of the immigrant / American label so common in the States. This moniker was for those who embraced their new country in a way that implied a spiritual birthright, a sense of true belonging as if it were fate.

.   .   .

When Jacoby got home, the full moon was high and porcelain, throwing silver light on the barn and its surrounding property, like a street lamp that covered everything around. Kids could still play ball in such light, Jacoby thought as he crossed the terrace, holding a case of wine on one shoulder, the keys to the barn in the opposite hand. He worked the lock on both doors and lurched inside with the precious yet heavy weight burdening his shoulders and neck. He maneuvered the case onto the table in the front room, concealing the letter from the law firm.

Jacoby sat in the silence on the couch, torn between thoughts of his spectacular day and a tomorrow that had no real plan or promise. He'd have to get to a bank to check his accounts, and he'd have to see a travel agent, but tomorrow was Sunday and surely all businesses would be closed, even the internet cafes he passed in Florence. Maybe Bill would be around. What else could he do? And what could he do now, not ready for bed, not in the mood to read. He unsealed the case of wine and stored the bottles upright on the banquette beyond the table that held glasses and kitchen accoutrement. The bottles looked nice up there; Jacoby loved the aesthetic of wine bottles: official and orderly, adorned with lovely labels and caps sealed in thick foil. Someday, somewhere, he'd have a wine rack, full of beautiful bottles that he would share with people he loved.

For now, though, he would drink alone. He unsealed and uncorked a bottle, grabbed a glass and headed for the patio outside the barn doors. On the way past the front table, he picked up the letter from the law firm. After a few glasses of wine, he could read the no-news and get that disappointment out of the way while under the spell of Brunello di Montalcino. He folded the envelope, put it in his back pocket and went outside with his wine bottle and a single glass.

The moonlight splashed onto the patio, so bright Jacoby's shadow proceeded him as he walked to the table beside the wall draped with rosemary but silent in the cool night. The air smelled of fruit and earth. Jacoby sensed a strong crop of olives maturing on the branch. A fig fell from the tree and toppled down the ancient stairs that turned toward the grove above. Hunger pinged in Jacoby's belly. He picked a handful of figs from the tree and slipped back inside to wash them in the kitchen sink. There was some prosciutto in the fridge, left from Paolo's welcome basket, which Jacoby brought back outside along with a platter that now held the figs.

He poured some wine and swirled it on table; the moon appeared like a polished pearl on the wine's dark surface when he brought it to his nose for a sniff. The majestic fragrance wafted out and aroused Jacoby's sense of hunger. He wrapped a fig in a prosciutto blanket and took a bite; the cured meat contained the explosion of fleshy pulp from the fig, meshing the dispirit flavors in his mouth. The sweet and salty made a perfect balance and filled Jacoby with contentment and the simple pleasure he sought in life. Washing it down with Brunello felt like utter decadence.

After the figs were gone, along with most of the bottle of wine, he lit a cigarette and blew smoke at the moon, feeling the heady wine and the nicotine in his nervous system, and the pleasure it brought to his mouth. It was late. Jacoby grew groggy and finished the cigarette with the last of the wine. He tipped the sturdy chair back against the stone wall, crossed his arms and stared at the sky. The moon sank beyond the trees and darkness arrived along with a sky rung with stars. Jacoby dropped off into sleep and dreamed of hot and crowded subways in the rat infested tunnels below New York.

•   •   •

He woke to the sound of a squeal, fierce and feral, from beyond the hedge. It was almost morning, and shapes were visible in the fake dawn. Jacoby's body was cloaked in cold from sleeping uncovered outside. A shiver of fear sliced through him; he shot to his feet. The door to the barn was close by, an easy escape. But another sound began, a keening whimper from the same area beyond the hedge. It sounded so helpless. Desperate. The grunts repeated, overriding the whimper. Jacoby walked carefully around the barn toward the carport. He followed the familiar trail up to the shed, squinting in the half light. The sounds grew louder. Jacoby's heart walloped inside his chest and reverberated throughout his whole cavity. It reminded him of being too close to amplifier stacks.

The sun edged upward beyond the horizon as Jacoby appeared in the shed, streaks of faint light shot through the slots in the wall boards. The hunter's dog cowered in the far corner, against the stacked wood, tucked almost into itself in defense against the massive cinghiale with a twitching nose, beady eyes, and jagged tusks, wiry fur like the boogey man. If it charged, the dog would be gored, probably killed, and Jacoby thought of the bull fights he'd read about in Hemingway novels. Now he understood. His body jetted sweat through every pore as he reached for the ax handle. The dog noticed Jacoby and raced toward him, eluding the swipe of the wild boar's tusk. The hound yelped in fear and scurried out of the shed just as Jacoby got a grip on the handle and raised the ax. He thought to drop it and run, but the cinghiale turned toward him and grunted through a huge, round nose of darkest brown with gaping nostrils. Jacoby had never seen anything so ugly. Malevolent and beady eyes. A body like a woolly barrel. It even smelled vicious, of swine and mottled fur. It lowered its head and raised its tusks, and charged at him on little legs.

The surge of adrenalin, inspired by the deep desire to survive, aided the familiar ax turn as it swung around his shoulder and over his head. He brought it straight down, his muscle memory focused on the thousands of strokes recently performed, thinking of wood being split, not the skull of a charging living beast that connected with the flat ax side. Jacoby let out a primal scream that propelled the ax through the initial resistance of contact and seemed to have come from a place as far back as he could remember, stored in his conscience throughout his life as if waiting for this single moment to explode. It held all of his hurt and longing and sense of mistreatment, but also his desire to live.

The wild boar crashed to the ground, and Jacoby collapsed by its side. Their heads only a few feet apart. No breath came from the giant nostrils, no movement of its body at all. Jacoby pushed himself away frantically and sat sideways, staring in shock at the fallen beast. He felt sick and happy to be alive. The dirt from the floor stuck to his hands. He smelled shit and hoped it wasn't his. More light entered the shed, and he could hear movement outside, footsteps and barking.

Paolo arrived in the doorway, breathing heavy, wearing pajamas, wide-eyed, a shotgun at the ready. He must have heard Jacoby's scream. His big dog was by his side, barking at the dead animal. Paolo assessed the situation and raised the gun.

"Don't," Jacoby said, his voice dry and cracked yet calm. "It's dead."

"Are you certain?" Paolo asked, still aiming the gun.

Jacoby nodded and gathered his feet. Paolo lowered his weapon and helped him up. The dog stopped barking.

"Are you all right? OK? Not hurt?"

Jacoby's head spun, and his stomach churned. He knew he had done something very bold, something that he could talk about for the rest of his life, but he did not like the feeling of having killed something, and that something was lying next to him in a dead heap. Jacoby walked outside the shed to shake off the shock and breathe sweet morning air. Paolo followed closely behind.

"I'm fine," Jacoby said, between slow breaths.

Paolo motioned toward the shed.

"What do we do with this?"

The answer hit Jacoby in an instant, as if divinely delivered. He felt himself expand and then explode into a million pieces. "We'll have to give it away."

Chapter 32

Paolo went for the three-wheeled "Ape" while Jacoby roamed the property looking for the lost dog. Poor thing was so scared, but it was alive and Jacoby had saved it, and that made him feel a little heroic, something he'd never truly felt before. He wondered if the hunter and his crew were still up in the hills or if they'd gone home without their pet. He'd have to check in at the cafe after they got to the village and delivered the cinghiale to the butcher as a present for Bill. He couldn't wait. He even had a line rehearsed to explain such an unusual gift. He walked the grounds feeling that the land, in a way, now belonged to him.

Coming back from the property's perimeter, Jacoby stopped by the hedge just beyond the barn and rummaged through its thick branches. Snapped pieces and misshaped surfaces revealed an attempt at entry which the cinghiale had most likely made. Jacoby got on his knees and crawled in, holding the firm branches aside. A few feet within, possibly out of reach of the cinghiale's snout but not its sense of smell, beyond a particularly dense set of thicket, was a trove of brown and odd-shaped nuggets clustered among the roots. With full extension, Jacoby was able to secure a half-dozen truffles that filled both palms after he came out. He held them like found treasure.

He carried them back around the hedge and into the barn, where he put them into a plastic bag, which he brought to the shed where

Paolo waited with the small vehicle, its bed opened toward the doorway. Jacoby held up the bag; Paolo squinted then began to nod.

"Ah," he said, smiling. "Tartuffo. Where did you find?"

Jacoby pointed toward the thick hedge.

"No wonder we have cinghiale."

Jacoby extended the bag to Paolo, but he refused.

"No. No," he said. "Give to your friend in the village, for the sagra."

Jacoby was pleased. He put the plastic bag on the passenger seat of the Ape and then stood over the dead beast. He grabbed it by the back huffs, and dragged it a few feet around, trying to turn its back to the doorway. It had to weigh 200 pounds. The enormity of the animal gave Jacoby pause, thinking the damage it could have wrought had it put its weight into the tusks as it charged. He made quick peace with the death. Better it than him. Or the dog.

"How are we gonna do this?" he asked Paolo.

"Slow," he said. "Very slow."

They worked inch by inch to maneuver the animal as close as possible to the vehicle's bed. It took 20 minutes that seemed like two hours, but they got the hind legs up on to the bed, and Jacoby lifted the head and torso off the ground by the solid tusks. It was disgusting, being close to the ugly eyes and ugly snout; the sound of crushed skull moving beneath the fur. What he assumed was brain fluid leaked from one ear. Jacoby thought he was going to puke, but he desperately wanted the beast in the bed and to bring it to the village, so he couched his queasiness and called on the prospect of his potential hero status, riding into town with the bounty for the feast which he had killed with his own hands.

He bent his knees and raised the tusks, propelling it upward with all of his strength as Paolo pulled from up on the bed. The body slowly slid, in incremental progress, across the metal bed of the vehicle, until it flopped unceremoniously on its own, enough of its weight in place to be bound by ropes that Paolo produced and fastened. Jacoby gasped for breath and watched, feeling the accomplishment rise like the new sun above, shining its soft orange light.

In the new day, he felt very, very dirty, layered with sweat and filth, his white t-shirt stained by earth and beast, his jeans stuck to his legs. He thought to request time to shower before heading to town, but he couldn't really deliver a beast killed with his own hands while wearing a fresh set of clothes. He had to show up looking like the hunter he now was. Then he'd shower. For a long time.

Paolo cranked up the engine, and Jacoby climbed in. They bumped back down the hill, to the driveway, and out the gate that swung open on its mechanical hinges as they approached. The dirt road was busy with life, and many of the insects swarmed to the fallen beast in the back of the small vehicle. The wind felt good through the open windows. In the valley, Jacoby noticed movement among the wild grass. Something was cutting across in their direction. The coloring became clear against the verdant ground, and Jacoby knew what it was.

"Stop," he said, holding up his hand.

Paolo slowed the vehicle to a halt, turning to check on the cinghiale.

"What? What?" he asked. "Is it come loose?"

"No. No," Jacoby said, pointing out the front window. "It's the dog."

He got out and watched it bound across the valley. Its head up and tongue wagging. It scampered up the incline and stopped on the road, breathing heavy, staring at Jacoby who got down on one knee.

"Come here, boy," he said.

The dog remained in place, shaking from exertion but committed to not moving.

"Come here," Jacoby asked again, even more kindness in his voice.

"Ja-co-bey," Paolo called from the driver's seat. "Come back. The dog will follow the cinghiale."

That made sense, but Jacoby wanted to hold the dog, to pet it and deliver it back to town himself. To make sure it felt safe and loved. He called it again, but Paolo was right. Jacoby got back in the passenger seat and watched the dog follow the moving vehicle with its eyes and then assume pace from behind. Jacoby laughed to himself, thinking that the damn dog was taking some credit for the kill.

They crossed the paved road that led to Florence and traveled on gravel paths through olive groves. They caught the road leading to the village, only a few hundred meters out of town, and Jacoby swelled with pride when they took the turn and the piazza came into view. Paolo worked the bleating horn of the vehicle and hopped the curb to the piazza, where he stopped on its high side, between the church and the hotel, directly across from the butcher shop.

Paolo climbed out and said he would go wake the butcher.

Jacoby got out just as the dog caught up to sit proudly next to the vehicle's bed. No one was around. Except Bill, who appeared as if an apparition from behind the precipice of the statue, with a cup of demitasse and a newspaper. Jacoby was so happy to see him. He looked well and rested, dressed for a morning forage.

"My, my," Bill said as he approached. "What do we have here?"

Jacoby swallowed hard and tried not to rush his line.

"It's found money," he said, his voice true and clear.

"What?"

"I found this in my backyard, and I'm giving it to you, to avoid bad luck."

Bill smiled. Jacoby held up the bag of truffles.

"Find those, too?" Bill asked.

"Afraid so."

Bill sized up Jacoby's appearance. "You look like a man who has found himself a country."

Chapter 33

Jacoby told Bill the whole story of his encounter with the cinghiale while they waited for Paolo to return with the butcher. It seemed even more incredible to Jacoby once put into words and delivered from his own mouth. Bill did not hide his awe at Jacoby's courage nor his gratitude for the generosity which saved the sagra. He even mentioned special plans for the truffles to gild the lily on his secret cinghiale recipe. Jacoby promised to help Bill with the preparations. The sagra would be Tuesday, the day after the next, when the city of Florence fetes its patron saint.

The village started to slowly appear on this bright Sunday morning. By the time the church bells rang eight, word had spread, and soon a crowd gathered around Jacoby and his cinghiale. People took pictures with actual cameras and smart phones. Some who recognized him from the ceci-episode at the forno came up to smile and clutch his arm. It became difficult for Bill to explain to them all individually what had happened, so he climbed up on the back of the vehicle and stood in the small space not occupied by the giant beast. He called for calm with his outstretched arms and told them all the story in Italian that Jacoby had just told him in English. And he told the story with flourish, like a performer, his voice deepened and slow, his hands and body in motion, pointing at Jacoby and mimicking the action.

Faces stared with amazement, and Jacoby felt uncomfortable from all the attention, but he liked not being anonymous for a change, especially here, where he so wanted to be welcomed. To quell the discomfort of silence, he picked up the hound and petted it as a distraction. Nicoletta appeared, surveyed the scene, and made an impassioned call on her cell phone.

By the time Paolo returned with the butcher, the crowd filled half the piazza and Bill had told the story three times. A party atmosphere was building as Paolo, the butcher and a few other men of seeming import stood around the beast arguing with their hands about how to get it across the street and into the shop.

The priest even came out of the church to investigate after noticing how few of his parishioners had entered for the morning's first mass. He gleaned the story from someone who had heard it numerous times already. The crowd parted and fell silent as the priest, an elderly man in full cloak, approached the dead animal, to which he offered some sort of last rights. He then turned towards Jacoby, who put the dog down and felt very thirsty. And dirty. The priest asked his name. Jacoby told him. Then the priest asked him again.

"Jake, il americano," Bill yelled to the priest, who nodded and took Jacoby's hand and held it in the air like the winner of a boxing match.

"A Jake, il americano!"

The crowd roared, and Jacoby felt like a rock star for the first time in his life. The parishioners followed the priest into the church and others began to seek offerings of the few shops that were open on Sunday, including the cafe. A dozen or so people hung around the site, still interested in talking about the spectacle before them, a wild cinghiale felled by an ax-wielding American. Younger residents appeared to take selfies with and pictures of the dead beast. Jacoby picked up the dog again, which had not left his side. Bill was in conversation with a small group, and the others were still making a plan for the transport of the beast. None of them, except Jacoby and the dog, saw the hunter's jeep come flying from the opposite side of the piazza, up over the curb and skid to a halt, dead center in the piazza. Everyone turned to see the hunter storm from the driver's side and approach the scene, his hair mussed and his eyes enlarged. He seemed bigger than Jacoby remembered, especially as he approached and the dog whimpered in Jacoby's arms.

Paolo, backed by a few other men, interrupted the hunter before he could reach Jacoby. In a show of impressive bravery, Paolo berated the hunter, his hands flailing towards the hills beyond the village and the cinghiale in the bed of his vehicle. The hunter seethed but was silent, contrition etched into his crooked mouth until Paolo turned abruptly away and returned to his conversation with the butcher. The hunter shot Bill a malevolent look and approached Jacoby, holding out his arms for the dog. Jacoby tried to extend the dog, but it curled closer to him and ducked its head. The hunter lunged for the animal and ripped it from Jacoby's arms, undeterred by the animal's whimper. He stomped back to the jeep and chirped away as people cursed at him and cried shame, shame.

Paolo took the three-wheeler to the side street beside the butcher shop, where a few men awaited with a wheelbarrow. They began unloading the beast while the butcher expertly sharpened a massive knife. The crowd in the piazza dispersed, leaving only Bill and Jacoby.

"That was fun," Jacoby declared.

"Yes," Bill agreed. "It was."

"What's going to happen?" Jacoby asked, looking toward the butcher shop.

"Lorenzo is going to spend most of his Sunday slaughtering the enormous animal that you killed this morning. He's going to find use for almost all of its parts, saving the meat for me, which I will begin preparing a brine for right after I make you a Texan breakfast."

"Sounds good."

"You can help make the brine and marinade, if you'd like."

"Sure."

"I'll need to speak with you about the woman we sought, Fillipo's mother," Bill said, squinting with compassion and underlying sadness. "Your great-grandmother."

"She's dead."

"How'd you know?"

"Paolo told me."

Bill nodded. "I was there."

"Where?"

"With her, when she died. I heard you'd been looking for me."

"I was getting worried."

Bill laughed. "Sorry about that, but I have to admit, it's nice to be worried about."

"So, what happened?"

"Come inside," Bill said, motioning toward the hotel. "Let's get you cleaned up first, then I'll tell you everything over breakfast."

•   •   •

Bill opened a second floor room for Jacoby. It was a well-adorned and well-lit, with elegant materials and ample sun streaming in through the windows that overlooked the back garden. Bill told Jacoby to leave his clothes in a laundry bag outside the door and to come down after showering, dressed in a white, fluffy robe that hung in the closet. Jacoby followed the instructions, lingering under the hot water, washing his body again and again to remove what he perceived to be stench from the nasty beast. Once clean and dry, wrapped in the comfy robe, he felt very sleepy. He laid his tired body on top of the silk duvet and fell asleep for a few precious hours uninterrupted by dreams.

When he came downstairs, Giovanni the shoemaker was alone at a table in the dining hall. He jumped up when Jacoby entered.

"Oh!" he cried. "Jake, il americano! Come stai? Come stai?"

Giovanni rushed over to enthusiastically shake Jacoby's hand with two of his own. Jacoby smiled and nodded, followed the shoemakers gesture to enter the room and sit.

Bill came from the kitchen with an apron around his torso and a kitchen towel over his shoulder. "I'm afraid young Giovanni ate your breakfast."

Giovanni shrugged in apology; Jacoby shrugged back in acceptance.

"I'm also afraid," Bill continued, "that I'm too busy at the moment preparing the brine for your cinghiale to make another plate. Is there anything else I can get you?"

"I'd love just a pastry, and maybe a cup of coffee or even a cappuccino."

"Ah," Bill said, with a finger in the air. "Your timing is perfect."

He walked through the dining area to the front desk to make a call from the house phone.

"Your order will arrive momentarily," Bill said upon return. "Delivered by our dear Nicoletta who is due here any moment to, ah, change the sheets, if you will."

Bill smiled and motioned for Jacoby to sit at a table. Giovanni seemed excited about her arrival but also excited about something else. He looked at Bill and stammered a moment before blurting out an elongated question clearly intended for Jacoby. Bill listened closely, and Jacoby tried to follow; although he wasn't catching a word, the context was obvious.

"So," Bill prompted, addressing Jacoby, "our crooning cobbler would like to know if you were able to repair his instrument."

"Si," Jacoby said.

"And, also, if you were able to practice any of the songs that you discussed."

"Si," Jacoby said, looking now at Giovanni, who clenched two fists in exuberance.

Giovanni circled an open hand in front of him, encouraging Bill to continue.

"And what he'd like to know most of all is if you would accompany him for a small concert during the upcoming sagra."

Giovanni looked frozen in marble, his hands across his chest, his mouth open. Jacoby asked Bill for a pen and paper. Bill said something to Giovanni, who hurried to the front desk and returned with the request. Jacoby slowly wrote down the names of five Pearl Jam songs, which he handed to Giovanni.

"These songs," he said to Bill.

"Queste canzoni," he translated.

"Si, si," Giovanni muttered at first, and then began to repeat with more enthusiasm. "Si! Si! Si!"

The front buzzer rang, and Bill walked away smiling. Giovanni jumped around the room, stopping to shake supporting fists of solidarity at Jacoby. Nicoletta entered holding a tray with a cappuccino and two golden, crusty pastries.

"Buongiorno, americano," she said.

"Buongiorno, Nicoletta," he responded.

Her mouth opened to continue the conversation, but Giovanni whisked her away by the arm, toward the stairway off the lobby, talking very fast.

"I guess they've gotten beyond the back terrace," Jacoby said to Bill.

"Yes," he purred. "About time."

Jacoby laughed and sipped some foam from the top of his delicious cappuccino.

"Eat your breakfast and then come to the kitchen to help. I've got lots to tell you about."

Chapter 34

The kitchen was in full production mode, with industrial pots and pans on every burner. The counters were covered in aromatics, bottles of vinegar and oil and wine. The fog of chopped onions stung Jacoby's eyes. Crushed black pepper punched his nose. Bill stirred a massive pot with a long wooden spoon, conjuring a musty smell of vinegar with a hint of apple.

"Some set up," Jacoby observed.

"Indeed," Bill confirmed without turning around. "I've got ten gallons of brine to make, and an equal amount of marinade. All very last minute. Thanks to you."

"I'll try to slay your cinghiale earlier next year," he joked.

Bill laughed then stopped suddenly. "I'm not sure there's going to be a next year."

"For me?" Jacoby huffed, sickened by the thought that he might not be there at this time next week. "I'll say."

Bill stopped stirring and turned around. "For many of us," he said.

Bill explained to Jacoby that Bruna had come to the hotel to convey that Fillipo's mother had returned to the estate near the village, and that she was very ill and soon to die. Bruna told the matriarch about the visit of Jacoby and Bill. She had asked to see them both, but Bill had no way of finding Jacoby; so he went to her, alone, bringing the picture of Jacoby's that he had unwittingly kept after their night in Florence. He told her the story of the woman in the picture - her daughter - and that she had found great happiness in America and had been the original matriarch of a large and incredibly successful family, of which the grandson had recently come to pay her a visit.

"That's not right," Jacoby said, "about the large and successful family."

"Perhaps," Bill said, "but I certainly consider you a great success, and, besides, the woman was on her death bed, searching for peace. I told her what she wanted to hear."

"What did she say?" Jacoby asked. "How did she react?"

"She seemed uplifted by the news, truly, then she took my hand and told me she was sorry."

"Sorry about what?"

"About a lot of things, including shutting me out all these years and, most importantly, the status of the estate."

"What of it."

"It's bankrupt."

"Fuck."

"Everything must be sold to pay the back taxes owed."

"Everything?"

"Everything. The property in Florence, the villa here, the consortium and, most sadly, our dear hotel."

"What will you do?"

"I haven't the foggiest. She gave me my money back, though."

"What money?"

"The money in Fillipo's account. Basically, my savings under his name. It'd been frozen, and shielded from the government, more of a trust than an account. She transferred it to Bruna, who issued a statement of transfer to me."

"Is it a lot?"

"About what I figured - a decent amount, but not nearly enough."

"For what?"

"To buy a hotel, even a small one in an unknown village at government auction prices."

"What will you do?"

"I don't know. Wait and see what happens with the sale first. The Italian government is not known for expediency. It could be months, years before they move on the property if they don't find a buyer at auction."

"When's that?"

"Day after the sagra."

•　　　•　　　•

The butcher arrived with a small army of ad-hoc assistants, older men Jacoby recognized from the piazza, carrying long plastic containers of freshly butchered meat, neatly trimmed, in various configurations but mostly large pieces. The containers covered every available inch of counter space in the kitchen. Jacoby helped clear additional space to provide more room, as Bill and the butcher, who looked exhausted in a bloody apron over pajamas, had a serious conversation. The temporary assistants all nodded in deference to Jacoby and departed. The butcher shook Jacoby's hand and expressed appreciation in canned English. "Tank. You."

Bill and Jacoby surveyed the kitchen, newly decorated in a dozen containers of gamy meat.

"How'd we make out?" Jacoby asked.

"Quite well," Bill said. "This is about 50 pounds, which is more than enough for the sagra. Lorenzo says this is about half of the available meat. He's willing to provide some of his own wild boar prosciutto for the sagra in exchange for some of the remaining meat which he can begin curing immediately to replenish his stock."

"Works for me."

"And then freeze the rest for next year."

"If there is a next year."

"Oh, there will be a next year, my dear boy, with or without me."

Jacoby frowned and the blood flushed from his face.

"And what about you," Bill asked. "Will you be here next year?"

Jacoby screwed his mouth up to fight the emotion. He sniffed and smirked back tears. "I don't think I'll be here next week."

"But why not?" Bill asked, alarmed. "I thought you planned on a year?"

"Didn't work out," was all Jacoby could muster.

"You're not getting married, are you?"

"Nope."

Bill walked over slowly, wearing a wan smile. He gave Jacoby a hug that lasted 30 seconds but felt much longer. He couldn't remember ever being hugged like that. It felt awkward at first, but he could feel Bill's heart beating through the thick robe and absorb his empathy. When they parted, Bill kept his hands on Jacoby's shoulders and spoke while looking into his eyes.

"Help me dole out this brine, and I will thank you for your friendship and generosity with a late afternoon lunch at my favorite cantinetta in all of Tuscany."

"What's a cantinetta?"

"A country restaurant, of sorts."

"Sounds good."

"Just wait."

Chapter 35

After the gallons of brine were ladled over the meat in their containers, Bill and Jacoby carried them together, very carefully, to a walk-in storage area off the kitchen. The room was not refrigerated but dark and cool enough to keep the meat fresh, especially under liquid swimming with aromatics and seasoned with dissolved salt and sugar. The next day, they would have to be removed, the meat rinsed of the brine, dried and returned to the cleaned containers to be covered with a marinade for the last 24-hours before the sagra. Jacoby, of course, agreed to help. And he couldn't wait to taste the meat.

With the containers neatly stacked, they thoroughly cleaned the kitchen, a task performed in tandem yet in the silence that friendship affords. Jacoby used his good spirits to think optimistically about life back home, about starting over in a modest way, adapting, to the best of his ability, the lifestyle of Italy he so embraced. He would practice his brand of being an American-Italian at home. And he'd start saving and planning a return to Italy. That would be his real job. No matter how many years it took.

Their work behind them, Bill and Jacoby left the kitchen for the first time in hours. Before going upstairs to clean up and change, Bill told Jacoby where to find his clothes, air-dried on the back terrace. Jacoby fetched them and dressed in the empty dining area, then waited for Bill in the lobby. He thought to ask him for use of the computer to access the internet, but decided to save such an unpleasant task for an internet cafe the next day in Florence. Besides, he was hungry and his stomach jumped a bit when Bill came down the stairs.

"Well," he said in his charming bellow. "You look almost as comfortable as you did in that robe."

"I was thinking about wearing it out, but it smells like brine."

Bill laughed.

"Thanks for washing these," Jacoby said, pulling at his crisp, clean t-shirt that smelled of the back garden.

"Of course," Bill said and stepped toward the door before abruptly stopping. "Oh, and I have this for you, found in your jeans while hanging them on the line." Bill went behind the desk and pulled out the letter from the law firm, which Jacoby had tucked in his back pocket the night before. It was intact, sort of, wet and impossible to open without shredding. The ink was visible but spread all over the page, making the message indecipherable.

"Thanks," he said.

"Not anything important, I hope?"

"Nah," Jacoby said, throwing it into a trash bin. "Just a reminder that lawyers are useless, and that life is unfair."

"Well," Bill huffed. "I could have told you that."

●   ●   ●

The church bells clanged three times as they boarded Bill's motorini to put-put out of the village. They took a road Jacoby had yet to travel, a narrow, winding one cut through a forest of oak and pine. Jacoby smelled chestnuts as they climbed higher and Bill turned off onto an undulating dirt road bordered by birch trees. They soon arrived at a makeshift parking lot, a clearing of flattened crabgrass and dirt, with dozens of cars and rows of motorcycles scattered before the back of a spreading cabin of log and stone with smoke billowing from a gaping chimney. Bill pulled right in front, by a walkway of slate slabs marked by potted plants and ancient farming devices that led down and around to the front of a restaurant that overlooked swooning hills of a vineyard in bloom, large green leaves decorating the vines staked into the rich soil. A terrace was crowded with guests eating alfresco under a wooden canopy.

"Oh, man," Jacoby said, stopped in his tracks.

"Yes, indeed," Bill confirmed. "A sight of beauty, especially since it contains many of the vines that make our wine."

"Wow."

"You see how the sun is hitting them right now, at this hour?"

"Yes."

"This is the time, the special conditions here, the angles and light and soil, when they ripen so perfectly. It's happening right now."

"I know," Jacoby said without pause. "I can smell it."

Bill laughed. "I believe you can, young man. I believe you can."

They entered through a wooden side door into a dark room with walls of log and tables of wood. Lots of country bric-a-brac on display. A waiter greeted Bill with kisses on both cheeks and took them through the room, past the teeming kitchen, and into a corridor of wide windows overlooking the valley. The room was nearly full, with large groups of friends and families enjoying their Sunday afternoon together over a long meal. Their revelry filled the space with the symphony of a successful party. Bill and Jacoby were seated at the last available table, a picnic-style of worn oak vertical to a large window open to the breeze coming from the incredible panorama in front of them. Like so many views in Italy, the beauty bordered on surreal. Jacoby breathed and blinked and enjoyed the feeling of living in a still life.

A waitress approached with a big smile for Bill, who turned to Jacoby and asked, "Mind if I order for both of us?"

"Not at all."

Bill put on a faux-serious expression and tone. "May I assume you have no aversion to various courses of local products, succulent meats and fabulous wines?"

"Funny."

"Good then," he said, back to his own self. "Let's get started."

Bill addressed the waitress and ordered, extensively, in Italian. She wrote in all down and nodded, as if impressed.

"Care to know now what we're having or would you prefer to be surprised?" Bill asked.

"I'm pretty sure I already know."

"Do you?"

"Maybe," Jacoby said, with a mix of modesty and confidence. "A mixed plate of crostini, a salumi platter, tagliatelle with porcini mushrooms, followed by something with pork."

"Bravo."

"Oh, and the local wine, but a riserva."

Bill clapped and beamed. "Sometimes I wish I only understood enough Italian to order in restaurants. It'd be a great freedom."

"That's my goal," Jacoby said with pride.

"Well, you'd better hurry. How much time do we have left?"

"I'll find out tomorrow, I guess, when I find a travel agent who speaks English."

"I can help you with that, but you'd better go early. The offices of Florence will close at noon tomorrow for the holiday."

"The museums, too?"

"I imagine," Bill answered, head tilted with one eye squinted as if he were a marksman taking aim.

The waitress returned with an unlabeled bottle of wine with a small red sticker on the neck.

"That's how we know it's the riserva," Bill said.

"Fancy," Jacoby quipped.

"Indeed."

The cork was removed and two glasses were filled with a deep purple liquid that held a rust-colored tinge. Both men swirled the wine and raised their glasses.

"Truly," Bill said, "to one of the greatest times of my life, certainly since my dearest passed."

They chinked glasses.

"Agreed," Jacoby said. "It's been a hell of a few weeks."

Neither men wanted to play the "If only" game, but both were thinking that very thing as the waitress arrived with two platters that broke their forlorn spell.

The crostini plate had thin pieces of bread topped with chicken liver pate, lardo collonata, and traditional tomato bruschetta. The salumi platter had paper-thin prosciutto, slices of dried sausage, pickled artichokes, and pitted green olives. They ate slowly, nodding to agree that each offering was exceptional, sipping wine and looking over the magnificent countryside. In the distance, smoke billowed from a farm house; Jacoby envied those who'd made the fire.

Large clouds drifted past, casting slow-moving shadows over the luscious topography as they took a half plate each of fresh tagliatelle with silky mushroom sauté.

"How long does the riserva age?" Jacoby asked, after washing down his last twirl of pasta with a long sip of wine.

"Two years," Bill answered, after tilting the glass to his nose for inspection. "In oak."

"It's really good."

"Yes, I'd say as good if not better than anything that comes out of the Chianti Classico designation, but, of course, I'm afraid I've been here too long to be objective. I've become just as provincial and biased as everyone else."

"Hell, I'm not sure I can be objective at this point," Jacoby laughed, "but I'd say it's as good as anything I've tasted in Tuscany, short of Brunello, of course."

"Of course," Bill concurred.

"Speaking of Brunello..." Jacoby began as the waitress arrived with their next course.

Over a platter of enormous, flame-roasted pork ribs, adorned with fresh-squeezed lemon, Jacoby told Bill, between meaty bites, of his adventure south of Siena in the Val d'Orcia and its three hilltop towns. And the case of Brunello he brought home and promised to share. Bill nodded along, licking his fingers and washing the succulent pork down with long sips of wine.

When they were finished with the ribs and the riserva, they agreed on a plate of Pecorino and pear along with a half-carafe of the local table wine. After that, as the restaurant began to empty of its Sunday afternoon revelers and the sun started its descent, they shared a plate of Tuscan cookies dipped in sweet Vin Santo. Jacoby drank his amber dessert wine and savored the nutty crumbs at the bottom. He felt warm and heady. Content as could be.

"Here," Bill said, pushing his beveled glass to Jacoby. "Have mine. I don't want to steer us into a tree on the way home."

Jacoby smiled and deferred, "No, really, I couldn't," he said, taking the glass and tossing it down. He wiped his mouth with the back of his hand, inhaling clean air and exhaling flavorful fumes. "That was incredible."

Bill made a face of modest impression and flicked a wrist in the air. "Cucina tipica," he said.

"Do you have any clue of what a meal like that would cost, with the wine and everything, anywhere near New York City?"

"That, I'm afraid, I couldn't begin to estimate, though this meal here will cost you exactly nothing."

"No."

"Yes. You saved the sagra and were of enormous help in the kitchen. You deserve to be feted for months on end, if not indefinitely."

"This will do," Jacoby said. "Thank you."

Bill grew wistful and squinted as he stared at Jacoby.

"I wonder if this is what it feels like to have a son," he said. "I've often wondered."

Jacoby was caught off guard and didn't know what to say besides, "I don't know," though he'd been wondering if this is what it felt like to have a best friend.

Bill huffed out of his nose and used his palms on the table to propel him up. "Shall we?" he asked with a warm smile.

Jacoby nodded. "We shall."

They slowly walked the parameter of the property, in and around vestiges of a former farm, on dirt paths through meadows sown with timothy and edged with wild flowers. Bill foraged around a briar patch and Jacoby sat on a stump, trying to memorize the vision of the valley in front of him, soft and golden and full of life.

In the patina of late afternoon, through shaded back roads pierced by blades of sun, they returned to the village at a modest pace. The cool air of early evening felt nice on Jacoby's face. He felt full and content and happy to be home as they bumped up the dirt track toward Paolo's villa. The front gate was propped open; shiny coupes and sedans were parked all around the drive and the open areas that fronted the villa. Bill cut the engine as Jacoby climbed off the motorini.

"I'd be tempted to crash the party if I weren't so already sated," Bill said with mischief in his eyes.

"Yeah," Jacoby agreed, a willing partner. "But he does have really good grappa."

Bill smiled. "I better not," he said, tapping the motorini. "I might not make it home."

Jacoby nodded. Before leaving, Bill told Jacoby how to find the travel agency he'd mentioned.

"It is quite close to the Uffizi," he yelled after starting the engine, "which will be open tomorrow!"

Jacoby waved and Bill took off down the dirt road in a small cloud of dust and fumes.

The smell of Paolo's forno accompanied Jacoby up the drive. He hoped not to be spotted on his way inside, having to make small conversation and possibly refuse an invitation to be social with Paolo and his cronies. Their voices didn't sound festive from beyond the fence, but rather serious, officious even, as if discussing an important matter. Probably soccer, Jacoby thought as he slipped across the terrace and turned toward the barn doors, where the hunter's dog slept, curled into itself.

"Hey," Jacoby said, as if bumping into an old friend.

The dog jumped up, spun around once, and scampered to Jacoby's side, whimpering with utmost urgency. He picked it up and petted under its chin and around the neck. "Good boy," he said. "Good boy."

Jacoby was happy and flattered to see the dog, but he also knew that he couldn't keep it. But he also couldn't return it now: His car was blocked in and the cafe was surely closed at this hour on a Sunday night. Oh, well. He rationalized his way into keeping the dog for one night. It was still fairly early, and he so didn't want to be alone.

They went inside, and as the dog ran around the barn, sniffing around the edges, investigating every room, Jacoby rummaged through the fridge for something to feed the poor animal. It lapped up a bowl of water as Jacoby cooked some eggs and prosciutto, which he plated once cool and put on the floor. The dog ate quickly and then followed Jacoby upstairs, into the bathroom, into the bedroom to change and back downstairs where it curled up next to him on the couch while he read for an hour before falling asleep. It was exactly how Jacoby had imagined his life would be.

Chapter 36

In the morning, Jacoby took the dog for a walk behind the property. It stayed by his side and adhered to his orders. They crested the hill in the back of the property and watched the sun rise over the elevated ramparts east of the city. He petted the dog vigorously and wished so badly that he could stay. That this could be his routine. That fate was real and it would deposit him here forever.

They returned to the barn. Jacoby showered while the dog curled on the bed but kept its eyes open. Jacoby dressed in a white tennis shirt, a pair of khaki slacks and his brown Blundstone boots. He carried the dog to the car, and it sat on the passenger seat, its paws on the dash to see out the front window. Jacoby drove slowly and dreaded every passing meter on their way down to the village. He parked by the hotel and carried the dog under one arm across the empty piazza. Its heart beat hard, and it began to whimper as they grew closer. Jacoby could feel his own heart beating and breaking inside his body.

Nicoletta was setting up the bar when he entered, her back to the door.

"Ciao," Jacoby said softly.

She turned, gasped then frowned. With a sour countenance she came from behind the bar, her eyes big and brown and sad. "Mi dispiace, americano."

She took the dog from Jacoby, scolding it without any real heat as it continued to whimper and lunge for Jacoby. Nicoletta grew frustrated and took the dog to the back, through the dining area, where a door slammed and the sound of whimpering stopped.

Nicoletta returned and convinced Jacoby through body language that everything was alright. "Caffè?" she asked.

"Si."

"Cornetto?"

"Si."

She put a pastry on a plate and served Jacoby at the bar while she clanked and banged out his espresso. When she put the demitasse cup in front of him, she held the saucer for a moment and looked at Jacoby with great kindness until she popped up with wide eyes.

"Voui il cane?" she asked with enthusiasm.

Jacoby knew she had asked if he wanted the dog, but was too dumbfounded to indicate understanding.

"Prendi," she insisted he take the animal with a flick of her wrist and a mischievous slant of her eyes. "Prendi. Perchè no?"

"Impossibile," Jacoby answered.

"Perchè?"

"Io non ho un posto," he said slowly, feeling the currency of the words sink through his sternum: He had no place.

Nicoletta slouched and turned away as if she couldn't bear to witness such a sad sight. Jacoby could hear the dog's faint whimper as he ate small pieces of his pastry, reminding him of his first encounter with the hound. It was too much for him to bear, his whole body aching with each cry. He left some money on the counter and walked out of the cafe under the gaze of Nicoletta's sympathetic stare, crossing the piazza like a heartbroken zombie. He quickly started the car and roared out of the village as if the pain he felt could be escaped.

He drove with the windows down, and the fresh Tuscan morning soothed him somewhat. By the time he reached Piazza Michelangelo, he was thinking about his mission in town. Much of the piazza was portioned off, and there was lots of equipment and a platform being built with large pieces of wood. A man in a uniform said something to

Jacoby as he crossed the asphalt after parking at the far end of the piazza. The words were delivered quickly with an imperative tone, and Jacoby didn't catch the meaning, but he just nodded and kept walking as if it were all perfectly clear.

The city felt different. It was mostly empty, except for workers on ladders or even higher in cherry pickers decorating facades or stringing ornaments across the streets. It had the feeling of a looming party, and Jacoby hoped to get out of town before the festivities began.

He found the travel agent on a side street off of Piazza Signoria. She was a fashionable woman in her 60s who dressed like a woman in her 30s, and Jacoby couldn't help but be attracted to her elegant appearance and attention to detail. Her perfume didn't hurt either.

She poked around the internet for a while, typing in bursts and periodically declaring, "Allora," but then waiving it off after further inspection. There were apparently restrictions on his seat and complications regarding airport of departure which made the task all the more difficult. Eventually, after the scent of perfume began to sting at Jacoby's temples, a seat was secured on a flight leaving Florence with a stop in Paris before departing for New York. The flight was on Wednesday. Two days from then.

Jacoby left the travel agency with his ticket and a sense of desolation. But he also had things to do, a reality made evident by the plane ticket in his hand, so he searched for an internet cafe to check his bank account and look into some storage facilities back in Brooklyn. He also wanted to reach out to the bass player from his former band who now lived in Providence and built boats. There were also some bartending gigs to look into around Boston.

The only internet cafe he found was closed for the holiday, and he gleaned from the many shuttered storefronts that the travel agency was among the exceptions. He returned there to see if the fancy and fragrance-laden woman would let him use her computer, but she had closed already. Near Piazza Signoria, he found a Bancomat where he withdrew some cash.

As the receipt slipped out, Jacoby took a deep breath and prepared to confirm the modest four figure amount of his net worth, but before his eyes could focus on the tiny print, a bicycle skidded to a halt a mere few feet from where he stood.

"My, my," Helen Dempsey said, "if it isn't my hot mess, returned to town in all his glory."

She straddled her bike frame and had a lovely smile accompanying her bright eyes and rose cheeks. She shook her bob a little to one side. Jacoby crumpled the unread bank receipt as he shoved it into his wallet with the Euros and tried to think of something clever to say.

"Hi," is all he could come up with.

"Hi, yourself," Helen said. "Have you come for the festivities? Is Bill with you? Did you ever find the old woman? My god, I feel like I've run into a long lost friend."

"Uh, actually, no, on the festivities and Bill and the woman," Jacoby answered, a bit overwhelmed by her barrage and presence. She was wearing all white, a sleeveless button up tied at her naval over white clam diggers with white boat shoes. "Are you going sailing or something?"

"Pardon?"

"Why all the white?"

"I'm going to the final match of the calcio storico. It's this afternoon. Have you heard of it?"

"No."

"Oh, it's fantastic. Best sport in the world. Kind of like rugby meets American football with a bit of fighting mixed in, actually, more than a bit. Quite a lot of fighting."

"Really?"

"50 minutes of straight play. No substitutions. No rules. Well, there's no choking or kicks to the head."

"That's good."

"Do you like sports?"

"I do."

"Are you free for the rest of the afternoon?"

"I am."

"Well, then, this is your lucky day. My girlfriend is married to one of the players and she has refused to go. The semi-finals were just

Saturday, and it was a bloody mess. She just can't stand to watch another match. So, I have an extra ticket. Care to join, or is your life still too complicated?"

"I don't know," he fumbled but regained his footing. "Yes."

"Yes to what? The complications or the match?

Jacoby liked the way she wrinkled her nose when she asked playful questions. Her company felt so comfortable.

"Yes, to the match."

"Super. There's a parade starting at 2:00, and the procession goes from Santa Maria Novella to Santa Croce where they play in the piazza around 4:00."

"On the stones?"

"No!" Helen climbed off her bike and pushed Jacoby along. "Come on, we're going to return my bike home and go to the procession. I'll explain everything along the way."

Chapter 37

They walked through Piazza Signoria and crossed the Ponte Vecchio into the Oltrarno section of the city, where they strolled down the middle of shaded, narrow streets nearly empty of vehicles. Helen explained the history of the calcio storico, from its origins with Roman legionnaires to its adaptation by Florentine aristocrats during the Renaissance, where the game has essentially remained the same, with the four quarters of Florence, each designated a color and affiliation with a local church, fielding a team of amateurs for a 3-game tournament every June, on a sand-packed Piazza Santa Croce. The final match is played as part of the celebration on the 24th for St. John the Baptist. Helen lived in the Santo Spirito section of the city and, therefore, rooted, passionately, for the Bianchi (white) of her home quarter.

"Good thing you're wearing some white," she said. "Or I'd have to find another date."

"Good thing," Jacoby added, loving the idea of him being her date.

After a silent walk down a minuscule alley, a tiny piazza opened that couldn't have been more than 100 strides around its oblong perimeter bordered entirely by eateries or artisan shops. After crossing the stone surface, Helen fastened her bike to a crowded rack and led Jacoby back toward the river on foot.

"Wait a minute," Jacoby said. "This is where you live?"

"Yes," she said pointing toward a shuttered window. "Just above that tiny jeweler."

"It's, it's..." he stammered. "Too cute to even call cute. Or quaint. Or cutesy-quaint."

"I know!" Helen beamed. "There's not really a modifier that could capture this reality. And the best part is that it's almost entirely sufficient. There's the bar there, which has extraordinary cocktails, and a coffee shop in back. A gelateria there, that has, arguably, the best gelato in the city, and we have two restaurants, one an old establishment that serves the classics, wonderfully, bisteccas and all that, and this tiny one off the far corner that I just adore because it's a little more adventurous and fun. It's about as funky as Florence gets, I think."

Jacoby found it very exciting, though it saddened him to think of all the small treasures of Florence and Tuscany and beyond that he would probably never discover.

The midday sun slapped high heat on their skin, so they stayed as much as possible in the shadows while snaking back toward the historic center, crossing Ponte Santa Trinita which offered a lovely view of the silver river reflecting the sky and the Ponte Vecchio in its pastel and cubist glory. They walked the wide Via de'Tornabouni past elegant palazzos with carved stone facades. The famous retail shops on the ground level were all closed for the holiday. The Duomo's crushed-orange cupola popped in and out of view as if it were playing peek-a-boo with them.

They arrived at Piazza Santa Maria Novella just as the procession began. All the participants were dressed in Renaissance attire, from shoes to feathered hats. There were maidens and noblemen, soldiers and drum brigades. Many men, adorned with sheathed swords, plodded along high on saddled horses as well-groomed as their riders.

Helen looked around furiously, rising on her toes often, shading her eyes, taking it all in. She waved on occasion to people who waved enthusiastically back. The sun beat down on the open piazza, and the smell of horse manure rose in the heat. Jacoby felt a little bored and kind of excluded. Parades had never been part of his past, and they were kind of silly from his decidedly un-civic perspective. Men in costumes, any costumes, just looked stupid to him. Besides being bored, he wanted Helen's attention.

"What do you say we skip all this pageantry and get a panino?" Helen asked. "I could certainly use a bite before the game."

"Sure," Jacoby said, thinking that Helen had actually read his mind.

She took his arm and confirmed his suspicion as they walked. "Don't worry, Jacoby Pines. Plenty of excitement awaits."

They cut through the parade route and bee-lined past the Uffizi to shaded walkways beneath the loggias of buildings that buttressed the banks of the Arno. On a side street, they entered an open and modern space that looked to Jacoby like something more akin to hipster New York than Florence, Italy. Pop music played. There was lots of stainless steel and counter space, though the old bones of the building were evident in the washed out walls and antique ceiling. People were lingering and people were in line, reading the menu off hand-written sheets of paper.

"Share one with me?" Helen asked, holding her belly. "I don't want to be stuffed."

"Sure," Jacoby said. "You pick."

"I'm a purist, you know. Just simple prosciutto with a spread of cheese."

"Works for me."

"Grab some drinks, sparkling water for me, and find us a spot?"

Jacoby pulled two bottles of seltzer from a refrigerated merchandiser and studied Helen, who stood in line patiently, turning around on occasion to check in on Jacoby. He sat on a high stool with his back to a counter that fronted plate glass windows. He tapped his foot to the bad music and sipped his sparkling water.

The sandwich was overstuffed with prosciutto on soft country bread with a spread of tangy cheese and a hint of an acidic topping.

"I had them add some marinated artichokes," Helen said as she watched Jacoby consider his first bite. "I couldn't resist."

"Good call," Jacoby said before asking, "What kind of cheese is this?"

"Robiola," she said. "From Piemonte, in the north. Have you been?"

"Where?"

"To the north, to Piemonte in particular?"

"No."

"Oh, it's spectacular," Helen declared, putting down her sandwich. "It's even more mountainous that Tuscany, with big red wines that rival ours, and these quaint villages and ancient cities. Oh, and they have white truffles in the autumn, which they shave into mounds on plates of fresh, yellow pasta..."

Helen carried on about Piemonte while Jacoby chewed his sandwich and endured the torture of learning of yet another place he wouldn't visit, made all the worse by the fact that he wouldn't visit this place in particular with Helen.

"Am I talking too much?" Helen blurted, recognizing that Jacoby had finished his half of the panino while hers was hardly touched.

"Not at all," Jacoby lied, impressed by her awareness and consideration.

Helen huffed out of her nose, corrected her posture and ate her sandwich slowly and silently as Jacoby stared out at the street. When she was nearly finished, Jacoby took the receipt off the tray and went to the counter to pay.

"Thank you," Helen said upon his return. "You didn't have to pay for lunch."

"It's the least I could do," Jacoby said with charm. "You're taking me to the world's greatest sporting event."

"I am," Helen chirped. "And we should get moving."

Chapter 38

All roads leading to Piazza Santa Croce were blocked by metal barricades manned by burly security details. Helen ferried them through small streets in order to approach from the far side of the piazza, adjacent to the cloisters and the basilica. The majority of the people using this method of entry wore white, of both genders, mostly in their 20s and 30s, their excitement palpable in hurried steps and rapid dialogue as they crowded the narrow road to the piazza.

Temporary stands surrounded the piazza, blocking view of the playing field within. Helen presented two tickets to a silent security guard who parted the barricades to allow entry. In an alley of shadows between the back of high grandstands and the piazza's closed storefronts, Jacoby noticed an army of paramedics in bright yellow coats with medical kits and a dozen stretchers. His mouth went dry. And then the sound of drums arrived from the distance.

"Come on," Helen cried. "Let's get our seats before the procession arrives."

They passed through another security checkpoint and climbed the aluminum stairs of the stands set up in front of the basilica's facade, just before the church steps where Dante stood above the highest row. Their section backed a narrow end of the pitch, which ran about 20 yards across, bordered the entire length by a four-foot wall with loose netting above and behind. Helen explained that the walls were goals that ran the width of the field, like an end zone in American football that was breached by depositing the ball above the wall but below the netting in an opening of about five feet. Balls that landed above the netting were ½ goals for the defending team.

Every single person in their section wore white, and even though they sat quietly on the numbered bench rows, their nervous intensity was evident. On the opposite side of the piazza, about 80 yards away, across moistened and hard-packed sand, behind a similar waist-high wall, the stands were full of green, their section more crowded and rowdy, with green smoke bombs going off and green flags unfurled. They chanted something that Jacoby couldn't make out.

"Who are we playing anyway?" Jacoby asked once they settled into their spaces in the middle of a row about halfway up the bleachers, which were now filling quickly to capacity.

"San Lorenzo," Helen spoke over the din. "The quartiere beyond the Duomo, near the Mercato Centrale."

Jacoby nodded while studying their fans' raucous antics.

"They're a little low brow, if that's what you're wondering," Helen said without discretion. "And they also haven't won the tournament since 1996, so they are mad with desperation."

"Yikes."

"Yes," Helen concurred with a hint of suspicion in her voice. "There are rumors that they've brought in some hired muscle from Poland."

"Poland?'

"Yes. Professional fighters or something, I've heard."

"Isn't that against the rules?"

"Absolutely, all of the players are supposed to be from the quarter, but they allow them to recruit outside a bit just to keep it competitive, but going beyond the country is something I've never heard of before."

"How will they get away with it?"

"It's Italy after all, Jacoby. Corruption knows no bounds, especially for something as important as this."

"What do the winners get?"

"A prized cow from the countryside, and a steak dinner."

"That's it? One cow for all of them?"

"The cow's really more symbolic than anything else. I'm not even sure if they still actually provide it, but the dinner is real. A feast is more like it."

"And that's it? No money or anything."

"That's it. And, of course, bragging rights throughout the city and hero status in their home quarter for an entire year, which is – as they say - priceless."

"If you say so," Jacoby quipped, but her words had the currency of tradition and pride as opposed to the greed and ego which seemed to dominate American sports.

The drums grew louder, abetted by a small army of horns who were the first of the procession to enter the arena. They set up along the far length, where the bleachers that ran vertically along the pitch were mostly empty. The rest of the procession entered, each section announced over a loud speaker. Soon the entire pitch was covered in various factions of Renaissance society.

The mood shifted from ceremonious and respectful to intense and dangerous once players from respective teams began entering the arena. First came groups from the two teams not playing in the finals, large men in red or blue tops over wool Renaissance trousers. They were big and mean-looking, like pirates or bikers, lots of tattoos and bitter expressions from being denied the opportunity to play. They did a half-turn around the perimeter of the pitch. The crowd treated them respectfully, though none of their faithful were in attendance. Not a spec of blue or red anywhere in the crowd.

The music played on and announcements continued. Clouds mercifully covered the high sun on occasion, and a kind breeze swept in from the nearby river, but it was hot, and Jacoby felt parched and already unsettled by the atmosphere under an unforgiving sun. There was a visceral and malevolent energy in the air, like in a bar before a brawl breaks out. He and Helen had been silent for a while. She had taken a straw sun hat from her bag and seemed to be hiding under it.

Once both sets of non-participants had done their tour and been announced, everyone on the pitch made their way into the stands that lined either sideline of the playing field, which were soon filled with people in costume, players not in green or white, and a lot of photographers and journalists.

Then the green team entered. Fans on both sides stood on their seats. The players first passed by the stands of Bianchi supporters, who hurled invective at them which Jacoby was happy not to understand, though the intentions were clear. The stands rocked with rage, and Jacoby fought to keep his balance as people behind him lurched their bodies forward. All sense of seating assignment, as half-assed as it was, disappeared and the entire section felt like one big crush.

"There!" Helen yelled, pointing at two enormous men with shaved heads and baleful glares. "They must be the Poles."

"Holy shit balls," Jacoby said. "They're huge."

Helen stood perfectly still with a hand on each cheek. Jacoby felt her concern and began to grow worried himself. He sizzled inside and kind of wanted to leave, to rid himself of this helpless feeling, though he couldn't imagine how he could possible defy the energy keeping everyone where they were. The exits were essentially closed. No wonder Helen's friend couldn't watch her husband play. Jacoby felt tremendous empathy for all the mothers and wives of the players surely sequestered and clutching rosaries, praying for their sons and husbands to be safe. For this day to pass.

The whole green squad was notably larger than the two that had already entered, and there was a villainous vibe to the whole lot. They sneered as they passed the Bianchi bleachers, not bothered by their taunts and disdain. The opposite stands erupted as their players approached. Green smoke bombs went off in tandem and their chant cracked the air.

"Picche Verdi! Picche Verdi! EH! EH!"

"Picche Verdi! Picche Verdi! EH! EH!"

"Picche Verdi! Picche Verdi! EH! EH!"

"What are they saying?" Jacoby asked Helen.

"Their encouraging their players, the 'verdi' or green, to punch, punch."

"Nice," Jacoby said sarcastically.

"Oh, look," Helen said as the white team entered.

Jacoby felt a little reprieve as the stands around him erupted in positive energy and a chant of their own.

"Forza Bianchi! Forza Bianchi! EH! EH!"

"Forza Bianchi! Forza Bianchi! EH! EH!"

"Forza Bianchi! Forza Bianchi! EH! EH!"

Jacoby didn't need a translation here to understand that strength was being encouraged in the white team. He was surely the only person not contributing to the cacophony as he studied the white team, who were somewhat smaller though pretty damn formidable. They had some psychos themselves, wide-eyed and muscular men covered in tattoos who looked ready for war. They even had a few players of color, which Jacoby found interesting.

"That's Rodrigue there," Helen yelled, pointing at a black man with a faux fro-hawk and a shiny body seemingly carved from onyx. "Mariangela's husband."

"Damn," Jacoby said. "He work out?"

Helen laughed. "He has a doctorate in physical science, earned here at university in Florence, and was a championship rugby player back in Cameroon."

"Nice guy?"

"Incredibly nice. A total sweetheart, except on the pitch, of course, where he's quite a force."

Jacoby started to feel better. The white team looked capable, their fans seemed confident, and now he had someone in particular to follow and cheer on, a magnificent looking man who had the potential for heroism.

Once all the players were announced, most of the men took off their shirts, leaving only stripes on their trousers to indicate affiliation. Every single player, all 27 from each team, lined up in various positions of four designations, with about half of the squad, big brawler types, on the front lines and the small portion of men of agility and speed way in the back. Helen's friend Rodrigue was in the row one back from the front, in what appeared to be a halfback or linebacker position. All the men bounced and jabbed and vented adrenalin in some way. Many of the men upfront stared hard at their adversaries. The two giants from Poland were front and center for the green, dwarfing their counterparts who were big men.

This is what war must feel like, somewhat, Jacoby thought, trying to empathize with the men waiting for battle and how the churning inside must feel.

"No one has ever died during this, have they?" Jacoby suddenly thought to ask Helen.

"No. No," she said, not taking her eyes from the pitch. "But someone did lose a spleen once."

Jacoby shuddered at the thought, though unsure of what the loss of a spleen would involve.

"Oh, and someone had their ear bitten off," Helen added.

That was easier to imagine. Jacoby studied the statue of Dante, a mere 10 yards away, wondering what he'd make of all this.

The arena, so amped and eager, inflated with toxicity, felt like a plump red boil ready to burst. *Jesus Christ*, Jacoby thought. *Get on with it*.

And then a cannon fired and the ball - that looked like a soft soccer ball - was thrown into the air, and the game began. Jacoby's heart swooned with a blast of adrenalin, and he found himself, like everyone else, standing on his toes and trying to elongate his neck. It was both hard to watch and hard not to watch. Men along the front lines immediately began fighting, like a mixed martial arts rumble. Helen jumped up and down, holding his arm for support, reminding Jacoby of her pogo move at the secret dance club.

The ball went to the Verdi. They lateraled it to their back line, and the strategy became evident: wait for your guys to conquer ground ahead, in order to advance less-molested. The Verdi held the ball as their aggressive front line went to work. The two battering rams were mean as they were massive. One, in particular, was possibly the largest human being Jacoby had ever seen, in both height and width. And he displayed perfect boxing form, roundhouse kicks, and utter contempt for his opponent. His wing man was only slightly shorter if not a bit wider. Equally as intimidating. Jacoby felt bad for the Bianchi. They were getting the crap kicked out of them upfront, while everyone else stood ground, waiting for their part in the action. The crowd roared without pause and broke into chant on occasion.

First blood came from the faces of the Bianchi front line. They stood tall, but were taking shots to the face and kicks to the side and getting the majority of medical attention administered by the swarming paramedics. The Verdi front line pushed them back slowly and encroached towards the Bianchi goal. As a result, the Verdi scored the game's first points. Their fans went ballistic: chanting, waving flags, igniting green smoke bombs and sensing the upset-narrative taking shape. A sickness crept through Jacoby, but it was belied somewhat by the confidence still displayed by those around him. Helen squeezed his bicep in a gesture of not-to-worry.

And the Bianchi hung tough. The courageous front line regained their footing, stood tall and kept fighting; and soon the bloodshed and bodies pinned to the ground equaled out. Even the monster from Poland showed signs of battery upon his hard face. There was no clock on the field, and Jacoby kept wondering how many minutes of the 50 had elapsed. He had no clue.

After a reckless Bianchi advance - featuring missed shots, ill-advised passes and a lucky bounce - the white team scored the equalizer. And then, the tide would turn for the Bianchi, inspired, it seemed clearly to Jacoby, by a bunch of massive hits by Rodrigue, the first of which - a blindsided flattening of the Verdi ball carrier - would have been an endless loop on ESPN had it happened on American turf, administered by a millionaire, in helmet and pads, on any given Sunday. The second one, only moments after, was a full body slam of the WWF variety, followed by a midfield exchange of upper torsos that left a Verdi player supine on the ground. The Rodrigue show coincided with Bianchi control of the ball and the game, including two quick goals. As the shadows stretched across the playing field, even before a perfunctory and final goal the for whites, the Bianchi faithful were singing their victory song and taunting the Verdi fans across the length of the pitch, beyond the opposite goal, with a profane and mocking directive which Jacoby didn't understand but fully supported. In the waning moments, Rodrigue, his chiseled black body and handsome face covered in fair sand, appeared in front of the stands and sought out Helen's wave. With her cell phone, she took his picture as he gave a thumb's up pose. She quickly forwarded the photo on to his wife. Jacoby tried to imagine her sense of relief, and pride, and joy. It all really did make sense to him now, in the game's final moments among the exuberant fans, all of whom were congratulating each other as if they had been part of the victory. Jacoby had never experienced such a thing, and it was so much fun.

A celebration on the field spread into the stands, with a few of the players jumping the wall and climbing over the netting to revel with their faithful supporters. Then the team ran together back to the Piazza Santo Spirito, chanting all the way, carrying flags, over the Ponte Grazie, their voices echoing through the narrow alleys of Oltrarno. Helen and Jacoby followed at their own pace, a speed-walk of sorts.

When they arrived in Piazza Santo Spirito, the players were gathered on the steps of their namesake church, surrounded by a mass of local supporters and curious tourists. Lots of photos were being taken, and the players went through a collection of chants, returning often to the familiar refrain of "Forza Bianchi! Forza Bianchi!" arm in arm, spraying beer and Prosecco on each other and the crowd.

Helen and Jacoby stood just beyond the reach of the spray and quietly watched the celebration which slowly broke up after a short while, and the players began limping off in different directions.

"Where's Rodrigue?" Jacoby asked.

"Oh, I'm sure he's gone home already," Helen said. "To confirm his safety for Mariangela."

"Not a party guy?"

"I imagine he'll meet up with them later for dinner. There's a restaurant nearby owned by a former player. It's sort of their clubhouse. They'll surely be there late into the night."

"Do the fans go, too?"

"No. No. It's strictly for the players. There will be a public celebration here, in the piazza, in a few weeks. Once the players have had a chance to heal."

Jacoby watched the last of the players vanish into the fading light. The people in the piazza returned to their cafes and spots for sitting in the open air. A sense of ambivalence came over him.

"You're perplexed by the whole thing, aren't you?" Helen asked.

"How'd you know?"

"Happens to all people with a sense of humanity. It's odd, I know, these giant men beating each other up, but it's not like imbeciles in a bar or something, fighting over a squashed toe or a silly girl. These men fight together. A fair fight, for the most part. And they do it for their neighborhood. For the sense of community, and the brotherhood of the men. I think it's quite noble."

"Not ironic at all?"

"How's that?'

"I mean, the game is being played here, in lovely Florence, birthplace of the Renaissance, in front of the church where Italy's greatest inventors and artists and noblemen are memorialized. The statue of Dante is standing right there, looking over it all."

Jacoby felt astute and articulate, for a moment.

"I'll inform you, Jacoby Pines, that Dante Alighieri was not just a poet. He fought in war. As did many others in there. How do you even think the Renaissance happened? Through poetry readings? Michelangelo had a bent nose from battle. Those artists knew what it felt like to fight. All men did. So few of any sort do anymore. The calcio storico is not the same as actual war, of course, but these men who play know what it's like to fight, with nothing but their bodies, for their community, for their brothers, at great risk to themselves. That's so rare. I find it amazing."

"That's quite an argument," Jacoby said. "You should be a lawyer."

"Never!" Helen laughed and smacked him hard on the arm.

Jacoby put up his fists; Helen did the same. They danced around each other for a moment, until the sun sunk below the low roof line. Cool air swept through the piazza. Jacoby dropped his hands and looked Helen in the eye.

"So, I hear there's a cutesy quaint piazzetta around here with a funky osteria."

"There is!" Helen confirmed. "Care to try?"

Jacoby shrugged with feigned indifference. "I guess."

Helen hooked him by the arm and led them out of the Piazza Santo Spirito towards the magical little piazza where she lived.

Chapter 39

The sky held the remnants of light above the piazzetta as dusk slowly approached. The tables outside the larger restaurant were full under the awning. Light twinkled and lingered, as if fighting off darkness, not wanting the day to end. An old man with his back to an ancient wall played slow, whimsical songs on an accordion. Helen led Jacoby into an antique storefront and leaned into the bar after hugging the bartender and exchanging kisses on both cheeks.

"Let's have martinis!" she cried.

"Sure," Jacoby agreed.

"Vodka or gin?"

"Definitely vodka - gin is like injecting me with douche bag serum."

"Wouldn't want that," Helen quipped. "Could make for a long evening."

"I'll say."

"Or a short one."

Helen ordered the drinks in Italian with enthused pomp and then ushered Jacoby out of the bar and into the piazza.

"Where are we going?" he asked.

"To our table."

They sat on a bench on the far side of the tiny piazza. Helen crossed her legs. Jacoby studied the perfect scene, of so much beauty and peace and promise.

"Couldn't you just stay right here, at this precise moment, forever?" Helen asked without a bit of whimsy.

"Yep."

A man from the bar in a tailored shirt and faded jeans - middle-aged, hip and handsome - crossed the piazza with a tray balanced on one hand; it held a glass pitcher full of clear liquid swimming in ice and two large martini glasses foggy with frozen condensation.

"Buonasera," the man said cordially upon arrival.

"Buonasera, Michele," Helen answered. "Questo è il mioamico,Jacoby."

The two men shook hands. Michele gave each one of them a glass to hold before filling each with the cocktail, the ice restrained by a long metal spoon. Helen shook her shoulders in excitement and Jacoby recalled the moments of joy tending bar. Michele topped off both glasses and left the pitcher on the ground with the long spoon stuck in the ice and remaining liquid. He nodded pleasantly before taking the tray back across the piazza and into the bar.

"Cheers!" Helen sang, holding up her glass.

"Cheers," Jacoby responded with a giant smile.

They chinked glasses and took sips of the icy liquid. Jacoby's eyes popped a bit at the strong content, yet smooth and mellowed by the vermouth. Good martini.

Helen leaned back, carefully balancing her drink, and crossed her legs for maximum comfort. "OK, Jacoby Pines, my charming mate of great mystery, it's time to tell me everything."

"Everything?"

"Well, not everything," Helen said, wrinkling her nose. "Just the parts that would matter to me."

Over martini cocktails in the sifting twilight, through abridged and efficient storytelling, Jacoby was able to inform Helen of his itinerant childhood accompanying his melancholy and widowed father from college teaching post to college teaching post, to his own college years in Boston and subsequent role as a guitarist in an acclaimed rock band that flamed out after one album, which led to his new haircut and new

career as a PR account executive in New York City where he was soon
engaged to the travel writer Claire St. James who brought him to Italy
for what was supposed to be a year of recovery after he was fired for a
indiscretion that left him an unemployable pariah in the professional
ranks of America, but now he was no longer engaged and returning on
Wednesday to America even though he so didn't want to go and had
no real sense of what he'd do once he got there.

"Wow," Helen said, finishing off her martini. "You're like your very
own Lost Generation."

Jacoby laughed, impressed by the comparison and wondering if he
left anything of importance out.

"Oh," he quickly added, "and I killed a cinghiale with an ax
yesterday."

"Did you now?"

"Yep."

"Good for you."

"Thanks."

"I'm hungry," Helen declared. "Let's eat."

"Sounds good."

Jacoby brought the glasses and the pitcher back to the bar while
Helen secured a table for two at Lo Sprone, the tiny restaurant just off
the tiny piazza that she loved so much. The room was sparse and
festive, a charming hole-in-the wall, with conversations bouncing off
the faded pastel walls and a cat making circles around the ankles of
diners. A man, who Helen identified as the owner, sat in a chair by the
front window and played Flamenco on an old guitar.

With separate forks, they took a single plate of cacio e pepe, fresh
noodles dressed in cheese and pepper, followed by a plate of charred
octopus with potatoes then a stuffed and roasted pigeon which was the
most flavorful bird Jacoby had ever tasted. They drank white wine all
along and shared a piece of chocolate cake for dessert.

They split the check and went back to their bench outside and sat
in the darkness in the small lights of the piazzetta under the jet black
sky. Helen had told Jacoby her story over dinner, of growing up
outside Melbourne with three older and athletic brothers who she

loved but longed to get out from under their protection, which sent her to London to study and explore art, which led her to Florence to further her studies and acquire a desire to never live anywhere else. She'd dated plenty of Italian men but never found love. They were all too attached to their mothers, she believed. But she was incredibly content with her life in Florence, with friends and food and art and beauty everywhere all the time.

Jacoby envied Helen and told her so as they sat on the bench, his arm around her shoulder.

"Seriously. What will you do back in the States?" she asked.

"I don't know," he said, trying not to seem too pathetic. "I'll figure something out."

"Will you come back to visit?"

"I hope so," he said and stood up to leave, suddenly overwhelmed with emotion and the desire to run.

"Where are you going?"

"I should leave," he said. "It's late."

Church bells rang nine.

"I'm afraid you're not going anywhere."

"Why not?"

A burst of fireworks rippled and popped in the sky behind Jacoby. He turned around to study the explosion. More blooms of color and bursts of sound.

"That's why," Helen said. "They're being shot off from Piazza Michelangelo, where a few thousand people are gathered around your car."

"Oh," is all Jacoby could think to say.

"I meant to tell you earlier," Helen said with feigned sincerity, "but it must have slipped my mind."

Fireworks filled the sky, and Jacoby turned again to see them. When he turned back, Helen was standing right in front of him, her eyes locked on his, her mouth open just a little bit. She took his hands and kissed him softly on the mouth as the fireworks exploded overhead.

• • •

They kissed for a long time in the piazzetta, under the sky filled with color and an orchestra of pop and sizzle. Upstairs, in Helen's lovely apartment above the jewelry store, with her bedroom window open to the piazza, they made love until exhaustion demanded sleep. A breeze blew in the open window; Jacoby slept soundly with Helen's head on his chest, the touch of her skin all along his body. At first light, Helen got out of bed to close the window, secure the shudders, and return to bed. They slept until bells rang ten and then stayed in bed with their eyes open, not speaking, bodies touching, for a while longer.

Jacoby did not want to get out of bed. He did not want to leave Italy or Helen's apartment or Helen's arms. He wondered how long he could just lie there, nestled next to her.

"Holy shit," he cried, springing upright.

"What is it?" Helen asked.

"The sagra."

"What sagra?"

"The one in the village. It's today. I promised to help Bill."

Jacoby jumped out of bed and collected his clothes.

"What's he making?"

"What?"

"What's Bill making for the sagra?"

Helen had sat up in bed, holding the bed sheets across her chest. She looked genuinely interested and Jacoby so wanted to jump back in bed and make love with her some more.

"Cinghiale," Jacoby said, hopping into his pants.

"The one you killed?"

"Yep."

Jacoby hurried into Helen's bathroom to pee and wash his face, brush his teeth with a finger. "You know," Helen yelled from the bedroom. "They say cinghiale tastes better when you kill it yourself."

Jacoby walked slowly out of the bathroom and sat next to Helen on the bed. He knew that he was already in love with her.

"I'm going to find my way back here," he said. "I don't know how, but I will, and I will find you at the museum."

Helen bunched her mouth into a rose bud. "You could just come find me here, you know, where I live. Might be easier. Maybe even send an email ahead of time letting me know what time to expect you."

"Yeah, I know," Jacoby said, "but the whole finding you at the museum thing sounds more romantic."

Helen laughed and smacked his face lightly two times. "Yes. Yes, it does."

Jacoby slipped into his boots and bent over to kiss Helen on the forehead. She let the sheets slip down to cover her lap, and he savored the image of her upright and topless on the bed, like she was posing for a portrait. Or modeling for a statue. Then he walked out of her room and her apartment. The streets were quiet, the city slow to start after its big day and night. Jacoby hurried along, fighting off the swarming emotions, walking at a brisk clip in the cool morning air under another perfect sky of the most beautiful string of June days, of any days, he'd ever experienced.

Chapter 40

At Piazza Michelangelo, Jacoby's car - the only one in the vast lot - was covered in soot from the fireworks, and there was a ticket stuck under the windshield wiper, which he dumped in a garbage bin before roaring off down the hill back toward home. Most of the soot blew off as he drove, leaving only a thin dusting on the car.

Back at the barn, he savored his memory of being with Helen while he showered until the hot water ran out. Then he changed into jeans and a black t-shirt and packed the old Samsonite with the rest of his things. He loaded the car with the suitcase, Giovanni's guitar, and the case of Brunello di Montalcino. He drove down the drive and through the gate with a plan to return the remote and say his goodbye to Paolo at the sagra. He'd sleep at the hotel that night and text Claire with the location of her car. Bill could hold the keys. Jacoby went through the painful motions with the emotional detachment he used as an adolescent when leaving one place he lived for another, with the mindset of just getting through it. The difficulties of leaving Italy were somewhat eased by the fact that he still had a last hurrah of the sagra.

The village was active, and Jacoby got the final parking space alongside the piazza. In front of the hotel, Bill - in a large chef's hat - was under a tent directly across from the hotel, taking up a large piece of piazza real estate. In the shade, on a large wooden table, he set up trays over unlit burners until he noticed Jacoby's approach, carrying the case of wine.

"Good lord," Bill yelled, sounding more southern than usual. "I thought we'd lost you."

"Sorry," Jacoby said. "I got tied up in town."

"Sounds like fun," Bill quipped.

"It was," Jacoby confirmed. "How can I help?"

"The first thing you can do is go into the kitchen and let Giovanni know you are here. The poor boy is worried nearly out of his mind that his accompanist has disappeared."

"Where should I put this?" Jacoby asked, pointing his chin at the wine. "It's the Brunello I told you about."

"Oh my," Bill sighed. "Just put it on the bar for now. We'll get some bottles breathing soon enough. Door's open."

Bill went back to work, and Jacoby crossed the small side street and shouldered open the hotel door. The aroma had wafted out on to the street, but it hit Jacoby with full force inside the hotel. The humid smell of braised meat had a visceral effect on him. His jowls sluiced, and he hurried toward the kitchen, stopping quickly in the dining area to drop the case of wine on the bar, before kicking open the kitchen door, where the smell was even more pungent.

"Wow!" Jacoby yelled.

Giovanni jerked around from the sink, where he filled an enormous pot with water.

"Jake!!" he screamed and ran over to bear hug him. "Dov'eri? Dov'eri?" he asked of Jacoby's whereabouts while still holding him tight, afraid he might vanish.

Jacoby wrestled himself free and held up his hands to confirm everything was OK.

"Pronto? Pronto?" Giovanni asked, squeezing his own fingers.

"Si," Jacoby confirmed. "I am ready. Sono pronto."

"Dov'è la chitarra?" Giovanni asked of the guitar's whereabouts.

"In the car," Jacoby said before translating. "In macchina."

"Vai. Vai," Giovanni ordered. "Dobbiamo praticare."

Jacoby got the gist of the imperative, and the simple translation of "to practice." He nodded and requested patience with both hands held up. Jacoby had to chase the source of the smell first. On top of the stove, there was a contraption cobbled together which included a bunch of large roasting pans pushed together and covered in a hood of foil from where the fragrant steam escaped through vent holes. Jacoby so wanted to peek inside but he was afraid to touch it.

Giovanni made wide eyes and twisted a finger in his jolly cheek. Jacoby nodded and returned the gesture. He held up a hand again then pantomimed strumming a guitar. Giovanni clenched his fists in triumph, and Jacoby left the kitchen for the piazza.

●   ●   ●

"What'cha got going back there?" he asked Bill, who was stacking thick paper plates on a table that faced the piazza.

Bill smiled conspiratorially. "I'd never tell this to anyone here, for it would offend their traditions so, but I've basically rigged up a giant crock pot, a basic humidor of flavor that breaks the meat down gently, rendering it to one of the most flavorful things I or anyone around here has ever tasted."

"It smells incredible."

"There's the brine and the marinade, too, which help tremendously, but the technique is not one they practice here in Tuscany."

"What do you serve with it?"

"Polenta is the perfect pairing, for which I have another secret technique that makes it magnificently fluffy."

Jacoby draped a hand over his heart. "I cannot wait to try this."

"Why wait?" Bill said, a wink on his lips. "I've made some already. It required two batches, there's so much meat. The previous batch has been shredded and is under a little broth in the oven over very low heat." He handed Jacoby a firm paper plate.

Jacoby spun around and bolted for the hotel, stopping in his tracks to go back and grab the guitar from the car before hurrying for the front door.

"Giovanni's starting the polenta now," Bill yelled. "Try it out for me, would you?"

Jacoby waived over his shoulder with his free hand just as he pushed open the hotel door to cruise through the lobby then place the guitar across a table in the dining salon. In the kitchen, Giovanni stood on a small step ladder and used a giant blending stick to stir the polenta that percolated in a large pot.

Jacoby shook the plate like a tambourine, and Giovanni smiled in return. He grabbed a large wooden spoon and doled out a portion of polenta on to Jacoby's plate. It was heavy, but more cloud-like in shape than the polenta he'd had before that resembled oatmeal. Giovanni went back to work on the polenta as Jacoby eased open the oven door. On baking sheets, under foil cover, the meat glistened with moisture. Jacoby tried to fork some out but the meat broke on the tines. He grabbed a metal serving spoon and scooped up some meat and its flavorful broth colored by tomato and spiked by seasonings, including whole black peppercorns. He covered the polenta with the concoction and then walked slowly to the dining salon, where he placed the plate on a table.

With great patience, he walked to the bar, removed a bottle of Brunello and popped the cork, filling a glass before returning to his table. He took a deep breath, and thought to himself that this may be his last meaningful meal in Italy. He swirled the wine with vigor and took a sip. It needed to breath some more, but he couldn't wait.

The meat was as tender as it was flavorful, filling his mouth with silky decadence buttressed by layers of flavor only attainable through days of preparation that proceed slow, slow cooking. Jacoby could pick out the aspects of the brine as compared to the marinade. He loved the whole peppercorns that stood up to the fulsome meat, stripped of game and flavored by melted collagen. The meat was so delicate, he could mash it against the tines of a plastic fork, though he was careful to keep it intact to maximize mouth feel. Jacoby's first favorite meal was his father's beef bourguignon, and this made that taste memory seem childish, though he so wished his father was there with him at that moment. And he had the nostalgic rush of appreciating his father for introducing him to the pleasures of eating.

He toasted his father with a sip of the rare wine that could compliment such exquisite meat, cleansing his palate for another bite.

The polenta absorbed the broth and held many of the aromatics. It was of perfect texture but in need of some salt since the corn flavor wasn't quite there. Jacoby would tell Giovanni once he finished this plate and before they rehearsed for their one and only gig that would take place that afternoon.

•   •   •

Jacoby and Giovanni rehearsed their five songs in one of the hotel rooms. Both had prepared, and their sound was in time and tight. They did each song three times, improving with each pass. Giovanni declared them ready and then went home to change.

The piazza was active when Jacoby went outside. All of the food related businesses had set up stands, and it reminded Jacoby of the open air food markets they had in Brooklyn every weekend, except the offerings here were free and not commercially motivated but inspired by community. In that way, this was more like the best block party ever.

After taking a tour of the piazza, accepting offerings and smiles, Jacoby returned to Bill's camp and began to help. The line snaked around to the side street, and both men work furiously. In the back of the tent, Jacoby loaded each plate with an acceptable portion, being careful, as Bill warned, not to overdo it and offend his fellow sagra contributors. Bill delivered each plate personally and was exceedingly polite to all who approached; he even seemed a bit nervous, as if trying to impress. Jacoby remembered Bill's previous comment about the sagra being the only day he really feels like part of the village.

Nicoletta walked up to the counter with a sheepish look on her face. She ignored the line and whispered something to Bill while looking over her shoulder at the cafe, where her husband and his cronies sat under the awning, gigantic glasses of beer covering their table. Bill smiled kindly at her and shook his head with certitude and motioned toward the end of the line. Nicoletta shrugged, touched

Bill's arm and walked back to the cafe to report the news, which was not taken well. Her husband stood and glared across the piazza, but Bill paid him no mind.

People with plates of cinghiale and polenta began to congregate in the middle of the piazza, conferring with each other with enthusiasm for what they ate. Once finished, many would return to compliment Bill, or yell "Bravo" across the piazza, and he would graciously nod and continue serving his fellow villagers. People who arrived were directed toward the hotel with encouraging gestures.

"Looks like you're killing," Jacoby called.

It was mid-afternoon, and they were nearly out of plates.

"Indeed," Bill declared back over his shoulder.

The butcher came over, and Bill directed him around back, where Jacoby handed him a plate. He was back ten minutes later for a refill.

A herd of clouds roamed overhead, mercifully blocking the sun for long periods at a time. The mood in the piazza was festive, full of laughter and people touching each other on the shoulders and arms as they talked and laughed and indulged. Lots of people held fiascos or unmarked bottles of wine, which they generously poured out for each other.

When the demand for cinghiale and polenta finally ended, Jacoby had a seat in a folding chair under the tent. He was worn out, sweat sticking to his black t-shirt. Bill brought him a bottle of water.

"Thanks."

"No. Thank you," Bill said with great sincerity. "This sagra is very much dedicated to you."

"My pleasure," Jacoby responded. "Truly."

"You will be back some day, won't you?"

"I hope so."

"I can feel it," Bill said. "Like fate. You belong here."

Giovanni appeared, dressed in a crisp, gray button down, untucked, with a pattern of large black skulls. His hair was heavy with product and parted around his face and over his ears. His jeans were faded and ripped at the knees. Very rock-n-roll, Jacoby thought, sort of Meatloaf meets Eddie Vedder. Jacoby gave Giovanni thumbs up, and the shoemaker smiled and clenched his fists. Bill gave Giovanni some direction involving the tent and then led Jacoby into the hotel.

"I think we deserve a break," Bill said as they entered the cool foyer. "Are you hungry?"

"I could eat," Jacoby said, following Bill down the corridor to the dining area and kitchen.

"Have you had enough cinghiale for one day?"

"Nope."

Bill laughed and tapped a table for them to sit. He went into the kitchen and Jacoby fetched the opened bottle of Brunello and two glasses. They met back at the table to share yet another meal. Bill had returned from the kitchen with two ceramic plates piled with the sagra meal, real silverware, and cloth napkins.

"Food always tastes better when served properly," Bill said, laying a napkin across his lap.

"I don't know," Jacoby responded. "I could eat this stuff off the curb, and it would still be outrageous."

Bill smiled and raised his glass of Brunello. "Salute," he toasted.

"We do have our health," Jacoby noted. "Got that going for us."

"And all this," Bill said, gesturing with his hands to the room and the meal and the company.

Jacoby smiled at the wisdom and grace of his friend and then dug into the meat.

"Holy fuck balls," he said, as if punched in the palate. "This is better than before."

"It's not the place settings, actually," Bill said with a coy smile. "I gilded the lily a bit on this last batch set aside for us."

"How?" Jacoby asked though he had just figured it out.

"The truffles," both men said together.

"You're insane," Jacoby insisted.

"I slivered them thin as paper and added most at the end of the braise and saved some fresh for the finish. It shouldn't be too overwhelming but they do show up."

Jacoby nodded as he chewed and swallowed, took a big sip of Brunello. "They show up all right, and what they do to the wine is ridiculous."

"I know," Bill purred. "This is what heaven must be like."

"I hope so," Jacoby added.

They ate slowly without speaking, only exchanging looks of wonder and absolute contentment. When they finished, Bill poured each of them a small glass of grappa.

"And how about a quick nap before returning to the party?"

"Can we do that?" Jacoby asked, feeling somewhat fatigued and heady.

"Of course we can," Bill confirmed. "Giovanni can handle things outside, and you will be well-rested for your little show."

"Works for me," Jacoby said.

Chapter 41

After an hour of rest in the front parlor, sitting upright on the couch with his eyes closed and hands on his lap, Jacoby woke just as Bill entered the room. He stood up quickly, feeling fresh and vigorous.

"The riposa treated you right?" Bill asked rhetorically.

Jacoby nodded with exaggeration.

"Good. Let's get your instrument and make Giovanni's dreams come true."

The importance of the event to Giovanni hadn't really registered with Jacoby before. Obviously, he was aware of how much it meant to the man, but he'd been too concerned with doing his part, and not screwing it up, to fully appreciate the stakes for the shoemaker in the little Tuscan village with dreams rooted in American mythology. This was Giovanni's big night. Jacoby was ready. With the guitar up on his shoulder like an ax, he exited the hotel and made for the piazza.

The sun had sunk behind the hills, and the open piazza horded magical light that flitted around the large crowd gathered as if in someone's backyard. Kids played soccer and adults drank, smoked, and chatted amiably. The clamor was pleasant, more of a hum than a din. It felt, for Jacoby, like walking into a gig where the crowd was in good spirits. Vibes matter when playing a room.

Giovanni hustled up to Jacoby and shook him by the shoulders. "Pronto? Pronto?"

"Si," Jacoby said, looking into Giovanni's big brown eyes. "Let's rock."

Giovanni bounced on his toes and made for the statue in the middle of the piazza. He hopped up on the precipice and threw his hands in the air. "Buona sera!" he bellowed as the villagers turned their attention to him. "Sono Giovanni Anguzza, e sono qui cantara per voi con il mio amico dagli Stati Uniti." He held out a hand toward Jacoby who stepped up onto the precipice suddenly aware of a problem: The guitar had no strap. He'd been playing solely in sitting position, though there was nowhere for him to sit, except on the side of the statue's base which would kill much of the acoustic guitar's projection. Giovanni recognized the problem and looked around frantically. He spotted Nicoletta out front of the cafe. He called a directive to her, and she grabbed a metal chair from under the awning and walked it through the crowd to Giovanni.

He beamed as she approached to hand him the chair. "Gente! Gente!" he called to the people. "Grazie alla bellissima Nicoletta!"

The people laughed and cheered the mock-pageantry. The hunters had risen from their table and stood, unamused, at the edge of the piazza, arms crossed, faces stern. Nicoletta's husband whispered something with urgency to her upon return, but she blew him off with a raised hand and kept her eyes on the statue which had become a stage.

Jacoby sat on the chair but was still a little low for projection, so he balanced himself on the backing with his feet on the seat. Now he was above the crowd, and he could see the goodwill and interest in their eyes. Giovanni gestured a concerned pantomime of balance, and Jacoby assured him he was ready.

"Allora," Giovanni said. "Suona la chitarra."

Jacoby rubbed his hands on the thighs of his jeans, readied his fingers and secured the pick. And then he began the opening refrain of "Alive," a slow, somber riff of single notes in two parts, with slides and hammers, repeated four times, whereupon Giovanni jumped in as the chord progression began to deliver the lyrics with a perfect growl, his baritone projecting over the piazza, his upper torso tensed and hinged, back and forth, over his hips. The duo made it to the chorus and back around to the second verse, and Jacoby knew they were killing. He threw in a jazzy solo to compensate for the rock progression his acoustic wouldn't allow, but Giovanni's energy and movement made it feel electric. The lyrics rejoined in an exclamatory refrain for the song's building culmination, which Giovanni accompanied through jumps that had the beefy shoemaker high off the ground, his hair flying like a flag on a pirate ship's mast. Jacoby felt the chair shifting under his own impetus, so he steadied himself to nail the ending.

A fairly large group of young people, many who knew Giovanni by name, had come close to the stage/statue. Their explosion of cheers and calls was nicely complimented by the elders in back and the pack of sweaty adolescents who had abandoned their soccer game and maneuvered to Jacoby's immediate left. He recognized the one holding the ball from their game aside the cafe. The boy stared with wonder at Jacoby, who winked at him quickly before breaking into the opening chords of "Elderly Woman behind the Counter in a Small Town."

Giovanni carried this strum-along with its mix of visceral emotion as if he were a bard delivering a 1st Person narration. While he made eye contact with the crowd, he dedicated much of his delivery to Nicoletta, who now stood in front, swaying and wide-eyed with her arms locked under her chest. Some of the younger audience sang along with the bridge and yelled "Hello!" at the exact point where audiences around the world often join in. Jacoby was shaken by a wave of chills but kept his strumming steady till the song's end.

His heart raced and adrenalin pulsed through his system in a way he hadn't felt on stage in a very long time. He was completely locked in the moment, his brain seemingly on autopilot while also almost super aware of the surroundings. He could see faces and expressions, and he certainly noticed the look of fawning adoration on Nicoletta who had come even closer to the stage and now stood only a few feet below Giovanni.

They kicked through a version of "Corduroy," which was tough on acoustic but Jacoby's favorite Pearl Jam song, so he hammered out the staccato riff, careful not to break any strings. "Even Flow" was easier physically, and towards the end, Jacoby started regretting not preparing more songs or even an encore.

The final song was "Better Man" and Giovanni sang it almost entirely to Nicoletta, which was foolish and a clear sign that Giovanni was experiencing the type of hubris that made rock star a dangerous vocation. About halfway through the song, the hunter approached Nicoletta from behind and tried to lead her back to the cafe by her arm. She refused. He pulled harder, and she smacked him across the face. He pushed her to the ground and drew back a fist. The crowd reacted and Jacoby - who saw the whole thing - stopped playing. No one moved or made a sound. Everything felt like it was made of glass; the moment was broken by Giovanni diving from the stage onto the hunter. Both men crashed to the ground. The hunter got up first and began yelling at Giovanni and kicking him hard in the sides. Nicoletta screamed and attacked her husband, but he held her off with a long, powerful arm. Jacoby, inspired and outraged, jumped from the stage, still holding the guitar, and smashed it across the hunter's broad back, sending him down in a spray of splinters. The hunter's friends appeared and teamed up on Jacoby, punching and kicking him wildly as Jacoby threw punches back, powered by adrenalin that felt almost super human, feeling some of his punches land while many landed hard on his face and neck and head. Still, he kept swinging. It felt, in a way, like he was winning.

The younger members of the audience joined in and helped rescue both Giovanni and Jacoby from the gang of hunters. The warring sides were separated by villagers, the open space marked by a broken guitar. Nicoletta appeared defiant under the arm of Giovanni, who winced with pain, his eyes alive with suffering, one side of his face battered. The butcher showed up with a shotgun, fired once into the distance and declared the sagra over. The hunter and his crew made for the cafe, while Jacoby and Giovanni and Nicoletta went to Bill who waived from the hotel's entrance. As they made their way through the crowd, they were treated like heroes, with supportive words and slaps on the shoulder. Jacoby tasted blood.

Jacoby felt signs of damage all over his body, but especially in his left eye that was busy swelling shut as they crossed the side street and entered the cool and dark safety of the hotel. In the dining salon, Bill left the warriors at a table and hurried into the kitchen for ice and other triage materials. Nicoletta went to the bar and returned with a bottle of Wild Turkey. She poured three shots and held up her glass, but no words came.

"Rock and roll!" Jacoby howled.

"Rock and roll!!" they repeated.

Bill came out of the kitchen, his hands full of ice bags and bandages. "I guess I can assume there are no life threatening wounds?"

"I think we're good," Jacoby said, sincerely. "Thanks."

"Tutto a posto?" Bill asked Giovanni if everything was OK.

"Si," he said, taking Nicoletta's hand. "Tutto a posto."

"Good then," Bill said. "I'm going to bed. Big day tomorrow. Jacoby, you are free to stay on the couch if you'd like."

"Thanks," he said. "Think I will."

Bill went up to bed while Jacoby, Giovanni, and Nicoletta got rip-roaring drunk on American whiskey, reminiscing about their afternoon of rock and roll, until night fell and sleep beckoned. It was his last night in Italy, and Jacoby drifted off, fully dressed, in a drunken stupor thinking about how he had fought for his village. And how Helen would be proud.

Chapter 42

Daylight framed the shutters, but the parlor was still dark and cool when Jacoby reluctantly woke. His eyes were crusted with gunk and backed by pain. The side of his face throbbed. His mouth tasted of dry blood and stale whiskey. Standing up would definitely bring new pain: bruises on his body and around his head from the hunters' beating; residue from the whiskey poisoning his system. So he stayed supine as long as he could, the booze and bruises too much for an early morning.

He'd heard Bill move around the hotel a few hours earlier, but Jacoby kept his eyes closed when his friend approached, playing dead, basically. Jacoby had promised to accompany Bill to the auction, but he simply couldn't bear the thought of it in his condition. So he feigned sleep when Bill tip-toed into the room. He understood. And Jacoby went back to sleep, for real, after Bill departed.

He woke hours later at the sound of the hotel buzzer ringing. He ignored it, but the buzzing repeated. He couldn't make out the chatter on the other side of the door, of women's voices, speaking English, it seemed. Convinced it wasn't the hunter and his friends after a rematch, Jacoby stood up, let the head rush subside, and then dragged his ragged ass to the hotel's entrance. He undid the only lock and let his eyes adjust to the streaming light where two figures, arms akimbo, slowly came into focus, like twin femme fatales.

"Jesus Christ," Claire blurted. "The hell happened to you?"

Dolores nudged Claire aside and took Jacoby's bruised face in one hand. "Looks like he's been ravaged. Who was she?"

"And poisoned with alcohol," Claire added, waiving away his stench.

They were dressed stylishly, and both in good spirits with bemused smiles and shifting postures. Behind them, the piazza was in disarray, the detritus from the sagra still evident. Even Bill's tent stood, as if abandoned. Someone had piled the broken guitar by the side of the hotel's door.

"Must have been some party," Dolores declared. "You should have called. Claire and I are great fun at parties."

"Yes, Jacoby," Claire picked up on the riff but not with the same mirth. "You should have called. I haven't heard from you at all, actually. I was getting worried."

"You're here for the car," Jacoby said, his voice scratched and raw. "Aren't you?"

"Yes," Claire said. "I am. But I'm also here to check on you. Get a sense of your plans. We still need to keep each other informed. You know that, right?"

The sunlight was killing Jacoby, and Claire's pedantic (and appropriate) lecture wasn't helping. He invited them inside.

"How charming," Dolores announced sincerely as they followed him through the lobby into the dining salon. On a table, a carefully written note had been left, which Dolores snatched up and read aloud:

Dearest Jacoby,

I've gone to the auction without you. Thought you would be better served by sleep. I've taken your car. If you could be so kind as to help me breakdown the tent when I return. I will still get you to the airport on time.

Your friend,
Bill

- There is a plate of cinghiale ragu for you in the oven.

"Cinghiale ragu!?!" Dolores squealed. "Where's the oven?"

Jacoby pointed to the swinging door, which Dolores was quickly through.

"You're leaving today?" Claire asked.

The look of deep disappointment sickened Jacoby some. She wasn't bothered by his leaving, just that he hadn't bothered to tell her. She was the responsible one, the one who kept her job and her appointments and had command of her affairs.

"I was going to text you later," Jacoby said, sounding like a child even to his own ears. "The car would be here with Bill."

"And who the hell is Bill?" Claire asked, irritation firing her voice. "Some stranger you trust with my car?"

"He's my friend."

"Oh, good," Claire snapped. "I'm glad you've made a friend at least."

That was mean, and Jacoby knew she felt badly by the way she took a deep breath and blew the bangs off her forehead. "I'm sorry," she said, looking tired all of the sudden.

"It's OK," Jacoby said. "You're right to be mad. I'm just having a hard time accepting all this. Guess I'm in denial. And a little freaked out."

Claire walked over wearing a pursed smile and gave him a hug. Jacoby let it linger, feeling its faith and support.

"My God!" Dolores' voice shot from the kitchen. "This is the best thing I've ever tasted in my life!"

Jacoby and Claire cracked up and parted their hug.

"Bring it in here," Jacoby called.

"No fucking way!" Dolores called back.

"There's plenty," Jacoby assured her. "I promise."

While they waited for Dolores, Jacoby went to the bar and uncorked a bottle of Brunello. He brought it with two glasses to a table.

"None for you?" Claire asked sarcastically.

He shook his battered head and rubbed his sour belly. "Think I'll pass."

He filled two goblets as Dolores crept from the kitchen, the plate tucked safely under her arm. "Certain there's more?"

Jacoby nodded and motioned for her to join them. Jacoby went to the kitchen for more utensils and another plate. He smiled upon hearing the cousins passing the lone fork back and forth, trading sounds of exultation with each bite and sip.

Jacoby came back out and watched them eat, no need for the additional utensils. The plate was overstuffed to begin with, a portion really for two.

When they finished eating, Claire pulled out her iPhone and tapped away in a familiar manner.

"Oh," she said to Jacoby. "Have you been checking your messages?"

"Not really."

"Not really or not at all?"

"Not at all. I'm not even sure where the phone is. The car, I think."

Claire shook her head but kept her criticism quiet. "Mums been asking about some letter."

"What letter?"

"I don't know. We've been in a tiff about this whole Alistair Haxby thing, so I've been avoiding her somewhat, but she's texted me twice now, specifically asking if you received a letter from the lawyers in New York."

"I did," he said, curiosity mounting ever so slightly. "But I figured it was like all the others."

"Might want to read it."

"I can't."

"Why not?"

"Went through the laundry."

"What are you, 12?"

Jacoby glared at Claire, feeling happy that this would be one of their last arguments.

"Have you checked your emails, at least?" she asked.

"No, Claire," he said with all the sanctimony he could muster. "I don't live my life through the internet."

"Be that way," she said, resuming her tapping. "But you might want to check back in with the real world when you have a matter with a New York law firm, and they are looking for you. Just sayin'."

"Sounds reasonable," Dolores added, filling her glass with more Brunello. "I don't go for all this head up the arse, narcissistic nonsense with the phone like my dear cousin, but respectable people do check in once in a while."

"Thanks, Dolores," Jacoby said, "for filling me in on how respectable people behave."

"You're very welcome," she said. "Thank you for the wine. And be sure to thank this Bill character for the marvelous lunch. I might have to stick around and show some gratitude in the flesh. Think he might like a piece of Dolores pie?"

"Only if it comes with a penis on top."

"Too bad," Dolores rued. "Though penis pie does sound yummy."

Jacoby tried to remember where he put his phone, thinking to check the car, and then realizing Bill had the car. Then a thought, from out of nowhere, inspired him to check his wallet for the receipt he'd received from the Bancomat. Maybe there was some connection to the news from New York.

His wallet had survived the fight and the drunken night; it was still in his back pocket, and he pulled it out quickly to rifle through the folds, looking for the receipt he'd stuffed in there with some Euros upon Helen's surprise appearance two days before.

He studied the number printed for the balance. He blinked repeatedly and studied it harder. He took a huge breath through his nose and made extra sure to count the figures, all six of them, numerous times. Adrenalin jolted him out of his hangover and into a frenzy of decisive action and ecstasy.

"Come on! Come on! Come on!" Jacoby screamed, feeling like he could jump out of his clothes. "We have to go!!"

"Go where?" Dolores asked.

Claire put down her phone. Jacoby's heart thumped like a trapped animal's. His pores opened and sweat broke out all over his body.

"To the auction! To the auction! I'll explain on the way. You have to drive me. I swear it will be the last thing I ever ask of you. You have to take me; and you have to take me now!!"

The cousins exchanged intrigued looks and hurried to do as they'd been asked.

Chapter 43

With the top down on Dolores' Audi that blitzed the countryside at Jacoby's direction, he had to yell to explain how his bank statement showed 50 times what he assumed to be his balance, which must have had something to do with the letter from the firm. He told Claire his gmail account name and password, and she quickly accessed it on her phone. She soon found an email from the law firm, which confirmed that they'd settled the suit for wrongful termination and settled a separate suit for slander. The total amount, minus legal fees, had been deposited in his account on a recent date.

Jacoby pumped his fists and pounded his feet on the floorboards in the back seat. Joy rocketed like a pinball around his cavity. He thought of Giovanni before his big show, pumped full of life and meaning.

"It also says here," Claire added, looking impressed, "that you've got your job back, too, mister. How about them apples?"

"Fuck those apples!" Jacoby screamed to the dense forest whipping past. "I don't want those apples. I want a hotel."

"What hotel?" Dolores asked over her shoulder. "Where are we going anyway?"

Jacoby tried his best to explain everything about the picture and the heiress and the bankrupt family to whom he was actually related, and how he could save at least a part of his family history by getting to the auction at the property on time.

"My god," Claire exclaimed. "Why didn't you tell me any of this?"

"I don't know," Jacoby shrugged. "I don't know."

"You, my former husband-to-be, are an asshole."

"I am," he yelled. "And I'm sorry I am."

He pointed out the next turn and held on as the car bumped along the dirt track that led to the abbey-turned-consortium and the villa. "There," he said, motioning to the cars parked outside the consortium. "It must be there."

"Look at that villa," Dolores gasped as they approached. "How magnificent."

"I know!" Jacoby shouted, even there was no longer a need. "It belonged to my family until a few days ago."

They hurried from the convertible to where a dozen people gathered in a half-circle around a man in a fine suit standing behind a podium on a make-shift platform. They were just outside the open doors to the section of the abbey where the wine aged in huge chrome vats. He was speaking officiously with a young, female assistant next to him, well-dressed and erect, holding a tablet with a finger ready to input data.

Paolo was there, within a small group of men of similar age and similar attire. Bill stood to the side, his arm around a somber Bruna. Jacoby ran up and nearly knocked him over.

"Whoa, easy Jacoby," Bill said, taken back by the enthusiasm. "You didn't need to come to this. You remember Bruna, don't you?"

Jacoby shook her hand quickly and turned back to Bill. "How much do you need for the hotel?"

"What?"

"How much do you need?"

"Well, I'm not sure," he said. "They are about to read the amounts where the bids are to begin – anything below that will not be accepted."

"Do you think you'll have enough?"

"Hardly," Bill sighed. "Maybe half. I just really came for the symbolism of it all. And to be here with Bruna."

Jacoby checked in again with her, gently grasping her forearm. She smiled sweetly and bowed her head, touched his swollen cheek, sympathizing with his ragged appearance.

"Look," Jacoby said, uttering words he'd never imagine the opportunity to share. "I've come into a shit load of money. I want in."

"In on what?"

"The hotel!"

"Are you still drunk?" Bill asked, taking in Jacoby's wild-eyed exuberance.

"No, man. No. Maybe a little, but I want to be your partner. In the hotel."

"Do you have the money?"

"How much do you have?"

"About 50,000 Euro. We'd need another 50, at least. Do you have it?"

"Oh, yeah."

Bill put a hand to his chest. "Are you sure you want to do this?"

"How long have we known each other?"

"A little more than a week."

"So you know that I want to stay here the rest of my life."

"I certainly do."

"Then let's do this."

"Come on, Jacoby," Bill said slowly, a sobriety informing his words. "I know we get along wonderfully, but we're, we're..."

"Family."

"What?"

"Do you believe all that about me and the picture?"

"I do."

"Well, then, you were essentially married to my great uncle, right? Fillipo was my grandmother's brother. Right?"

"I hadn't thought of it that way."

"I have. From the moment we figured it out. It's fate. And our fate is a gift. It can't be taken from us."

Bill's chest and face swelled with majesty. "Perhaps it is so."

"And here we are," Jacoby said just as the man in the suit began to speak into a small microphone. Bill grabbed Jacoby's hand and squeezed it tight, looking ahead at the proceedings. Jacoby's body tingled, each breath felt like a gift. His senses heightened and carried him to a level of existence he'd never felt; he had to resist the overwhelming joy in order to stay focused.

The man spoke quickly with bored formality. Jacoby gathered that three items were up for auction: the "villa," the "fattoria" and the "albergo."

"Albergo" is the hotel," Bill whispered in Jacoby's ear.

"I know. I know," Jacoby responded.

"The fattoria is this here, and the villa is, of course, the villa. The palazzo in Florence must be auctioned at a different time."

Jacoby nodded and tried to follow along, not concerned with any of the other offerings. They began with the "albergo." It was described and offered at a price of 120,000 Euro. Jacoby jerked, but Bill held him still. "Wait," he said. "Aspetta."

The silence was like mercury teeming through Jacoby's veins. Breath came in and out of his nose, and he thought of what the players must have felt like moments before the cannon fired to start the calcio storico. The stillness shimmered in the blessed space, where his fate hung like the nearby hawk hovering above the tree tops, seeking salvation below. Jacoby bent to one knee, pinched the bridge of his nose, and held his breath, trying not to let it out until the silence broke.

After a torturous moment, Bill called "Qui," with great confidence. Jacoby stood up. All heads turned toward them: the two Americans and the withered Italian woman off to the side. Jacoby nearly shattered into pieces and fought the need to pee his pants.

Bill calmly approached the auctioneer, who leaned forward to hear his words. Bill produced some paperwork and then turned to waive Jacoby over. His feet didn't seem to entirely touch the ground, as if he were stepping on the automated walkways of airport terminals. The auctioneer shook Jacoby's hand with kind formality.

"He wants to know if you have means of providing your contribution," Bill said, serious and somber.

"Right now?"

"Of course," Bill said, agitated but with dignity. "This is the only moment we have."

Like an idiot, Jacoby patted his pockets and looked around. He noticed the young assistant had a device attached to her tablet, one that restaurants and bars back in the States used to take payment.

"You take debit card?" he asked.

The man looked confused. Bill translated.

"Si," he said with assurance. "Certamente."

With a shaky hand, Jacoby pulled his wallet and handed over his bank card. The young woman smiled and nodded, took the card and swiped it through her device. She poked information into the tablet's screen. Jacoby had a slash of panic, thinking he'd read the statement amount wrong, and that he was about to make a colossal fool out of himself. And Bill. In front of Claire and Dolores and Paolo and everyone else. He'd be a laughing stock in two countries. But he knew he hadn't read it wrong. He knew he hadn't. He feared a glitch of technology, some sort of international banking bullshit. Or the device couldn't read his band or something. He held his breath and thought of the times in his younger years when he was hard up for cash, and the intolerable moments waiting in the silence for an ATM to churn and spit out much needed money instead of flashing insufficient funds on the screen. He swooned with thoughts of disgust and contempt, his moments of failure. He clucked his tongue and fought the burn of agita. A river of purged whiskey ran down his back.

Every major organ, every pore of his body churned, thumped, pulsed. The hair inside his nostrils wiggled. Bill smiled confidently and kindly. Claire and Dolores, in the back of the crowd, held each other nervously, as if the kicker from their beloved football team was about to attempt a last second field goal in the big game. Paolo came up alongside Jacoby and put a thick hand on his shoulder. Suddenly, he felt loved. And redeemed. It sent waves through his body, shattering the tension enough for him to wonder why Paolo was even there, when the woman looked up from her device and smiled.

"Auguri," she said. "Tanti auguri."

A receipt churned out and she ripped it off, handing it to Jacoby with a pen. With a shaking hand, he scribbled his signature, feeling electric and alive. And then he and Bill hugged. They hugged until announcements began again, talk of the fattoria and the villa.

Bill and Jacoby and Bruna walked to the back of the small crowd. Claire and Dolores grabbed Jacoby in tandem. He held them for a moment before breaking the hug to introduce the respective strangers.

Claire chatted up Bruna in Italian while Dolores stepped right up to Bill.

"Are you the Bill responsible for that cinghiale ragu I had earlier?" she asked.

"I am," he said, beaming with cordial delight.

"You, sir, are a genius."

"Why thank you," he said with a small bow. "I am also the co-owner of a lovely hotel with this fine gentleman here."

Jacoby was speechless and numb, his whole existence validated in such spectacular form, he couldn't fathom its reality. He looked around and felt, for the first time in his life, that he had been delivered home.

Paolo was huddled nearby with a small group of men. Feeling inspired and invincible, Jacoby walked up and interrupted with a hand on the older man's shoulder.

"Ciao, Paolo," Jacoby said.

"Ah, ciao, Ja-co-bey. Tanti auguri," Paolo congratulated him on his new enterprise. "You will now stay on in the barn?"

"Yes," Jacoby beamed. "But only if I can have a dog."

"A dog?"

"Yes. The one that helped deliver the cinghiale."

"Certo," Paolo confirmed, of course.

Jacoby smiled and shook Paolo's hand before rejoining his friends to celebrate the best day of his life, but Dolores refused to leave.

"Wait a minute," she quipped. "I want to stick around and see how this plays out."

"How what plays out?" Claire huffed, her tone threaded with impatience.

"Hush, cousin," she said. "I sense an opportunity here, like a flash sale at Bergdorf."

The man in charge stated a price for the consortium and villa, together. Paolo and his cohorts charged the makeshift stage and began a rather heated conversation without raised voices.

"Can you make out what they're saying?" Dolores asked.

Bill walked up to the gathering; Dolores followed a few steps behind.

"The hell is she doing?" Claire asked, her impatience now replaced with admiration, a bemused appreciation of her ballsy cousin.

Bill listened to the conversation and then interrupted with a tap on Paolo's arm. He called Dolores over and introduced her. Paolo began to speak to Bill, but Dolores stepped in front and took charge. She spoke quickly in Italian to Paolo and then motioned him aside so she could speak with the man in charge. He listened. And then nodded. Dolores turned back to Paolo and spoke to him and his cohorts at length with a finger wagging and the men nodding in unison. Bill stood a few feet aside, an impressed smile creasing his face.

Jacoby looked on, exchanging baffled but amused glances with Bruna while Claire clutched his arm and mumbled, "The hell is she doing?" every 30 seconds or so. Jacoby recognized the cars from those parked in Paolo's drive the other day, and he now assumed they were not at Paolo's house for a party but to discuss a business venture. What he couldn't figure out was the matter at hand, and how in the hell Dolores had taken charge of it all.

When she stopped speaking, Dolores shook Paolo's hand formally, and then shook the hand of each of the men in his collective. They looked dumbstruck yet impressed. She turned to the woman with the tablet and read from a booklet pulled from her purse. The woman tapped furiously and produced a cellphone to make a call. Dolores waited patiently, squeezing off quick smiles of reassurance to Paolo and company. She whispered something to Bill, who nodded and returned to where Jacoby and Claire and Bruna waited, their eyes wide with wonder and demand.

Bill spoke quietly to Bruna. When he was done, she planted her head against his chest and began to cry. Bill smiled and held her tight.

"What happened?" Jacoby mouthed.

"She just saved Bruna's job. And her home. Many others', too."

"So, I guess you've told her then," Dolores announced with her arrival.

"My god!" Claire squealed. "What's going on?"

"There was a bit of a hang up with the property. Paolo is it? Yes, Paolo and his cronies cobbled some funds together with plans of running the consortium here, where they make the local wine and press the oil and such. Is it any good?" she stopped to ask Jacoby.

"Spectacular," Jacoby confirmed.

"Well, that's good," Dolores acknowledged before carrying on. "But they had no interest in the villa, or the means of paying for it, for that matter, but the properties were not being offered separately, so that's where I came in. I took the villa and a share of the fattoria business, at an absolute song, really, for all of it – truly, I've blown more on a weekend in Canary than I've spent today - and they will run the fattoria with me as a partner. We'll need to work it out with the local comune, square it all away."

Claire blurted, "But what will you do with it?"

"Dear cousin," Dolores said, straightening her shoulders. "Do you realize that we are mere miles from Florence proper? Out here in the gorgeous hills near a charming village, with apparently amazing products. And not a lousy tourist in sight. We have stumbled upon a gold mine. And we shall put it on the map by converting it into a plush vacation spot."

"We?" Claire asked. "I'm going back to New York as soon as I can."

"Please do," Dolores said with a wry smile. "Can't wait for that, but first you shall do the rest of us a little favor with your writing. That would actually suit your needs, as well, if I'm not mistaken, as I understand you still have some obligations to Alistair Haxby."

Claire put her hands on her hips and smiled knowingly. "You're not nearly as awful and stupid as everyone says."

Dolores smiled like a school girl and gave her cousin the finger.

"And Jacoby," Dolores broached, "once we finish the renovation,

I'd like you to come on and manage the place, as long as it doesn't interfere with your work with dear Bill here and the hotel."

"Could I live here?" he asked.

"Eventually, sure."

No words came to Jacoby, just a feeling of fate being delivered.

"Shall I begin teaching you the hotel business tomorrow?" Bill asked Jacoby.

"Can we start the day after?"

Bill looked amenable but somewhat perplexed.

"Need to get to the museum, you know, to share the news."

Bill smiled and clasped Jacoby on the shoulder. "Perfectly understood. Take all the time you need."

Jacoby's heart was suddenly everywhere all at once, thinking of his surprise reunion with Helen, the story he would share and the plans they might make.

"Why don't we go out to really celebrate and discuss our new endeavors?" Bill suggested to the group.

"Fabulous idea," Dolores concurred. "Fabulous. I could use a vat of Prosecco at this point. Where do you have in mind?"

"There's a local cantinetta, not more than a mile from here."

"Perfect," Dolores said and turned to Jacoby. "How's the food? Decent?"

"Oh, it's way better than decent," Jacoby said. "More like typical."

The End

Thank you so much for reading one of our **Literary Fiction** novels.
If you enjoyed our book, please check out our recommended title for your
next great read!

The Five Wishes by Mr. Murray McBride by Joe Siple

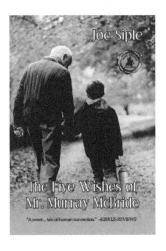

2018 Maxy Award "Book of the Year"

"A sweet...tale of human connection...will feel familiar to fans of Hallmark

movies." *–KIRKUS REVIEWS*

"An emotional story that will leave readers meditating on the life-saving

magic of kindness." *–Indie Reader*

Made in the USA
Las Vegas, NV
11 May 2021